TAUGHT BY THE DRAGON

Stonefire Dragons
Book 15

JESSIE DONOVAN

Mythical Lake Press, LLC

Taught by the Dragon

Copyright © 2023 Laura Hoak-Kagey

Mythical Lake Press, LLC

Print Edition

www.JessieDonovan.com

Cover Art by Laura Hoak-Kagey of Mythical Lake Design

ISBN: 978-1944776657

The Stonefire and Lochguard series intertwine with one another. (As well as with one Tahoe Dragon Mates book.) Since so many readers ask for the overall reading order, I've included it with this book. (This list is as of May 2023 and you can view the most up-to-date version at JessieDonovan.com)

Treasured by the Dragon (Stonefire Dragons #13)
The Dragon Collective (Lochguard Highland Dragons #8)
The Dragon's Bidder (Tahoe Dragon Mates #3)
The Dragon's Chance (Lochguard Highland Dragons #9)
Summer at Lochguard (Dragon Clan Gatherings #1)
Trusting the Dragon (Stonefire Dragons #14)
The Dragon's Memory (Lochguard Highland Dragons #10)
Finding Dragon's Court (Stonefire Dragon's Universe #3)
Taught by the Dragon (Stonefire Dragons #15)
Winter at Stonefire (Dragon Clan Gatherings #2 / August 3, 2023)

Short stories that lead up to *Persuading the Dragon* / *Treasured by the Dragon*:

Meeting the Humans (Stonefire Dragons Shorts #1)
The Dragon Camp (Stonefire Dragons Shorts #2)
The Dragon Play (Stonefire Dragons Shorts #3)
Dragon's First Christmas (Stonefire Dragons Shorts #4)

Semi-related dragon stories set in the USA, beginning sometime around *The Dragon's Discovery* / *Transforming Snowridge*:

The Dragon's Choice (Tahoe Dragon Mates #1)
The Dragon's Need (Tahoe Dragon Mates #2)
The Dragon's Bidder (Tahoe Dragon Mates #3)
The Dragon's Charge (Tahoe Dragon Mates #4)
The Dragon's Weakness (Tahoe Dragon Mates #5)
The Dragon's Find (Tahoe Dragon Mates #6)
The Dragon's Surprise (Tahoe Dragon Mates #7 / TBD)

Chapter One

Even through the thick walls of the prison, roars pierced the air, and Persephone "Percy" Smith paused while making a snack for the two kids sitting across from her.

For a beat, hope flooded her body. Had the girl's uncle finally come to rescue them, like Ava had said he would? Percy's cynical side said of course he hadn't, but as more roars echoed from somewhere above, her heart skipped a beat. Maybe he had followed through, which was something she'd never experienced before. Well, at least in a positive light—threats and punishments, she knew well enough.

Still, she wasn't going to completely rely on strangers and hope for the best. She needed to protect herself and her two bargaining chips. They were her chance at freedom.

One of the two kids who'd been handed into her care the day before, the little dragon girl named Ava Moore-Llewellyn, stood up and met Percy's gaze.

"That's them. I told you my uncle would come save me."

The younger human boy, Joey Carter, frowned. "What? I thought they couldn't help us. You said so."

Ava's flashing dragon eyes met hers. Percy's inner dragon had been silent for years, and even if she'd hidden the pain, the sight still made her long for the days when she'd actually had a friend. Her dragon had been her only friend, ever.

Until she'd been taken from her.

More roars sounded—as if a whole fleet or group or whatever they called a flock of dragons was in the air—and the long-dead emotion of hope tried to break free.

Joey leaned forward. "Is someone from Stonefire coming, then? Did my stepdad send help?"

The human boy looked to be on the verge of tears —he was so fucking young and innocent—but Percy didn't know the first thing about comforting someone.

After all, no one had comforted her since her dragon had fallen silent all those years ago. All she could do was be her normal, straight-to-the-point self. "Maybe."

Joey looked at the door exiting into the hallway, which was locked from the outside, and blurted, "Can we go looking for them? Or shout until they hear us? I want to see my mum."

Ava sat up straighter. "They'll find us, no matter what, Joey. I'm sure of it. My uncle would do anything to protect me."

Percy nearly barked out a laugh. In her experience,

people only cared about themselves. That was why she only trusted one person: herself.

Still, as the noise in the hallway grew louder, she wanted to be prepared. If—and that was a big if—someone had stormed the facility to rescue Ava and Joey, then the guards might come to take her or the kids away.

And she needed to keep the kids alive. After all, they would be her only ticket out of this hellhole.

She laid down the butter knife and walked to the other side of the counter. "Whoever it is, it's dangerous to be out here, in the bigger room. Come on. You'll be safer in the back bedroom, where there's only one door in or out."

Joey eyed the food on the counter. "Can we take a snack? I'm hungry."

He was young, quite young, and Percy tried to remind herself that these two had lived sheltered lives with family who wanted them. Complaining about a snack seemed normal, even if to her, a woman who'd been sold at thirteen to become an experimental subject for a bunch of sadistic arseholes, it seemed ridiculous.

Remember, if you help them and keep them safe, Ava's uncle might, just might, let you stay with their dragon clan until you can figure out what to do with freedom.

Percy was skeptical as hell that Ava's uncle would hold up his word, but it was all she had.

She gestured toward the back room. "It's either hide to try and not get hurt, or stay and have a snack and maybe have someone kill you. You're human, Joey.

And they only keep dragon-shifters here. Do you know what that means?"

Joey's eyes widened, but Ava spoke to the boy before he could say anything. "Come on, Joey. It's just for a bit. Remember, Percy knows this place. And we have to follow her orders if we want to stay safe."

The little human boy's eyes were wet, as if he were about to cry, and he was probably one step away from falling into hysterics. But Percy didn't know how to be nice or kind or how to care about other people's feelings.

At one point she had, but she'd learned rather fucking quickly how dangerous that was.

Shouts filled the hallway, as did a cacophony of boots hitting the tiles. She gently pushed the kids toward the bedroom. "Go. I'll carry you in there and tie you up if I need to."

Ava murmured some nonsense to Joey about how everything would be all right.

Oh, to be young and naïve.

But as more roars sounded, and the shouting from outside her locked set of apartments grew even louder, that flicker of hope came to life inside her again.

Once they were all inside her bedroom, Percy crouched until she was at eye level with the little human boy. She looked from him to the dragon girl and back again. "Now, listen carefully. I need you two to stay in this room and not open that door to anyone until I say it's okay. Understand?"

Ava asked, "But what if it's my—"

"If your uncle shows up, then of course. But if the guards say to open it, even if they threaten me, you keep it locked and put a chair under the door handle. If they start banging against it, then use these." Percy went to the attached bath, pried open the tile where she stashed things she'd stolen over the years, and returned to the kids. She put the phone in Joey's hand and held out a stun gun to Ava. "You press that trigger, and this will fire a little wire thing that will shock whoever it attaches to. Got it?"

Ava stared at the stun gun, speechless.

Percy gently placed a finger under the girl's chin and made her look up. "It's scary—and hard—but the people here are monsters. It's better to fight them, even if it means you die trying. Don't let them take you away, Ava. I mean it. It'll be hell."

The dragon girl blinked, her pupils flashing, and nodded.

Joey just stared at her with his mouth open.

Maybe normal people would have felt bad or guilty or some shite like that. But Percy didn't. Survival was everything, and feelings only ever got in the way.

She nodded. "Right, then I'm going to stand watch in the kitchen. Lock the door after me, okay?"

Joey blurted, "Will you be okay or get hurt, Percy?"

Considering how young he was—she couldn't judge ages well since she hadn't seen a young child in years, but he was maybe six or seven—he would still care about others, even strangers like her.

Something flared in her heart, but she ignored it.

She shrugged nonchalantly. "Maybe. Maybe not. But I have experience, and I need you two alive if I'm to escape this place."

Ava hugged Joey close to her side, her eyes

frightened. Good. The formerly pampered princess needed to learn that life was fucking unfair and awful, nothing like the fairy tales.

Percy rose and stopped inside the doorway. "I mean it—lock the door and put a chair under the handle."

Only after Ava nodded did Percy shut the door. As soon as the lock clicked and she could make out the scraping sound of the chair being put into place, she went to the kitchen. The knives provided to her were dull, but she'd stolen a few switchblades from the guards over the years—she'd learned to steal early on—and retrieved them from her second hiding place inside one of the cupboards.

With the blades extended, she crouched behind the little kitchen island to wait.

The roars were probably from dragons. And the male shouting and grunts in the hallway probably meant there was some kind of battle going on.

Maybe, just maybe, Ava's uncle had come to rescue his niece after all.

Percy's heart pounded at the thought. On the one hand, Percy wanted to leave this hellhole and all the rape, torture, and humiliation she'd suffered. However, if Ava's uncle held up his end of the bargain, it meant she would set foot into the territory of her first dragon clan.

A place where they'd hate someone like her—a half-human, half-dragon female with a silent dragon.

One of the first things she'd learned as a kid in the orphanage, before being sold to this prison, was that dragon-shifters hated mixed children, to such a degree that they often refused any children with human blood and sent them to the only orphanage in the UK that took in such bastards.

Percy had spent her first thirteen years there.

Buck up, Percy. She'd dealt with hatred for years, not to mention ridicule for being a freak with a massive birthmark on her neck and shoulder. After all the shite she'd endured, she could take a few sneers or jeers if it meant she could do the one thing she wanted to accomplish before she died—learn to talk to her dragon again and then fly. She didn't give a fuck what happened after that. But she was going to fly, damn it, no matter what it took to accomplish her only dream.

Suddenly, there was shouting right outside her door. However, the light soundproofing made it so she couldn't hear the words, not even with her supersensitive hearing.

Tightening her grip on her knives, she waited. She wasn't all altruistic, determined to save children for the sake of it. But it was definitely a bonus if she could fight any of the guards and doctors. Pissing them off and ruining their plans gave her life.

The lock on the front door turned, and it swung open hard enough to smack against the wall. Then her least favorite guard, Denny Browne, strode in and shut the door behind him. "Percy, get your arse out here. Don't bloody make me find you, or you won't like it."

She rolled her eyes. As if his threats were going to be any worse than some of the things that had been done to her inside this place.

Denny walked a few steps closer, and she rose, making sure to keep her hands with the knives hidden behind the kitchen island. "What the fuck do you want?"

The guard strode toward her. "We're evacuating, and you and that dragon girl are coming with me. If I have to punch you unconscious and carry you over my shoulder, I will." Lust flared in his eyes, and Percy willed herself not to gag. "But the boss said to try to keep you conscious first. Some plan of his I didn't question."

"Well, sorry to disappoint you, dickhead. But I'm not going anywhere. There's shouting and roars, and who the bloody hell knows what else is happening out there? It's safer in here."

Denny wasn't especially clever—he was valued for his willingness to do anything, without question, even to children—and liked to boast. "Some fucking dragons found us, but they won't be able to beat us." He took out a syringe. "Now, get over here, bitch. We need to leave. You can do it the easy way or the hard way."

She tightened her grip and readied herself to attack. Since she needed space to swing her weapon, she moved her hands behind her back and retreated a few feet. Denny only came closer.

When he was within three feet, she pounced, moving her arms in ways she'd practiced alone, trying to land a blow where she could make him bleed the most—places they'd discussed around her before, to make sure they didn't cut her there and kill her. Channeling the rage at all the stuff they'd done to her over the years, she swung hard. Denny managed to lean back from the first blow and gripped her wrist.

With her other knife, she cut his neck, but not in the right place, as it barely trickled.

Fuck. She tried to move her still-free arm and stab him somewhere, anywhere, to weaken him. However, for all his lack of brains, Denny was bloody strong. He squeezed her first wrist hard enough, it felt as if it might break, and the metal blade clanged against the tile floor.

He must've dropped the syringe at some point, because he finally took hold of her other wrist—the one belonging to the hand with the remaining blade— and twisted it away from him, toward her chest. He pushed, and she tried to keep it from stabbing her.

Despite her hellish existence, Percy had always held on to one dream—to be able to shift into her dragon form for the first time and finally feel the wind against her skin or scales or whatever.

To have the ultimate freedom, no matter how brief, and be in control of her life.

But as Denny moved the knife closer and closer to her neck, sweat trailed between her breasts and down her back. He might've been given orders not to kill her, but rage burned in his eyes. He might do it just to teach her a lesson.

And she'd never get the chance to be a real dragon-shifter.

For a brief second, she worried about the children. She shouldn't care—she really shouldn't—and yet the thought of this fucker getting his hands on them gave her a second wind. She managed to maneuver her thigh between his legs and jerked it upward, until she smashed her knee against his bollocks.

Denny howled and released her. The sudden movement made her drop the knife, and she cursed. There wasn't time to get it, so she dashed around Denny, heading for the stool on the other side of the island, and picked it up. If she had to smash the arsehole over the head, it might buy her enough time to tie him up—and maybe even kill him.

Denny finally turned toward her, his eyes narrowed. "You're going to fucking pay for that, you bitch."

Instead of moving closer, he took something from the utility belt all the guards wore, something she rarely saw, unless they were dealing with a dangerous prisoner. A tranquilizer gun. One shot, and she'd be helpless and unable to do a thing to safeguard the kids until the dragons could rescue them.

She backed up, trying to use the stool to protect herself as much as possible. If she could just reach the picture on the wall, the one she'd been given as a reward for fucking the catatonic dragonman a few months ago, she'd have a shield. And since he had one shot before he had to reload, that might give her enough time to attack.

Percy took one step back and then another. Everything slowed as she tried to reach her last chance at safety. Because if Denny hit her with the dart, she'd be out for hours.

Close enough to the wall, she turned to grab it, dropping the stool in the process. Just as she was about to turn back, pain radiated from her arse.

Fuck. He'd hit her.

She plucked it out, but that wouldn't make much difference. Her vision already blurred and swam, and the room began to tilt. Her legs wouldn't hold her, and she fell to the floor.

In the next second, Denny's rancid breath danced across her face. "I'm going to enjoy teaching you a lesson later, when the doctor issues your punishment. Maybe this time, he'll let me slice you as I fuck you, you dragon whore."

The drugs made her weak, and she whimpered—bloody whimpered. Then she murmured, "No."

Denny's smile turned smug. "Oh, yes, pet. We're going to have fun."

The edges of her vision darkened just as the door burst open. Just as Denny stood and turned, a tall, blond-haired man with flashing dragon eyes rushed over and took him by the throat. He growled, "If you've fucking touched them, you're going to pay."

As the dragonman—it had to be one, right?—slammed Denny against the wall, Percy tried to speak, but all that came out was a croak.

The dragonman heard it, though, and never taking his eyes off Denny, he said, "Don't worry. This bastard won't be bothering you any longer."

He did something, and Denny slumped to the floor. Before she could ask if her long-term tormentor was dead, the world finally went black.

Chapter Two

Bronx Wells paced the little meeting area inside one of the cabins used on the outskirts of Clan Stonefire. Sometimes the buildings were used for happy events, such as the dragon camp held between the human and dragon children in the summer. But today, it was going to be a holding cell of sorts, a place to interrogate the mysterious dragonwoman who'd been rescued from a hellish experimentation center. He'd received only the barest minimum of information about her, but it was enough —torture, drug trials, rape, and more.

In the past, he might've served as backup to Stonefire's team of Protectors for the rescue mission. But after losing his lower leg during a fire a while ago, he would be useless on such a job.

The pacing irritated his right leg, the one where he had a prosthetic on the lower half, but he couldn't bloody well sit still. He was as eager as his clan mates to find out more about the dragon female. She'd helped protect the clan leader's niece and the human son of Bronx's brother's mate, Sarah Carter-Wells.

But more than that, it was good to be a part of the team again. Ever since he'd lost part of his leg, he'd been forced to sit and let everyone else take charge. And to a male who'd been leading wings of dragons for more than a decade, he bloody well hated giving up control, let alone feeling useless.

His inner dragon, the second personality inside his head, grunted. *Why are you pacing and making our leg ache? She'll get here when Kai and his team get here. Unless you think Kai will fail the clan?*

Don't be ridiculous, dragon.

Kai Sutherland was the head Protector of Stonefire, in charge of clan security and related operations. Bronx, like everyone on Stonefire, trusted him implicitly.

His dragon replied, *Then sit the fuck down and save your strength. It's going to be a delicate situation, given what we know, and being in a temper or all worked up will probably scare her.*

Bronx knew his beast was correct. This Percy female was only one of a number of prisoners that Kai and his Protectors had rescued from a facility that conducted illegal experiments on dragon-shifters. As best he knew, it was loosely tied to the dragon hunters, who were Stonefire's nemesis and more and more recently, a pain in their arses.

And dragon hunters weren't known for treating dragon-shifters well. Hudson, one of Bronx's younger brothers, had lost his first mate to the bloody hunters a number of years ago.

Their reputation for harshness was why Bronx was

here at all. He wasn't involved with security but had previously been head of the fire and rescue team. After losing his leg, he'd had to find something to occupy his time, and researching how to work with trauma victims had become his focus.

Between working with the clan psychologist and the recommended texts, he would have to suffice until Dr. Rossi returned. Since she was currently away in Ireland —dragon psychologists were few and far between—he was the next best thing. His job was to ensure Zain, the clan's best interrogator, didn't push the rescued female too hard too soon while trying to figure out if she was a threat to Stonefire.

Bronx finally sat down, crossed his arms over his chest, and jostled his good leg up and down. He was just about to check in with his teenaged daughter when a knock sounded on the door.

In the next second, Kai Sutherland's tall, blond-haired, pale-skinned form strode in. He said without preamble, "She's unconscious, so I had to put her in the bedroom. Come with me."

"Unconscious?"

Kai nodded. "One of the prison guard fuckers shot her with a dart. I told Zain the interrogation would have to wait. Although I'm still trying to figure out what to do with her now. Resources are tight, and even if it'd probably be better to have a female watch over Percy, I'm reluctant to do so until we know more about her. The only two I'd trust to do so—and handle themselves —are both watching over the bastards at the facility until the Department of Dragon Affairs shows up to sort the mess."

He was talking about Nikki and Diana, two female Protectors who were part of Kai's team.

Hefting himself up, which took a little skill with his prosthetic, Bronx said, "I can watch over her for a little while, provided she remains unconscious. But I shouldn't be alone in a room with her until we know more about what happened during her imprisonment."

Kai nodded. "Ava and Joey's jumbled story said she not only handled the guards without blinking but did her best to protect them whilst they were there. I want to believe them, but children can be manipulated. We need to determine whose side she's on as soon as possible."

"I know, but you can't just shout at her or threaten to hurt her. She's not a fucking dragon hunter."

Kai grunted. "That we know of. Ivy was brainwashed by a similar group, and this dragonwoman is fucking young. It's possible they got to her too, especially since Ava said she never saw Percy's pupils flash the whole time she was there. And all of the inmates were dragon-shifters, so she has to be one too. Otherwise, it wouldn't make sense."

Bronx shrugged one shoulder. "Her dragon could have been silenced. Dr. Sid will know more after she examines her."

Kai nodded. "She's coming, but I wanted you to be in the room, just in case Dr. Sid needs help restraining her. And who knows? If she wakes up soon, maybe you can get her to chat a bit and open up."

He raised his brows. "Don't expect bloody miracles, Kai. I heard a little about the other prisoners, and it sounds like they were all abused, or worse."

Kai's face turned grim. "It wasn't for the faint of heart." He shook his head. "Regardless, I want to know more about her before we allow her inside Stonefire. And since Dr. Rossi isn't here, you'd better be able to do what you said you could."

The head Protector's words prickled at his ego. And even if he knew Kai was merely doing his job, he stood taller and stated, "I'll be able to handle her better than Zain, that's for bloody sure."

Kai merely raised an eyebrow. "Nice to see some of your confidence is back, Bronx."

Before Bronx could say a word, Kai opened the door and motioned for him to follow.

His dragon said, *He's not trying to provoke you. Kai is Kai; it's just his way.*

That meant the dragonman probably had some master plan Bronx had no clue about. *I know. Still, this is our chance to prove we're back to full fighting force and that we can do more than sit behind a desk. Maybe we can't fly into an inferno or locate someone trapped on a mountainside, but at least this way, I can help people again.*

That was something he needed to do, as if it would one day make up for what he'd done to his late mate, Edith.

Bronx's beast growled, but Kai motioned his chin toward a chair and whispered, "Sit there. I don't want any of us looming over her, except for Sid. If she wakes and starts to freak out, then you'll have to give her this." Kai handed over a capped syringe filled with a sedative.

Bronx wanted to toss it across the room. "I hope I

don't have to use it. I probably won't ever be able to earn her trust then."

"I know, but I also can't have a half-mad female running through Stonefire." Kai moved to the door and stopped to hold up his mobile phone. "Keep me in the loop."

With that, the dragonman left, keeping the door open.

After sitting, Bronx quickly tucked the sedative between his leg and the side of the chair and stared at the still female form on the bed.

Her chest moved up and down, but nothing else. Her face was partially turned toward him. She had brown hair and extremely pale skin, as if she'd never been outside, and he could make out the edges of a red birthmark on her neck, one that brushed the edges of her jaw.

He had no idea how old she was, but she was young. Too fucking young to have suffered all she probably had.

Just the thought of his only daughter, Violet, being held prisoner, raped, or tortured made his stomach turn. His daughter was only fifteen, and the female on the bed couldn't be more than ten years older than her.

His dragon said softly, *Violet is safe. But we can try to help this female as much as we can. She deserves a better life than what she's had to date.*

For a second, his confidence faltered. Dr. Serafina Rossi would've been a better choice—a female talking to a female survivor—but he was all they had. No one else even remotely possessed the training he had.

And for most dragon-shifters, their first instinct was

to push, and demand, and be a bit bossy. That would probably be counterproductive with someone like Percy.

Maybe once they'd figured out if she was friend or foe, he could bring in Nikki or another clan member to help her feel safe. Because being constantly surrounded by males probably wouldn't do it.

He was lost in thought, thinking of who might be able to help, when Dr. Sid strode into the room. Her mousy brown hair was in its usual ponytail, but she didn't have a white lab coat on like she usually wore at the surgery. Instead, she had on dark jeans and a short-sleeved blue top.

At his raised brow, Dr. Sid shrugged. "They said she'd been surrounded by so-called doctors in white coats. And given the state of the others and what little I've already learned, the white coat signaled hell and misery to them."

Bronx tucked away that bit of information, along with a note to find out what he could from anyone who'd been on the rescue mission. The more intel he had, the more easily he could form a plan for Percy. He nodded. "I'll need statements or reports about their experiences." Dr. Sid frowned, but he added quickly, "Just generalizations. It'll help me figure out who this female is a lot quicker."

Once Kai had sent a message that Percy had been imprisoned the longest, Bram, Stonefire's clan leader, had made the decision to assign Percy to Bronx. The others would go to those with lesser training.

That meant Percy was probably the most traumatized. Any of the inmates would've suffered, but this one had been clever enough to survive. Not only that, but she had been smart enough to come up with a plan once Ava and Joey were handed into her care.

To keep that kind of intelligence and calm intact, she'd probably had some sort of coping mechanism in place. If it failed her, it wouldn't be good.

And if they wanted to learn as much as possible from Percy, they needed to keep her from falling apart.

As Dr. Sid checked her over, Bronx stood and turned away, to give them privacy. It was hard to remain calm and still, since he wanted to get to work right away. However, he couldn't do anything that might set her off. She probably had triggers he needed to learn. Plus, if she'd been imprisoned a long time, she'd probably never had choices before.

He wanted to give them to her.

His dragon spoke up. *We will. And Kai and the others will make the bastards responsible for hurting her pay.*

Dr. Sid said, "You can turn around."

He did and saw Percy now was on her back, the covers tucked up to her neck.

"Kai found a dart near her body, and it was some kind of sedative. She'll be out for a while yet." She motioned toward the door. "We need to chat."

He glanced one last time at Percy and followed the dragon doctor down the hall and into the kitchen. She turned and didn't beat around the bush. "I still need to run tests on her blood, but if she's like the others, she's been given the sleeping dragon drug for years. I don't know if, or when, her dragon might return. The safest thing would be to keep her restrained, and yet I'm hesitant to do that." She lowered her voice. "Some of the others mentioned being used for fertility experiments and pain threshold tests and all other kinds of bloody barbaric practices. If that's true for Percy too, which I suspect it is, her dragon could wake up rogue and out of control. Especially if it's true she spent seven years in that hellhole, she would've been a child when she first set foot inside. She probably didn't even have proper training on how to control her dragon."

The thought of a girl younger than his own daughter being imprisoned, her dragon drugged silent, and who the bloody hell knew what kind of pain she'd endured, made both man and beast growl.

Dr. Sid nodded. "I feel the same way. I'll consult some of my fellow doctors to see if there's ever been a case like hers, or at least one that's been recorded. Until then, we might have to keep her dragon silent, administering it secretly via a food source instead of a syringe. But at the same time, I don't want to lose any possibility of trust. What do you suggest, Bronx?"

He tapped his fingers against his thigh. "I need to talk to her, but with other females present. Until I learn more about what she's gone through, what she suffered, or even how hostile or guarded she is, I can't form a plan. There are certain things that might trigger memories or bring back suppressed memories, so we need to be careful."

Dr. Sid nodded. "We'll have to discuss it with Dr. Rossi on the video conference Bram scheduled for later. Also, Dr. Layla McFarland is coming down from Lochguard to help for a few days. But for now, I have eight new patients to attend to. I wish Bram would allow them inside Stonefire and inside my surgery, although I understand why he's being cautious."

All of the rescued prisoners, apart from Ava and Joey, were in the various cabins located on the edge of the clan's land. It was stretching the Protectors and the medical staff thin.

Bronx nodded. "I'll work with Zain later. Maybe we can put some questions together to help figure out their loyalties. Although I'll be realistic with you—this kind of stuff could take a lifetime to fully move past, if she can at all."

Dr. Sid's lips thinned before she replied, "I know. But we'll just have to see what we can do." Her pupils flashed to slits and back. "And maybe once we find a way to stop the dragon hunters for good, we can finally focus more on the clan and our relations with the humans, to stop something like this from happening again. It'd be bloody nice to not always fight, recover, and fight some more, in an endless cycle."

They'd made great progress over the last four or so years, starting with the human sacrifice named Melanie Hall and to even Ivy Passmore, a former dragon enemy who had ended up mating with a dragon-shifter. "Thanks, Dr. Sid. If you have to leave, then I need to call another female over to sit with me. I won't risk being alone with her this early."

Sid raised her brows. "How about Melanie and Tristan, and maybe even your daughter? Tristan knows how to handle young or untrained dragons, and if there were ever two females who could make someone feel safe or be nonthreatening, it would be Melanie and Violet."

Melanie Hall was strong but kind and had a knack for getting along with nearly everyone. Provided her mate came, the pair would help in the worst-case scenario. And Violet could charm the spots off a leopard, if she tried hard enough.

Although the protective father side of him growled at the idea of exposing Violet to potential danger or even just to the harsh reality of Percy's past.

His dragon spoke up. *Our daughter's fifteen, on her way to being an adult. She's also shown an interest in becoming a doctor and would love this chance to watch Sid or the nurses work with Percy.*

It's still dangerous.

If we have to stick around long term, Violet will find a way to visit anyway.

His dragon was right—Violet often didn't like being told no and found a way to assuage her curiosity.

It was still dangerous, though.

His dragon sighed. *Tristan will also be here, and we can probably ask for a female nurse to stop by regularly to check for signs that her dragon might be coming out. Between that, us, and the doctors, no one will allow Violet to get hurt.*

Still, I wish we could have Nikki or even Diana.

Both were trained Protectors. And even if Diana was younger, not long back from her time with the British Army, she had training and experience his daughter didn't.

His beast grunted. *Both of them are still dealing with the criminal prisoners. Until the DDA takes them, they have to watch them closely and protect the clan.*

Accepting the inevitable, Bronx eyed the dragon doctor. "I know you're busy, but can someone check on

Percy at fixed intervals, just to make sure her dragon won't take charge and lash out?"

She replied, "Of course. I'd planned to do that anyway. I would never risk any of the clan members, Bronx, and you should bloody well know that."

He resisted a wince at Dr. Sid's glare. He put up a hand. "I'm sorry, Sid. But you have a mate and son, and I bet you're just as protective of them."

"Yes, you're right." She shook her head. "At any rate, will you see if Melanie, Tristan, and Violet will help you? I'd suggest some of the children, like Daisy, but she's currently on holiday with her mum and stepdad."

Daisy Chadwick was a human child who had the ability to make anyone smile. Although Bronx thought his daughter was nearly as good.

His dragon said, *Violet always wants to spend more time with us. Ever since the accident, you've been keeping her at more of a distance.*

Only at the beginning, as I didn't want her to see my leg.

His beast grunted. *More than that. Let her in, let her help, and you can protect her, if need be. You know how she wants to be a doctor, so this might be good practice at seeing that not all of medicine is easy.*

Dr. Sid had previously offered to allow Violet to observe her, but Bronx had wanted to protect his daughter for as long as possible. Although since she was fifteen now, he doubted he could think of her as a little girl much longer.

And he bloody well hated admitting his daughter was nearly a grown female.

He finally sighed. "All right, I will. But if Percy so

much as growls at them, I'm kicking them out of the room."

"Fair enough." Dr. Sid picked up her bag. "Call them and stand guard outside Percy's door until they arrive. I need to move on to the next patient and can't linger. I'm not about to let Gregor boast about seeing more patients than me today."

She smiled and exited the room. Dr. Gregor Innes was her mate, and even though Dr. Sid hadn't meant anything by the remark, it reminded him of when he'd had a mate and how they'd just started to have a loving, teasing relationship when Edith was taken away from him.

Before his dragon could growl, he took out his mobile and texted his daughter and then Melanie and Tristan. All replied that they would come, although Tristan said at the first sign of trouble, he would whisk Melanie away. Zain also said he'd be there soon, to discuss their plan to talk to Percy, once she was ready.

Putting away his phone, he went to stand in front of Percy's door. His gut said this was the right thing to do, and yet he couldn't help but worry if he should keep Percy isolated until they determined the state of her dragon.

His inner beast spoke up. *I'll keep a close watch. I would never let anything happen to Violet.*

I know. In an ideal world, we'd have weeks or months to help her before doing any sort of interrogation. But information about the dragon hunters is time sensitive, and if she knows anything, we need it now.

It was true—in the past, the hunters had sometimes

moved bases within hours, rendering their gathered intelligence useless.

So he'd just have to be vigilant and observant, and come up with questions to ask Dr. Rossi later.

For now, he waited for his daughter, Melanie, and Tristan to arrive and for his new job to begin.

Chapter Three

Some sort of cheering noise jolted Percy awake. She sat up and moved backward until she bumped against the wall. Blinking, she tried to adjust to the light. The first thing she noticed was no one was standing in front of her or over her or pointing a gun at her.

The room also smelled unfamiliar, and then her eyes finally latched on to the small group of people sitting around a table on the far side of the space.

Everyone stared at her.

There were two males, a younger female, and a slightly older female. Three out of the four had flashing pupils.

Dragon-shifters.

The only one without flashing dragon eyes, a short female with reddish-brown hair and green eyes, said, "You're awake. Sorry for all the noise. It was totally my fault. I never win, and I finally did and couldn't hold back my excitement."

Her accent was strange, one that Percy had heard only once or twice in her life.

But before she could ask anything or demand answers, the younger female stood, smiled, and said in an accent that sounded like Percy's, "Hi, my name's Violet! And it was also my fault. I'm kind of loud sometimes. My dad says most of the time, but..." She paused, put a hand to one side of her mouth, and whispered, "I don't believe him."

The two males both had dark hair, but one had gray eyes and the other brown. The one with gray eyes turned around more in his chair and said, "I'm Bronx, Violet's father. And this is Tristan and his mate, Melanie. What should we call you?"

She eyed each of the four people, looking for any signs of deceit, or forced smiles, or anything to suggest they might be part of some doctor's mad scheme, ones they used to test her on various shite.

But the flashing pupils were real, and if anything, the one named Bronx let his curiosity shine in his eyes, along with some sort of emotion she'd never seen in her life.

However, none of that crap mattered. She last remembered Denny shooting her with a tranquilizer dart, a blond dragonman, and then waking up here. She blurted, "Where am I?"

Percy expected them to tell her to shut the fuck up. However, the younger female, named Violet, spoke up, rocking on her toes and back to her heels. "This is Clan Stonefire. We're in the Lake District, not too far from Manchester. Do you know where either of those places are?"

For a second, shame rushed through her. She hadn't attended school since she was twelve, when she'd been sold to the facility, and hadn't been allowed to read anything over the last seven years except for the signs or notes on the wall.

She sure as hell hadn't been given a map or a guide to the UK. Although, to be honest, their accents didn't mean they were still in the UK. "No. Where the hell is this? England?"

Violet nodded. "Yes, but—"

Bronx cut off his daughter, his tone gentle. "This is Ava and Joey's home. Thank you for taking care of them."

No one had ever thanked Percy for anything. Ever. And she didn't know what to say.

Then she remembered she knew nothing about these bloody people and fell back on her take-no-shit armor. "If this is their home, then where's Ava's uncle? He made a deal with me, and I need to talk to him about it."

The female—human, yes, she smelled human, like all the guards and doctors—named Melanie spoke up. "Bram's super busy with all the cleanup from rescuing you and the others. He'll visit when he can, I'm sure. For now, we're just here to keep you company. Are you hungry? Need some new clothes? Want to play a card game with us? Just let us know, and we'll see what we can do."

The human's smile was so warm that Percy decided it had to be fake. No one was nice without wanting something. "Even if I wanted food, why should I trust you? I only eat food I make myself."

Violet jumped in. "Well, there's food in the kitchen, I think." She took a step toward her. "Are you strong enough to stand?"

Bronx murmured, "Violet."

"What, Dad? She's hungry. And maybe she just wants to get up and move a little. I can barely stand staying in bed, even when I'm sick. Maybe she's the same way." She turned back toward Percy. "Are you?"

She took a second to study the female, who was younger than she was. The girl had medium-brown hair and brown eyes, with a few freckles on her nose and a constant smile on her face. She wondered if this was what normal people looked like if they had families. Even if she didn't know anything about them, the looks shared between Bronx and Violet at least said they didn't hate each other.

And in all her time inside the prison, the younger ones had always been more honest. Scared as well, true. But after a while, prisoners learned not to feel anything so they could keep going.

Most did that, at any rate. The few who hadn't found a way to cope had taken their own lives.

But Percy had stayed strong, determined to make her dream of flying a reality, no matter what.

Before she could think better of it, she said, "The only thing I really think about is if I'll ever have my inner dragon again."

She paused, willing herself to keep it together. For a brief few months, her inner beast had been her only friend. But she couldn't show such weakness to strangers, so she continued, "I want to learn how to fly. How can I make that happen?"

For a beat, she waited to see if the males would growl, or yell, or stalk over and slap her—all stuff the guards had done any time she'd challenged them or spoken out of turn.

Unlike most of the other prisoners, she'd never lost that core spirit. Percy had always thought that pissing off the guards was a way to pass the time, a game to keep her sane.

And it'd worked.

Bronx spoke. "You need to talk to Bram, Ava's uncle and the clan leader, before we can answer any of that."

"So you lot are just my babysitters?"

Melanie took a few steps closer to Percy's bed. That stupid warm smile made Percy wary, but she didn't scurry away. She needed to feel out these people to figure out her new survival plan.

One of the males said, "Don't get any closer."

Melanie stopped, waved a hand in dismissal, and kept her gaze on Percy. "I don't think she'll hurt me."

Percy shook her head. "How the fuck do you know that?"

"Let's just say that I have a lot of practice with growly, outwardly asshole temperaments and know it often hides some wounds."

Percy blinked. "What the hell are you talking about?"

Melanie glanced at Tristan and back at her. "That's a story for later. But let's just say I don't think you'll hurt me. And even if you haven't talked to Bram yet, my mate is a teacher and helps young dragon-shifters learn how to control their beasts—how to shift, fly, all that kind of stuff. So if you have questions, I'm sure he can answer them."

She eyed the human and then the frowning dragonman, Tristan. Then she realized something. "Wait, he's your mate? But you're human. How's that possible? Dragon-shifters hate humans and abandon any half-babies like me."

Fuck. She hadn't meant to let that slip.

Melanie's eyes widened. "Why would you say that? Tristan and I have twins, and everyone here adores them, not caring that I'm their mother."

"You're just lying to make me feel better." She scooted away from the human. "Leave me the fuck alone. I'll wait for this clan leader bloke before I say anything else."

Violet chimed in. "My mother was human too. And you've met my dad here, who's a dragon-shifter. No one's ever scoffed at me for my parentage. Oh, some of the lads call me annoying, or some people say I talk too much or ask too many questions. But that's just who I am, and their words have nothing to do with my blood and DNA or whatever. Whoever told you that lied to you."

Percy looked between Violet and Melanie, trying to look for deceit or, at the very least, to figure out what sort of game they were playing. It would be perfect of them to tell her what she wanted to hear, that she wasn't a freak on so many levels.

Bronx said quietly, "Let's leave Percy alone. Violet can fetch some sandwich ingredients, and we can all make them in here. That way, Percy can see we're all eating the same food, and she can make it herself. How does that sound?"

He stared straight at her, his eyes flashing, but merely alert and not pissed off.

"You're asking me? Why?"

Some emotion flashed through his eyes, but then it was gone. "Because that's what normal people usually do. There are bastards who dictate, of course. But usually you ask a person if they want something, give them a choice, and try to respect their wishes." He glanced at his daughter. "If it's within reason. Sneaking out and trying to hitch a ride to a human city at twelve most definitely doesn't fit that category."

Violet shrugged. "I had to try. No one was telling me anything, and I wanted more information to add to my journal."

Bronx took his daughter's hand. "I'm sorry I dismissed your wishes as a waste of time. I had no idea that it was so important to you."

Violet smiled at her dad. "I know. You said so back then. And since then, you've helped me loads to fill up the notebook. Although I still need some information. And you promised when I turn sixteen and get my dragon-shifter tattoo, that we'd visit Birmingham." She looked at Percy. "That's the human city my mother was from."

Was. "She's dead?"

Violet nodded. "Yes. She died giving birth to me."

Percy's head swam from so much information: Bronx asking her a question and giving her a choice; learning Violet was also a half-human, half-dragon female; and watching a dad actually care about his daughter and, not only that, but freely apologizing to her. She had absolutely no bloody idea how to process it all. Their actions went against everything she'd been taught and told her whole life. Had someone lied to her on purpose? Or were these people part of an elaborate scheme to see if she would fall for kindness bullshit?

She never took her eyes from the four people as she rubbed the sides of her temples. For once, she wished she didn't have to second-guess every little thing.

But of course that would never fucking happen. Nothing good ever happened to her, and no one ever told her the truth.

Bronx cleared his throat. "Go get the sandwich stuff, Violet. And Tristan can go with you, to bring the drinks."

Tristan grunted. "There's no bloody way I'm leaving Melanie alone in here."

Melanie walked to her mate and placed a hand on his arm. "How about Tristan and I go get the stuff? You and Violet can stay here." She switched her gaze to Percy. "Sound good?"

Tired of trying to figure out whatever game these people were playing, Percy nodded.

As soon as Tristan and Melanie left, Violet moved a chair a little closer to the bed, facing her. Once she sat down, she swung her legs and said, "Percy's a pretty good name, better than being named for a flower."

She glanced at her dad and winked, and Bronx smiled. "Your mother wanted it, and you know that, so stop grumbling."

Violet laughed. "I know, I know." She moved her gaze back to Percy. "Still, it's pretty cool."

Percy wanted to hold back, to not give anything else away. But something about this teenaged girl made Percy want to trust her, which was bloody ridiculous.

However, her name wasn't going to give anything away; they could find it in the files from the research facility. So she took a deep breath and replied, "I was given the name Persephone Smith at the orphanage where I grew up. All of the kids had names from mythology."

Not that they'd taught them any of the mythology related to their names. No, Percy had barely learned to write and read simple books before she'd been sold off.

Violet said, "Well, Persephone was the wife of the ruler of the Underworld, Hades. I'm not sure if that's a good thing or a bad thing. I'm fairly sure she had to divide her time between worlds or something like that. Dad? Is that right?"

Percy moved her gaze to Bronx, and he nodded. "Yes. She spent half the time in the Underworld and half the time on Earth with her mother, or so one version goes. There are all sorts of conflicting points about whether she wanted to be there or her mother wanted her there, and it goes on and on. But she straddled two worlds." He nodded toward her. "Which fits, I think, if your mother was human but your father was a dragon-shifter."

She highly doubted the staff at the orphanage had thought that deeply about her name, especially since all of the children had been half and half like her.

Although she'd been the only one with a birthmark, or the mark of a freak, as the other kids had called it.

She nearly raised a hand to touch her neck where

the mark was the strongest, but resisted. She'd made that mistake in the early days at the research place, and the guards had quickly used it to belittle her.

Now, she didn't give as much of a fuck. But she wouldn't share even that little weakness with these strangers.

Used to silence, Percy merely sat on the bed, her knees pulled up to her chest, her arms wrapped around them.

Violet, on the other hand, didn't stay quiet for long. "Well, we have the half dragon-shifter thing in common. So you know, if you have any questions about being half-human and half-dragon, you can ask me. I don't know everything, although I know heaps. And there are lots of kids here now that are like us, more than when I was growing up. Maybe we could form a club or something." She lowered her voice. "Although we should maybe watch out for Mel and Tristan's twins. They're always getting into trouble."

Melanie's voice filled the room. "I heard that."

Percy expected the human to yell, or scold, or do something in retaliation. But Melanie merely smiled and shook her head before adding, "And it's true sometimes. But they're kind and giving, when they want to be. Give them some time to grow up. Maybe when their inner dragons start talking, it'll help tame some of their extra energy. Tristan says it can help since the inner dragon becomes a lifelong distraction, so I have my fingers crossed."

The way they all casually discussed their lives, their children, and even their inner dragons was weird to Percy. Even in the orphanage, everything had been about keeping or trading secrets, trying to find allies, and generally keeping most people at a distance.

Because if someone didn't know your weakness, they couldn't strike out and hurt you.

But already, Melanie had revealed a massive weakness—her children. And Percy guessed it was the same with Bronx and Violet.

Didn't they see how dangerous that could be? She blurted, "You know nothing about me, so why are you being so open? I could be here as some sort of spy, set up this whole thing, and will be rescued when I give the word."

Tristan narrowed his eyes. "Are you a spy?"

Why, oh why, had she opened her mouth? She didn't like the anger brewing in his brown-eyed gaze.

Although poking the bear might show her what she believed deep down—this place wouldn't be any better than the other two places she'd lived in her life.

And once she knew the truth, she could plan better and adapt, because no matter what, she would find a way to escape and be reunited with her inner dragon. "If I was, would I admit it?"

They stared at one another, but it was Violet who spoke up. "I don't think you're a spy."

She blinked. "What?"

"I think you're uncomfortable and angry and confused at everything that's happened. I know I would be. And you're not used to being around nice people, and so you see us like everyone else—the enemy. Getting us angry is what you know, right? So you want us angry with you. And, well, I'm not. I already know I want to be your friend, if you let me. You seem like you could use a friend."

Who the hell is this teenager? She was too bloody observant, which, indeed, made Percy uncomfortable. She could handle someone's anger—it was any other emotion she had trouble with. "I don't need any fucking friends. People only ever care about themselves."

Bronx spoke up. "I don't know about anyone else, but I'm starving. Let's make some sandwiches, and maybe by the time we're done, Bram will stop by to chat with you, Percy."

It was clearly a change in topic, but Percy was fine with it. Her stomach rumbled, and being hungry always triggered anxiety because food hadn't always been reliable for her.

And yet, she didn't think she could willingly walk over to the group of people. If it was a trap or experiment, they might grab her. One of them would pin her down, and they'd do whatever the fuck they wanted to her—probably rape her for more fucking fertility experiments.

So she stayed put.

She didn't think anyone noticed she hadn't moved until Violet called out, "What do you want—ham or turkey? And cheese? There's only cheddar. And salad?"

She paused, but at Violet's gaze, she murmured, "Ham, cheese, and tomato."

Violet gestured everyone to step back from the table and then looked at Percy. "Just so you can watch me take it from the same place as everyone else."

And as Violet dramatically took out the ingredients

and piled them on the plate, for a brief moment, Percy started to like this young female.

But then she pushed it aside. She still didn't know enough about any of them.

As she put together her sandwich and ate it, she watched the other four interact. None of them asked her any more questions. They merely joked, laughed, and bickered as if it were any other day.

She wondered yet again if this was how normal people acted. Maybe one day, she'd find out, but she doubted it. After all, no one had given a shit about her since the day she was born. There was no reason to ever think that would change.

Chapter Four

Bronx did his best to watch Percy from the corners of his eyes while he kept his main attention on the other three people in the room. She wore a permanently guarded look, with occasional flashes of longing, and the sight made his heart ache for her.

Not pity, as she'd been resourceful and a survivor, for sure, to have lasted so long. However, if she'd been told her heritage was shameful, disgusting, or any other such rubbish, she'd spent far too many years believing a lie.

His inner dragon spoke up. *She seems to do well with Violet.*

I know. But I'm still keeping a close eye on Percy, though. I wouldn't trust her alone with Violet.

Yet, is what you're thinking.

I want to believe she's not a spy or an enemy or a threat to our clan. But there's still far too much we don't know about her.

What we know is bad enough.

Even him just giving Percy a few choices had baffled the female. She clearly had never been in charge of anything, and he would make an extra effort to ask her opinion on things as much as possible.

She probably yearned for some kind of control over her life, but he couldn't give that until they knew she wasn't a threat.

Not wanting to overwhelm Percy, he focused on Violet, Melanie, and Tristan as they all ate. Ignoring her didn't sit right with him, though. He wanted to help her, even if he knew it would take time.

Still, part of him wished they could make her inner dragon return right away, show her how to shift, and maybe see happiness or joy in her eyes for the first time as she did it.

Not only because it would make her happy, but it would also prove he was still useful. Even if he couldn't lead rescue missions because of his leg, he could still help others.

His dragon growled. *Don't start. We're alive and here for Violet. That should be enough.*

Yes, he knew that. However, ever since he'd failed his late mate, Edith, he'd tried to make up for it by helping or saving as many people as possible. He could never fully erase his guilt surrounding Edith's fate, but at least he could try to make his late mate as proud as possible.

His dragon said gently, *She would be proud of us. And not just because of your rescue work over the years. Violet's happy —most of the time—and turning out to be a brilliant young female.*

Don't remind me. She'll get her dragon tattoo before you know it, and a couple of years later, she'll move out.

That's what happens to all children. Besides, that's the goal of being a parent—to teach them what they need to know to navigate life on their own, discover themselves, and to pass on beliefs, such as how kindness is better than cruelty.

Kindness was one of the things his mother had always instilled in her three sons. Sometimes his middle brother, Brooklyn, forgot that. He was a huge gossip, but even so, Brooklyn had never crossed the line into being malicious. His youngest brother, Hudson, was maybe the kindest of them all, and Bronx was grateful his little brother had found a second chance at happiness with Sarah. Bronx was content to live vicariously through his brothers and mates because he didn't deserve another chance himself.

Before his dragon could sigh and argue with him, there was a knock at the door. Bronx answered, opening it just a fraction so as to not overwhelm Percy any further, and saw it was Stonefire's clan leader, Bram.

Bram asked, "Is she well enough to chat?"

Bronx burned to ask what else Bram had discovered from the Protectors about Percy's former prison, but he would have to save those questions for later. "Let's ask her."

He opened the door and motioned for Bram to stay put. He met Percy's wary gaze. "This is Ava's uncle, Bram, who you talked with on the phone. You said earlier you wanted to chat with him. Are you still up for it?"

She frowned a beat, like she always did when he

asked her permission, and then nodded. "Yes. I want to sort out our agreement. The sooner I can embrace my dragon and learn to fly, the sooner I can leave."

Bronx glanced at Bram, asking with his eyes if he should mention how Percy would need to live with a dragon clan.

Violet spoke before either of them could. "But where would you go? Dragon-shifters have to live with a dragon clan. Well, unless you're one of the awful people who didn't want humans here. They were banished and live in a forest somewhere, probably. But you shouldn't do that. You should stay here with us. There's heaps to learn still, and I can help you."

Bram spoke up. "That's a brilliant idea, Violet."

Bronx blinked. "What are you talking about?"

"Well, if Percy wants to learn how to embrace and deal with her dragon, she'll need teachers. Tristan is busy with the school and can only help sometimes, and it's the same with the other teaching staff. However, you and Violet can do the bulk of her training, consulting with others when needed."

Bronx frowned. "I still don't understand why you want to include Violet."

Bram shrugged. "Violet's also a half-human dragon-shifter, and younger as well. Her memory will be fresher when it comes to the early days of talking with her beast. And, Bronx, you have long-term experience in how to build a relationship that's equal between the human and dragon halves, which Percy will need help with, given she's an adult already. The pair of you working together makes sense. So what do you say?"

Even though Bram had asked a question, Bronx sensed there really wasn't a choice. He'd known he'd be working with Percy a lot until Dr. Rossi returned, but he hadn't expected for his daughter to be so involved.

His dragon spoke up. *I think it's a good idea, and it'll distract Violet for a while from her human fact-finding mission.*

That mission could lead to the full truth about Edith's past, which Bronx had mostly kept from his daughter to protect her.

Violet clapped her hands. "Oh, please, Daddy. Can't I help?"

Bronx narrowed his eyes at her sweet tone. His daughter hadn't called him anything but Dad for years. She was buttering him up.

Percy asked, "Do I get a say in this?"

All eyes moved to her. She had curled up again, her legs close to her chest and her arms wrapped around them. Even Bronx knew that was a protective posture, as if by keeping as much distance as possible from everyone else, it would save her from harm.

He asked, "What do you think, then, Percy?"

She looked at Bram. "Even if you can easily break it, I want a promise that I can stay here until I learn how to talk with my dragon and shift. If I have to offer my body to anyone who wants it in exchange for food and a place to stay, I'll do it."

The room fell deathly silent. Bronx couldn't have been the only one struck dumb by her words.

Bram was the first to speak, his voice gentle. "There's no need for that, lass. You sleep with whoever you want or no one at all. That's up to you. I'm sure we can find something else for you to do inside the clan to pay your way. But not until you're better and the doctors give the all-clear. You need to heal, and once you're ready, talk to my security team more about the facility we rescued you from, if possible."

She frowned. "I don't know how much I can tell you, really. I only know my experience and a few days here or there with new inmates."

Bram replied, "Aye, but that's better than nothing. They're an enemy to us both, and the sooner I can find out who they're working for or with, and eradicate them, the better."

Percy studied Bram and looked at Violet and then at Bronx. For the first time, he noticed her eyes were hazel, but more gold than green.

Had they ever been filled with laughter or happiness? And why did he care so much?

Percy's response brought him back to the room. "I still need a promise I can stay here. And if you give it and let me have a place to stay and cook my own food, I'll do whatever you ask me to do, even if you change your mind about me needing to fuck some people to pay my way."

Bloody hell. Just how many bastards had taken advantage of her inside the facility, to the point she would so causally offer her body as if it didn't matter? Anger flared, and he quickly tamped it down. The last thing he wanted to do was frighten her.

Bram nodded. "You can stay here until you're ready to leave, provided you don't try to fuck over my clan. If you do, then I'll hand you over to the DDA." At her blank look, he explained, "The Department of Dragon Affairs. They're the human governmental agency who oversees and sometimes protects dragon-shifters."

She laughed bitterly. "I call bullshit. If they were supposed to protect dragon-shifters, then where the bloody hell have they been my entire life?"

Bram didn't bat an eyelash. "They're not perfect and have only really gotten on our good side in recent years, but they are more an ally than an enemy. And regardless of what you think, if you break the law, they'll put you in prison. So listen to what all your teachers say and take notes. We can also give you a book of the rules to memorize."

Percy said nothing, and Bronx swore she tensed.

But in the next moment, Percy shrugged. "I'm not going to kill anyone unless they attack me first. And I know how to keep to myself and stay out of trouble. I doubt I'll have to worry about this DDA or whatever."

She would have to talk to a few DDA staff soon enough, but he didn't breathe a word. Neither did Bram. And for once, Violet kept quiet too.

Bram said, "As for you having your own place, you can stay in this cabin until the doctor clears your health."

"My health? I feel fine. A little tired, but I've suffered a hell of a lot worse."

Bronx curled the fingers of one hand into a fist to keep from growling or frowning. The more hints he heard about her past, the angrier he got.

Bram didn't hesitate. "It'll be difficult when your dragon wakes up." *If* she wakes up, everyone else thought but didn't say. "And in case your dragon acts out or goes rogue, staying in this cabin will keep you from hurting my clan. I want you to come live with us some day, Percy. I do. But I'm sure you understand that if your dragon takes control and goes a bit mad, it could hurt a lot of people."

Her voice was so quiet, Bronx could barely hear her. "I only talked with my dragon for a month or two before she went away, so I have no idea how any of that works. We were too afraid, the both of us, to ever show emotions."

Both man and beast wanted to go over and comfort her. For a dragon-shifter to meet their dragon and then be torn away so soon after was cruel. And given what he knew of Percy's isolation so far, having her inner beast might've made a world of difference.

And right here, right now, she didn't look like a guarded, jaded female lashing out. She looked like a lonely and lost young female who didn't know what to do next.

Bronx spoke up. "Well, that's what me, Violet, Tristan, and the others will help with—we'll teach you how to be a dragon-shifter. Plus, there is someone in our clan who had a silent dragon for a while, and she was eventually reunited. They're good friends again. So it's possible."

He didn't think Dr. Sid would mind the vague story sharing since it was common knowledge on Stonefire. Maybe the doctor would eventually give more details about what to expect, if not to Percy, then at least to Bronx.

Hope flickered a second before Percy's usual wariness returned. "Well, I'm sure I'll find out."

Since Percy didn't say anything else, Bram

continued. "As I said, you can have this cabin. You have free rein over everything inside it and can go as far as the hedges around it, which gives you the back garden. However, don't wander anywhere else until we chat again. If you try to escape, then I'll have to be harsher, and I really don't want to do that, lass. Understand?"

Percy shrugged, which wasn't exactly an answer, but Bram nodded anyway. "Good. Then I need to go and tend to my niece. Thank you for helping her and Joey, Percy. I'll do my best to repay you, aye?"

She mumbled, "We'll see."

After another moment, Bram turned toward Bronx. "The nurse is waiting in the kitchen to come check on Percy. She said she'll stay the night to watch over her, although I hope you and Violet will stay in one of the cabins nearby."

He glanced at Violet, who was being more restrained than usual. Even she must sense how hurt and damaged Percy was.

His dragon growled. *We need to find out if Kai and the others taught those bastards a lesson.*

I doubt they'll have killed them, if it could be avoided. The DDA will only accept so many deaths for a rescue operation.

Regardless, the motherfuckers deserve to die.

His dragon's vehemence shocked him for a second, but then he pushed it away. *Let's focus our energy on Percy and not them. It'll be more worthwhile.*

His beast grumbled, which meant he'd try.

Bronx met Percy's gaze again. "Is that okay, for me and Violet to stay in a nearby cabin? Or would you rather someone else—maybe a female?—watch over you and we only come for lessons?"

He needed to stay close, and yet, he knew Percy needed to have some sort of say in the matter. If she said no, he'd have to work out a plan with Bram.

She replied, "I don't care. As long as I get some dragon lessons, that's all that matters."

He nodded. "I'll have some books sent over tonight so you can get started. I'll have to wait for Dr. Sid to clear you before you can do more than learn information. But once she does, then we'll really start your lessons and work on coaxing out your dragon and training her. Okay?"

She lifted one shoulder.

He gently turned Violet toward the door. "Then let's go, and we'll send the nurse in to take a look at you."

Percy grunted and stared at her toes, as if they were the most interesting thing in the world.

She was most definitely a puzzle he wanted to crack. Still, he didn't want to overwhelm her.

Once they went to the kitchen and sent the nurse to Percy's room, Melanie and Tristan left with Violet in tow.

When alone with Bronx, the clan leader said, "She doesn't even know what's coming, if she follows the same pathway as Sid or Killian."

Killian was an Irish dragon-shifter whose dragon had gone silent because of too many drugs. He'd ended up with one of the first recorded two-headed inner dragons as a result. Sid had also had a silent dragon because of too many drugs, and she had nearly gone insane before her beast burst forth and made her life difficult. If not for Sid finding her true mate in Dr.

Gregor Innes, Bronx had no idea what would've happened to her.

He was going to do his bloody best to use all the knowledge he could gather from others and ensure Percy could at least get her dragon back. Bronx replied, "We'll find out soon enough. Giving her the cabin and even some resources will help some, I think. She knows nothing about dragon-shifters, Bram. Almost nothing. Her whole life has been filled with lies."

Bram grimaced. "Aye, I've been learning that from what the Protectors discovered inside that facility. We're also looking into this orphanage, to see if it still exists. Once we know more, I'll share it with you."

Bronx nodded. "The more I know, the better plan I can craft. Although, I already fucking hate what I've learned."

Bram rubbed a hand over his face. "Aye, it's bloody awful. I think when we were focusing on taking down the Dragon Knights, the dragon hunters quietly amped-up their secret projects. I'm hoping Lucien and Nate can break the encryption on the computers and learn the full truth."

The two males were in charge of IT stuff for the Protectors.

Bronx said, "They'll also ask Arabella if they need more help."

Arabella MacLeod, Tristan's sister, was good with computers and had mated the Scottish dragon clan leader of Lochguard. They still relied on her sometimes to help the clan. She had also experienced troubles with her inner dragon due to trauma, and Bronx might have to ask her for help too.

Bram sighed. "Aye, and Finn will make sure I'm grateful enough for it." He sobered. "At any rate, thanks in advance to you and Violet. I thought it best not to overwhelm her with a single male. Besides, Violet has a way about her that makes people smile, and even from that brief encounter, I can tell Percy needs it." He gripped Bronx's shoulder, squeezed, and released it. "Since Dr. Rossi postponed the meeting until tomorrow, I need to go back to Ava. Evie has her in hand, but with her dad still in Ireland and recently losing her mum, she's struggling a bit. Keep me informed of what's going on and don't hesitate to ask for what you need."

With a nod, Bram left, and Bronx finally let out a long sigh as he ran his hands through his hair. It was going to be a long night, especially since he had so much to look up and to ask Dr. Rossi about. Even without the conference video meeting, she always took his calls or answered his emails. He would have plenty to ask in the coming days, no doubt.

As he left the cabin and headed back toward Stonefire so he could pack and collect his daughter, Bronx made a list of everything he'd need to cover with the female. He refused to miss an important detail, make her struggle or give up, and fail her. Even though it couldn't make up for his past, he wouldn't fail Percy if he could help it. She would befriend her dragon and shift one day, if it was the last thing he ever did.

Chapter Five

Even though Percy's whole body sagged with exhaustion once she was alone again, she couldn't sleep.

And not just because she kept eyeing the books on the side table, ones she could barely make sense of. She remembered easy words, but there were complicated ones that a twelve-year-old never would've known. Yes, she might've heard them at some point over the last eight years, but English pronunciations didn't always make sense.

Sighing, she stared back up at the ceiling. *Dragon, where are you? Will you come out?*

Silence.

Not that she'd expected anything else. Sometimes, when she'd come close to showing emotion when she shouldn't have, Percy had talked inside her head to her dragon as if she were still there. But while that had been for comfort, maybe now that she was free of the facility and all their tests, just regular talking would help bring out her beast.

The nurse had explained how she'd been given a drug for years to keep her inner dragon silent, and now without it, her dragon might burst through at any moment. However, no one knew what would happen if she did. If Percy's beast was out of control, they'd have to silence her again.

She rubbed her eyes with the heels of her hands, not wanting to think of that outcome. Her head pounded from both the aftereffects of the tranquilizer and the information overload. It was still weird how they'd revealed so much. It was almost as if things were going right for once in her life.

Although given her track record, shit would hit the fan when she stopped being careful or let her guard down for even a second.

The curtain fluttered, and a soft breeze brushed over her face. Even just the air against her skin was new, something she hadn't felt in years, and she took a second to memorize how it felt. Her eyes trailed to the window.

She'd been putting off this moment, not wanting to be disappointed if her first glimpse of the outside world in more than seven years didn't live up to her memories. But not looking was cowardly, and if nothing else, she was determined to avoid being weak since her dragon might need her strength.

Staring at the billowing curtain, she took a deep breath and finally rolled out of bed and padded toward it.

Peeling the curtains back, she looked at the bright

moon in the sky, the outline of the trees, and even the faint stars twinkling in the patches of sky not covered with clouds.

There was so much open space, it nearly overwhelmed her. Years of living inside essentially three rooms had taken a toll.

But she'd come this far and wouldn't stop now. Opening the window all the way, she pressed a hand against the screen and simply enjoyed the fresh air, the slight chill, and the view of something other than a manmade wall. It was so simple, and yet her eyes heated with tears as she watched something fly in the sky. Even if she couldn't make it out, just being able to see life in motion was special.

Although as she continued to memorize everything in sight, she grew greedy. After devouring this small slice of the outdoors with her eyes, she wanted more, so much more. And since the nurse had rushed off to attend an emergency, no one would see her in case she lost control of her emotions.

So Percy dashed out of the bedroom and to the kitchen and gripped the handle of the back door. For one beat, then two, she waited. It'd been so long, but she needed to stop being afraid of how maybe her memories had lied to her about how the earth would feel under her bare feet.

After opening the door, she stepped outside onto the small patio and stopped in the middle of it. The breeze blew stronger out here, and faint sounds of animal life filled her ears. She tilted her face toward the moon.

As a child, she'd often stared at the bright circle,

wishing she could be there, away from everything else. To start over someplace new, where she could welcome other outcasts like herself and finally fit in.

It was all naïve bullshit, of course. She'd never get to the moon—let alone be able to live there—and there was no little haven for those who were different from everyone else.

Since she was alone, Percy touched the birthmark on her neck. She would always stick out, no matter where she went.

She had no idea how long she stood there staring at the sky and memorizing the feel of the patio and then the nearby dirt under her toes, but eventually, she shivered and went back inside.

Leaning against the closed door, she shut her eyes and imagined flying through the night sky, soaring among the stars, and for the first time in her life, being free.

And that image, that wish, she fixed into her mind. She would accomplish it, no matter what. After all, she'd gone through hell over the years. How bad could it be to work with her inner dragon when she finally woke up?

Chapter Six

Bronx woke up early the next morning and headed to the kitchen of their temporary cabin. Violet usually slept later than he did, and he was a little relieved to find the room empty. He'd have time to think through his planned activities for the day as he made breakfast. Violet would be excited to go visit Percy again—his daughter had talked nonstop about it the night before—and would try to rush him out the cabin. But if she didn't eat, she'd be grumpy, and no one needed that complication.

He took out the ingredients for pancakes and went to work on the batter. Just as he placed the frying pan on the burner and went to grab some bacon, a piercing scream rang through the air, followed by another.

It sounded as if someone were being tortured.

Within seconds, he stood outside, scanning the surroundings. Another scream erupted, coming from the direction of Percy's cabin.

His beast spoke up. *If her dragon came out, we need to go help her. The nurse might not be able to handle her by herself.*

Violet asked sleepily from behind him, "Who's screaming?"

"Vi, stay here, okay? I need to go check on Percy."

"But I want to help."

More screaming rent the air. "And you can help by fetching a doctor and bringing them to Percy's place. Can you do that?" She nodded, and he added, "I'm going on ahead. Call me if you need to."

With that, he grabbed his mobile phone and ran out of the yard, down the path, and up the walkway to Percy's place.

The closer he went, the louder the cries grew.

He tried the front door, but it was locked. He reached above the door trim until he found the spare key and opened the door. The never-ending screaming reverberated through the house.

His dragon growled. *I don't like this. I thought the doctors said it'd take longer for her dragon to wake up? And where's the nurse?*

Bronx had noticed the lack of sound of someone else in the cabin, apart from Percy. *They said they weren't completely sure about her dragon. The inmates had been given loads of drugs, and who the hell knows what it's done to Percy's system? And maybe she knocked the nurse unconscious.*

Just help her.

If his dragon seemed overly concerned about Percy, he paid it no attention.

Bronx finally reached her room, knocked, and said, "I'm coming in, Percy."

He didn't expect a reply beyond the tortured cries,

and he was right. Rushing inside, he saw Percy on the bed, arching her back and scratching at the sides of her face. At the blood trailing down her face, both man and beast growled.

There was no sign of the nurse.

In two strides, he was on the bed. He took her wrists in his hands, pinning them to the mattress. "Percy, can you hear me? Percy!"

She screamed and writhed some more, bucking as if she were trying to get away from something.

If it were her dragon, she'd never be able to do that since her beast was a part of her.

If she was having a nightmare, then he'd deal with that later, once he calmed her down.

Fuck, fuck, fuck. But how? He kept his grip on her wrists firm yet as gentle as he could as he said, "Percy, listen to me. If you can hear me at all and if your dragon has woken up, you need to fight for control. Dragons usually respond to firm tones and strict instructions. Try giving her one and tell her to calm down. If that doesn't work, maybe try singing to her, or even imagine constructing an imaginary wall around her, to contain her."

She continued to squirm and pulled against his grip, and the actions hurt his heart.

"Percy, did you hear me?"

Her screams grew a little fainter, but it still felt as if someone were stabbing him with each and every one. All he could do was keep her wrists in place and pin her legs down so she wouldn't hurt herself.

His dragon said, *Try singing to her. That always worked with Edith.*

Their late mate had suffered nightmares about her ex-boyfriend for the entirety of their short mating. One time, he'd tried singing, and it had helped to wake her up.

Without thinking, he started crooning an old-fashioned dragon ballad about a dragonwoman who lost her clan and spent years searching for them. Eventually, she was reunited, found her true mate, and helped to forge ties with the other clans she'd met during her journey.

It was long, and at first, Bronx didn't think it was doing anything. However, as he neared the final verse, Percy struggled a little less and stopped screaming.

After he sang the final note, she acted up again. And so Bronx sang the same song over and over again, until Dr. Sid and Dr. Gregor Innes dashed into the room.

Dr. Sid stopped near Percy's head and quickly murmured, "I'm sorry I have to do this, Percy. I truly am." Then she took out a syringe, made sure there was no air, and injected the contents.

Within seconds, Percy went slack.

And as Bronx perched over Percy, staring at her scratched face, blood drying on her cheeks and jaw, he felt like he'd already failed her.

His dragon spoke up. *No, this is all because of those human bastards who hurt her. We'll look after her, and it'll help. You'll see.*

Dr. Innes put a hand on Bronx's shoulder, and he jumped a little. The doctor's familiar Scottish accent brought him back to reality. "It's all right, Bronx. You can release her now, aye? We'll look after her."

Slowly, ever so slowly, he released his grip on Percy's wrists. He almost brushed her cheeks but resisted. Not only because it was wrong on so many levels, but also because Bronx had no right to it. Percy deserved to choose who touched her when she wasn't in danger, either from herself or from others. Always.

He backed off the bed and watched as the two doctors examined Percy and tended to her wounds. He should've been patient, but he blurted, "What did you give her?"

Dr. Sid glanced at him before continuing her work on Percy. "A regular sedative. I probably should've given her the dragon silent drug, but I can't bring myself to do it. She's had too many doses as it is, and I don't want to give her the one that might steal her dragon away forever."

Since Dr. Sid had lived exactly that scenario—it'd been decades before her dragon had returned—he understood her reasoning. "But if it was her dragon just now, won't this just happen again when she wakes up?"

Dr. Sid sighed. "Maybe. Maybe not. We really should restrain her, Bronx, until we know how her dragon will act." He growled, but before he could say a word, the doctor continued, "I understand why you don't want us to do it, given her past. And I know you're protective, and always have been. However, what if you hadn't heard her cries and come to stop her from hurting herself? She might've scratched her eyes out, or if the dragon figured out how to extend a talon, maybe even sliced her throat." She met his gaze again. "And I can't risk that happening."

"Where was the bloody nurse who was supposed to watch over her?"

Sid replied, "We had an emergency with one of the other rescued prisoners. Ginny's still there, trying to hold things together whilst we're here."

He growled. "Someone needs to watch over Percy. You can't just leave her alone. Not just because she might hurt herself again, but someone needs to be here when she wakes up so she knows she's not alone and back in her prison quarters."

And hopefully she wouldn't think Stonefire was the same as her old living situation.

Dr. Sid raised an eyebrow. "Let me guess—you want it to be you? But that's not a good idea, Bronx. One of the newer prisoners we rescued shared how most of the guards—who were all male—abused her. If she wakes up out of sorts, she could easily think you're one of them. Who knows what might happen then."

Clenching his fingers into fists, he hated how the doctor was right. "It doesn't have to be me, but someone needs to sit with her."

Dr. Sid moved so Dr. Innes could finish patching up Percy. "Bram has been working on that already. As long as a male strong enough to restrain her if something happens stays in one of the other rooms, he'll rotate through various females in the clan. If she's restrained, she won't be able to hurt them. And if somehow she does break free, the male guard can protect them."

For some reason, the thought of another male watching over Percy didn't sit well with man or beast. "Who?"

Dr. Sid rolled her eyes. "The way you're acting

about Percy, it's as if you're her true mate or something."

He froze. No, that wouldn't happen. It couldn't. Bronx didn't deserve another mate, or another chance, after failing his Edith.

He asked his dragon, *Is she our true mate?*

I don't know. Without her dragon, she's not whole, and I can't even guess.

Since the doctor waited for an answer, he shook his head. "Not as far as I know."

She looked about ready to say something, but Gregor turned toward them and spoke up. "Aye, well, none of that matters right now. I don't see why Bronx couldn't stay in the other room. He's the one assigned to help her anyway. Although you might have to send your daughter to stay with one of your brothers."

Violet. "Where is she, by the way?"

Gregor pointed toward the door. "We told her to wait in the living room." The corner of his mouth kicked up. "She all but herded us over here, by the way. Given her level of dominance already, she's going to be a feisty one all grown up."

Maybe he should have sighed, but he was rather proud of his daughter. "Yes, which will help her since she wants to be a doctor."

Dr. Sid bobbed her head. "She'll need every bit of confidence and determination she can muster to deal with sick dragon males." She shared a look with her mate and smiled. The sight twisted Bronx's heart, but thankfully, Dr. Sid spoke again before any memories rushed forth. "Maybe Violet could stay here with you, if you think that's okay. She can help me, Layla, or

Gregor when we look after Percy. It's always best to ensure a dragon-shifter knows what to expect for this job before committing to so many years of training."

His first thought was to say no, that Violet should stay with her uncles. But knowing his daughter—who'd managed to get to a train station when she was younger, determined to visit a human city on her own, before he'd found her in time—she would find a way to sneak back here. It was better to keep her close and help channel her energy into something more productive.

"As long as I'm here, she can be too. But just vow that if it ever gets dangerous or becomes some sort of medical procedure that could traumatize someone as young as her that you'll send her away."

Dr. Sid nodded. "Of course I vow it. I've been Violet's doctor for nearly her whole life, and I'd never want to hurt her."

The affront in the doctor's voice made him say, "Sorry, Sid. But Violet's all I have, and I don't want anything to happen to her."

The doctor's face softened. "I know." She stood straight and gestured toward Percy. "She'll sleep for quite a while, thanks to the sedative. I'll stay here whilst Gregor fetches some restraints. Nurse Ginny will probably have to take over for a bit, at least until Layla gets here. And no matter how growly you get, I don't want you in the room when Percy wakes up."

He grunted. "Although if she starts screaming again, I won't stay away."

"Fine, but keep your distance as long as she's quiet and sane. It's going to be hard enough dealing with a probably unstable dragon. I don't need her thinking she's going to be abused too."

He clenched his fingers tighter, not wanting to dwell even more on how bloody awful Percy's past had been. "Will the drug you gave her affect her beast too?"

Dr. Sid shrugged. "I don't know. I've been testing new mixtures I've devised with other dragon doctors, to find something that will help calm both the human and dragon halves without making them go entirely silent. I hate using people as test subjects without their permission, but Percy and her fellow inmates are special cases. If I can't help them straight away, I might not be able to help them at all."

If any of their dragons were allowed to go rogue, they would be punished.

He nodded. "I'll go talk to Violet and make sure she's okay with staying here. I think so, but if not, I'll let you know."

Leaving the room, Bronx rubbed a hand down his face. He should be focused on what to say to his daughter or what kind of plan to have if Percy woke up and her dragon tried to take over. And yet, he kept thinking back to Sid asking if Percy was his true mate.

And bloody hell, he hoped not. Even if she could get past his missing lower leg or the fact he had a daughter not much younger than she was, Percy was far too young—and damaged. She deserved someone her own age who could protect her, be there for her, and wasn't her true mate. Anyone who turned out to be her true mate would make her life hell because once they kissed her, it would kick off a mate-claim frenzy.

The last thing Percy needed was someone fucking

her roughly and continuously, which would probably trigger unwanted memories.

No, she needed to be healed, taught how to embrace her dragon, and learn what it was to be a dragon-shifter. Maybe she'd find someone to care for, and maybe she wouldn't.

However, it wouldn't be him. Ever. Bronx refused to fail another mate, which meant never taking one again.

Chapter Seven

Something poked at Percy as she imagined flying through the clouds. She was a human, though, and not a dragon soaring through the air. But she didn't care. The breeze felt amazing, and she was so far up that everything below was tiny.

Up in the air, no one could hurt her, control her, or even bully her. No, she was alone.

Maybe too alone, because even in her dream, she yearned for that dragon she'd known briefly, the one who'd always had her back and had cared about her. The only one to ever do so.

Something nudged at her, but she ignored it, not wanting her flight to end. But the nudging continued over and over again, as if someone were repeatedly poking her head.

Eventually, the sky faded and turned dark, almost pitch-black. The only light was in the distance—a purple glow coming from who knew where. She wanted to follow the light, and yet her instincts said not to yet.

Pain, struggle, and the total loss of freedom waited at the end of that road.

Wanting away from the temptation, she opened her eyes. It took a second for her to recognize the room, the same dark-wood and dark-blue accents from earlier.

She was in the cabin where Bronx, Violet, Melanie, and Tristan had played games.

Percy tried to sit up, but her arms wouldn't go where she wanted. Looking down, she saw cuffs. While they were padded and less painful than the metal ones she'd often worn in the facility, they still held firm when she tugged against the small chains.

She growled, "What the fuck?"

A female with some accent she didn't recognize spoke up. "Aye, I know it's a bother and probably the last thing you want, but you nearly scratched your face off, lassie."

She met the female's gaze, her pupils flashing to slits once before remaining round. The dragonwoman had dark hair, brown eyes, and light-brown skin. "Who're you?"

The stranger smiled, and somehow, it made Percy feel a little better. "I'm Dr. Layla McFarland, from Clan Lochguard in Scotland. But there are far too many doctors around here, aye? So just call me Layla."

Percy tugged at the restraints again. "Well, Layla, take these off."

The doctor shook her head. "Not yet. I need you to tell me what you remember from yesterday morning, then I'll release you."

She frowned and echoed, "Yesterday morning?"

"Aye. You've slept a little more than a day, and it's

no doubt done you good. But back to my question: what do you remember?"

Percy kept tugging at her restraints—not hard enough to hurt herself, but as if the action helped her to focus—and searched her brain.

Now that she thought about it, her cheeks and the sides of her face were sore and overly warm. Not only that, but the tips of her fingers throbbed, as if something were stuck under her nails. Looking down, sure enough, she saw some of her fingernails had blood under them. "I don't remember anything beyond looking at the moon, late at night. I fell asleep after that."

Layla sat forward, bracing her elbows on her knees. "What about now? Is there any sort of presence in your head? Or a pressure building, as if trying to burst?"

She eyed the older female. Doctors had never been Percy's friends. Something about Layla's eyes and manner made her different from all the fuckers inside the testing facility, though, almost as if she didn't look at Percy like a thing but rather a person, one who had opinions and feelings.

Don't. Just don't. The last thing Percy needed was to lower her guard and think anyone gave a shit about her. That path had caused pain in the past, and she was too old to fall for it again. "Why should I tell you?"

Layla tapped her fingertips together. "Aye, why should you? I'm not even from Stonefire, where you might want to make a good impression. However, I came all this way, leaving my two bairns with my mate and mother-in-law, so I could help the lot of you. I want all of you to recover, be free, and never have to worry about some fake doctor abusing you. I'm not sure how to convince you of that, though. So I'm open to suggestions."

She should keep her bloody mouth shut, but she blurted, "Bairns? What's that?"

Layla smiled. "Oh, aye, Sid said you might not understand some Scottish terms. It means baby, or small child, I suppose. Although some parents will refer to their children as bairns even when they're older. At any rate, I have twin boys." She took out her mobile phone, punched something, and held it out to Percy. "Have a look for yourself."

The two small sleeping babies—one had dark hair and the other blond—each clutched some sort of toy dragon in their arms. Sleeping next to them was a full-grown male, his arm protectively curled around the two children.

Layla said, "That's my mate, Chase. He's younger than me and yet somehow always manages to fall asleep first. I think it's because I have heaps of practice of running on little sleep as a doctor."

Percy studied the picture some more. The sight of a male being protective of babies was strange to her. The orphanage had been run mostly by females, and the males at the facility—well, those arseholes should stay far, far away from any child.

She resisted shivering. Instead, she maneuvered until she could lean against the headboard and pull her knees against her chest. She burned to ask what it was like to have a child—this female seemed to want hers—but instead, she asked, "Are you my new guard then?"

Layla put away her phone. "No, lass, I'm not. We

just wanted a doctor present when you woke up, to see how you acted." She gestured toward Percy. "Because of how you hurt yourself, we had to give you a sedative to calm you down. And we had no idea how it'd affect your dragon."

Ah, familiar territory. "So I'm an experiment. Again."

Layla frowned. "Not for fun, Percy. We're trying to help you."

Memories flashed of her early days at the facility, when one doctor after another said they needed to try one more thing to try to bring her dragon back—all lies, of course. Back then, she'd actually bloody sobbed at her dragon being gone. She'd been weak. And Percy had vowed to never be that way again.

She pushed aside any curiosity about the female dragon doctor or even the momentary desire to think she was different than the others. "Whatever." She raised one arm. "Can you take these off now? I want to make something to eat."

Layla searched her gaze, her pupils flashing to slits and back, and Percy wanted to shout, to ask why she couldn't have her dragon, too, and get along with her.

But no, instead she'd apparently woken up with a crazy one.

Maybe her dream was naïve and stupid.

No. She wouldn't think that. At least, not yet.

For years, that had been her reason for putting up with all the horrors inside the facility. If there was even a small chance she could embrace her beast, she would do anything for it.

The doctor finally replied, "Aye, I'll release you as

long as you vow to stay inside the cabin or its back garden until Stonefire's clan leader says otherwise."

She barked a laugh. "You think a vow means anything?"

Layla studied her, and Percy did her best not to squirm.

The doctor finally stood. "To me, aye, they mean the world. But I understand they probably don't mean anything to you just yet."

Or ever will, she thought to herself.

Layla took out a key and undid her cuffs.

As soon as her arms were free, Percy rubbed where the restraints had been. "Where's Bronx and Violet? They're supposed to give me lessons."

The dragonwoman didn't bat an eyelash at the change of topic. "They're somewhere in the cabin, waiting for you to wake up. You have in-house teachers now since they'll be staying there with you full-time."

For a beat, she wondered if Bronx would barge into her room while she was restrained and hurt her. It'd happened too many times in the past. That meant she'd just have to keep herself out of the restraints or learn how to pick them.

She always liked to have an escape plan.

A knock sounded, and Violet's voice came through the door. "I hear you two chatting. Can I come in?"

Uneasy at someone asking her for permission, she nodded first and then realized she had to speak. "Yes."

The door swung open, and Violet sauntered inside, carrying a plate of biscuits.

Percy hadn't eaten any baked goods since her thirteenth birthday and almost asked for one. Then she remembered her rule. When Violet offered the plate, she said, "No, I don't want any."

Violet frowned and looked at the biscuits. "Well, we can do this." She set it on a side table, picked up a biscuit, broke it in half, and ate one of them. After swallowing, she held out the other half. "See? If we share, then you have to know it's safe."

She watched Violet closely, looking for any changes to her pupils or coloring or anything that might signal the treats were laced with something.

But the girl merely kept smiling, moving side-to-side as if she didn't like standing still. Violet waved the biscuit half toward her. "Here. I know the doctors said you need healthy food, but sometimes biscuits just make everything better. Or ice cream. But I made these and wanted to share."

"You made them?"

Violet nodded. "For you. If you start your day with something sweet, then hopefully, it chases away the bitter dreams or nightmares."

For a beat, Percy stared at the teenaged girl. She seemed so innocent, and caring, and many more emotions that the world would take advantage of and hurt her with.

Doesn't her father see that and want to protect her?

Something stirred at the back of her mind, a tiny speck of purple light flashing at the same time, but then it died out. Percy searched, wondering if it was her dragon. *Are you there? Do you remember me?*

Silence.

Tears prickled her eyes, and she willed herself to keep them from falling. The guards and doctors had always liked it when she cried, and denying them had been one of the only ways she could say, "Fuck you," to them.

Violet sighed and started to pull her hand back, then Percy plucked the biscuit from her. She sniffed, and the sugar-and-chocolate smell made her stomach rumble.

Her mouth watered, and she finally took a bite. The sweetness melted inside her mouth, a burst of pure bliss, and she quickly devoured the rest. Determined to get every last crumb, she licked her fingers. When done, she looked up to find that in addition to Layla and Violet staring at her, Bronx stood near the door, his pupils flashing rapidly.

Her cheeks burned. She hadn't wanted him to see her moment of weakness. Now he'd probably use it against her.

Bronx cleared his throat, walked toward the plate of biscuits, and took one. After he finished it, he said, "These are all well and good, but you need some proper food, Percy. If you're up to it, the refrigerator is stocked and waiting for you."

"Did you poison or contaminate any of it?" Not that she expected him to be honest.

But the three dragon-shifters in the room all had looks of horror pasted onto their faces.

Violet was the first to speak. "No, Percy. I can taste any of it first, if you want. My dad sometimes calls me a seagull because I take bits and pieces from anything and everyone, so it's not really anything different from normal."

Bronx put a hand on his daughter's shoulder and

squeezed, but he didn't say anything. Still, the small gesture and the way Violet grinned at her dad as they shared some sort of memory stirred jealousy inside Percy.

When she'd been younger, she was the perfect student. She'd kept to herself, stayed out of trouble, and earned good marks. And yet, none of that had mattered. She'd been sold to a bunch of sick bastards then continually punished each and every day for the last seven years.

Tears threatened to fall, and she willed them back. She wouldn't cry in front of these people. She wouldn't.

So she jumped out of bed, walked around them, and headed for the attached toilet. Once she was inside, she sat down, placed her head in her hands, and took deep breaths. She'd been so bloody good at keeping herself contained back at the facility, so why did unwanted emotions keep threatening to spill out now?

Something stirred in her mind but then died down.

After several minutes of deep breathing and pushing all her emotions deep, deep down inside her again, she did her business, washed her hands, and exited the toilet. Violet and Layla were chatting about something but stopped at her appearance.

Violet tilted her head. "Are you okay?"

With her inner shields back up, she shrugged. "Fine. Now, I want to eat. And yes, I need you to taste everything for me."

Violet saluted. "At your service, Miss Percy."

She almost smiled. Almost. "How old are you, Violet?"

"Fifteen. Why? How old are you?"

Yet another thing that would be inside her file anyway. "Twenty."

Most of the time, she felt twice that, though, given her life experiences to date.

Violet motioned toward the door. "Let's head to the kitchen. Layla's going to stay a bit before she has to go back to the clan's clinic. And if you have any questions for her, you can ask them."

And as they walked out of the room and down the hall, Percy tried to come up with a list of questions. One of her priorities should be learning everything she needed to know to be a dragon-shifter in this country. Once she could handle her beast and shift, she would leave. And she was clever enough to know she wouldn't survive with her current level of knowledge.

The more she asked, the better prepared she'd be. Even if she had no bloody idea where she'd make a home, at least she'd have her dragon. And at this point in her life, that was all she wanted.

The only thing that mattered.

Chapter Eight

Bronx took the rubbish bag to the bin outside and lingered, watching as the trio of females entered the kitchen. Percy hung back from the others, almost as if she were afraid to get too close to anyone.

Even with some more detailed reports from Bram and Kai about Percy's former situation, none of the words conveyed just how hurt and damaged she truly was. For fuck's sake, she'd asked if they'd poisoned the food in the kitchen or not.

His dragon spoke up. *I don't know why you would be so surprised. We had to be careful with Edith.*

Yes, but only because her arsehole ex had beat her. She never asked if I poisoned anything, let alone would be clawing her face to pieces.

Percy made a wide circle around Violet and Layla, until she reached the fridge. When she opened it, the angle still allowed him to see her eyes widen.

He would've bet everything he had they'd

sometimes fucking starved her as punishment—she was far too thin, in the sickly way of too many angles and jutting cheekbones. His first impulse was to charge into the kitchen, tell Percy to sit, and make her everything she asked for.

Violet was a good baker but only a so-so cook. Bronx was better. He didn't burn toast or overcook eggs like his daughter, not that he'd be able to make a grand feast or anything close to it.

And yet, he stayed put. Percy wanted to make her own food, and he would have to let her do it. But never in his life had giving someone a choice been so bloody difficult.

His dragon sighed. *We can't do everything for everyone.*

I know, but it's nice feeling useful again.

He tapped his prosthetic against his good leg before putting it back on the ground. He did it again as he continued to watch, until Violet spied him and waved enthusiastically. He barely kept his cheeks from heating as Percy frowned out at him.

Great, now she thinks I'm a fucking pervert.

His beast chuckled. *You are a little, right now.* He growled, and his dragon added, *I'm merely kidding. Let's go back inside. She'll never get used to our presence if we always maintain our distance. And we both want her to learn the ropes of being a dragon-shifter as quickly as possible.*

He grunted and joined the others in the kitchen.

Violet asked him, "Percy said she's never eaten pizza or curry or even scones before. She didn't even know what scones were! We have to add the ingredients to our shopping list and give her the recipes. Because scones with jam and clotted cream are even better than chocolate chip biscuits."

His lips twitched. "If you have a sweet tooth." He looked at Percy. "Do you prefer sweet or savory?"

Her familiar frown—the one that signaled no one ever asked her opinion about things—returned. "I'm just grateful to eat. It doesn't matter what it is."

Maybe he should leave it there, but he couldn't seem to stop himself from asking, "But if you knew you could eat every day, as much as you wanted, and then had to decide which thing to reach for first—would it be sweet like cake or savory like a roast and potatoes?"

"I've only had cake once, but I remember it being good. Potatoes, I ate almost every day, so if I can avoid them, I will."

That still wasn't a real answer. But his daughter beat him to the punch and blurted, "What about chips? You can't tell me you don't like chips? I mean, nothing beats deep-fried potatoes."

Percy shrugged. "I've never had them. Our potatoes were always boiled."

Violet leaned against the island counter. "Well, then you'll need some fish and chips, and soon. It's a bit hard to make, though. But maybe one day, I'll take you to the chippy on Stonefire, and you can rethink your position on *all* potatoes."

Bronx was about to tell Violet to tone it down when Percy almost smiled. "Maybe. For now, I'll just have a sandwich. My cooking skills aren't all that great."

Violet rushed to a cupboard, took out a book, and held it out to Percy. "I've been using this. It has some pictures to help and is pretty easy to follow. Well, if you remember to watch the food and not get distracted like I do. But you can borrow it, if you want."

Percy gingerly took the book and nodded before setting it aside. "Thank you."

Violet continued to list off all the things Percy needed to try—she really hadn't tried much in her life, which only fueled Bronx's anger at the bastards who'd kept her prisoner—as Layla approached him.

She gestured to the side, and once they were on the far side of the room, she whispered, "I already talked to Violet about not bringing up her past too often, although she seems to have forgotten that. Maybe chat to her yourself? Focusing on things like cooking or new hobbies is good, aye, but until we're more certain about her dragon and what she'll do, I'd rather not trigger her with memories of her imprisonment."

Bronx kept his voice low too, so the other two females wouldn't hear. "I'll talk with Violet. When will the test results for her bloodwork come back?"

"Soon. Trahern's being thorough, for good reason." Trahern was another doctor on Stonefire, originally from Clan Snowridge in Wales. "The results will tell us more about what she's been given, what we can try, and what to avoid." Layla glanced at Percy. "It's a miracle the sedative Sid gave her worked. Some of the other inmates didn't react as well."

Before he could ask what they did know so far— Bronx relied on text updates but hadn't had a chance to talk with anyone in person or on the phone yet, for fear of Percy overhearing him—Violet said, "Come on, Dad. I always forget which cheese goes best with which meat. And it really makes heaps of difference."

After Layla nodded, signaling that their conversation was done for now, they went over and helped plan out a few different toasties, until Percy admitted she liked the ham and Swiss one with tomatoes and onions.

She devoured it, confirming Bronx's suspicions that food had never been reliable for her.

Well, that was one thing he could guarantee she'd never want for again. He might be her teacher on the surface, but he kept adding to his list of duties—because he would help this female, no matter what it took.

He couldn't fail with her. Provided the drugs hadn't irrevocably changed her dragon or the ability to shift, he would see she accomplished that someday. But even if that was her only goal, he would take it further. For some bloody reason, he wanted to see her smile or laugh. Or maybe relax around others, play a game, and act a little more like her age.

Because on paper, she was fairly young. However, her heart and mind were older than some people twice her age.

An old soul in a young body or something like that.

His dragon spoke up. *If you want her to have some fun, then you're going to have to be the one to show her. If you still know how to do it.*

He grunted mentally. *I know how to have fun.*

Really? Because I can't remember the last time you did. Violet always asks us to take her off Stonefire, to visit other places, to see humans, and you say no.

Because humans can be bloody dangerous. Did you forget they killed Hudson's first mate? Or that one beat Edith so badly that if we hadn't found her in time, she would've died?

Of course I bloody well didn't forget. But what about all the humans on Stonefire? Are they evil or bad or just waiting to hurt us?

He sighed mentally. *No, of course not.*

Right, then stop equating what a few horrible bastards did to the rest of humankind. If Hudson can move past it and mate Sarah, we can help Violet get to know her mother's heritage a little better.

Maybe.

His dragon snapped his wings in triumph. *Good. I'm going to hold you to that.*

Then his beast curled up and went to sleep.

Bronx spent the rest of the hour helping to clean up and let Layla and Violet do most of the talking. He still needed to feel out how Percy acted around males in general. Edith had given him a lot of practice in being patient, but Percy's past was a hundred times worse.

Not that he'd let that stand in his way.

Chapter Nine

As soon as she could get away, Percy fled to her bedroom with the cookbook in hand and shut the door. Bronx and Violet had said it was fine for her to spend time alone, provided she let them know about any signs of her dragon waking up or anything else that might concern her.

She'd agreed even though she'd probably never say a word. If her dragon acted out or she started having some sort of reaction from the withdrawal—Layla had explained it could happen, given all the drugs administered to her over the years—she would tough it out on her own. No one had ever helped her when she asked for it in the past. To start doing it now would only make her weak and scared or release the emotions she didn't dare let out.

Percy relied on Percy; no one else gave a shit.

Sitting on the bed, she traced the title of the book, which she could read: *Easy Meals for Beginners.* Opening it, she looked at the pictures, her mouth watering at the variety of foods, and itched to make a list of things to try.

However, she resisted. Wanting certain foods or trying to learn to cook them would be a waste of her energy. She needed to save her strength for helping her dragon.

Still, the pictures almost made her happy, as she imagined eating one thing and then another. Some of the ingredients, she couldn't make out, and while she could understand most of the directions, sometimes key words kept it from making sense.

She shut the book and tossed it to her side, onto the bed. Somehow, some way, she'd have to hide her low-level reading skills from Bronx and his daughter. Given how her emotions kept breaking free, one well-aimed barb about her being an idiot could send her into tears.

Tears, like when she'd been eight and had tried to befriend one of the new orphans. The words still stung: *Of course your mum gave you up. You're a freak. That must be some kind of evil mark. Or a curse. Yeah, a curse. She had to give you up to avoid being hurt or killed.*

Even though Percy didn't believe in actual curses, not even when she'd been eight, she'd rushed away to cry alone in the toilet. None of the other kids had disfigurements like her, so she'd always been the easy target.

All grown up, she almost understood how the other orphans had been scared, and hurt, and uncertain like her. And to feel better about themselves, they'd put her down. Not that it made it okay. Regardless, that incident had been the final lesson she'd needed to stop trying to make friends.

Only her dragon had ever befriended and liked her, which was why she was so desperate to get her back.

A knock sounded on the door, and she jumped. Glancing at the clock, she saw it'd been nearly two hours already. "What do you want?"

Bronx's deep voice came through the door. "I have some new dragon-shifter textbooks for you. I can leave them outside the door, though, if you prefer. I just wanted to let you know they arrived."

She almost shouted, "Yes, leave them and go." But that would appear cowardly. The first sign of weakness had made her an instant target of the guards inside the facility, and she was determined to do better this time.

So she took a deep breath and replied, "Come in."

He entered, leaving the door open behind him. He placed the books on the small desk in the far corner and patted them. "Some of these are aimed for younger dragon-shifters, so I hope that's okay. Because usually the inner dragon emerges at six years old, give or take, and so that's when dragon-shifters teach their kids how to deal with them."

Relief washed over her. She could read books for kids a lot easier than ones meant for adults. "Thank you." She bit her lip and decided that if she wanted information, it might be faster to ask Bronx than wade slowly through the texts.

So even though she'd prefer to tell him to fuck off, lock the door, and not worry about anyone else, she asked, "I barely remember my dragon. What should I do if she comes back?"

If he noticed her use of *if* instead of *when*, Bronx didn't comment. He gestured toward the chair at the desk. "Can I sit down to chat?" She eyed the door, and he added, "I'll keep the door open. Violet is in hearing range too." He raised his voice a little. "Listening to every word, aren't you, Vi?"

Laughter filled the air. "Yeah, I'm not even going to pretend I'm not, Dad."

"Good. Now, get back to your homework. You're missing classes to help out here, and I won't have you falling behind."

"Okay."

Bronx smiled at Percy. "She's a bit nosey, so just fair warning."

Violet shouted, "I heard that!"

He chuckled. "And I love you just as you are. Now, get back to work."

There was some distant grumbling before silence.

His easy words, saying he loved his daughter, baffled Percy.

Not that she was going to waste her time asking about that. No, Percy studied Bronx, wondering if she'd have to repeat herself.

Then he cleared his throat and crossed one leg until his ankle rested on the opposite knee. "Your dragon. Well, the hardest part will be keeping control of her. Dragons sometimes try to take over when they're young. And no, you're not a child any longer. However, your dragon might be, or she might be a wild adult— we have no way of knowing. Either way, don't let her tell you what to do or give in too easily. That way lies disaster."

His pupils flashed, and that streak of jealousy shot through her again. She wanted to talk to her dragon too. Badly. Maybe even more than being able to fly. She'd seen so many dragon-shifters regularly talking to their inner beasts already, and it made her loneliness that much more acute.

"That's all well and good, but what can I do specifically?"

He jostled his leg perched atop his thigh. "Well, I think a better place to start is: what do you know already? What did you learn growing up?"

She pressed her lips into a line for a second, not wanting to vent about her bloody awful teachers inside the orphanage. Sharing her past would only open her up to more potential hurt.

After a second to think of what to reveal, she said calmly, "Very little. As I'm sure you can find out, the orphanage where I grew up was the only one in the UK for a long, long time." Or so they'd told her. That was something else she'd have to learn about, eventually. She continued, "The humans didn't want to deal with half-dragon-shifter children, and the clans didn't want us either. There wasn't a lot of money, so we used really old books, mostly from human schools, and were told that if our dragons didn't behave—and we didn't ensure they did—we'd be punished. Threats, beatings, and starving us worked most of the time." She shrugged. "If it didn't, the kid eventually disappeared."

They'd probably gone to the same sort of place Percy had been sold to, not that she knew that fact for certain.

Bronx sat still, preternaturally still, and his knuckles gripping his leg turned white. Did that mean he was angry or upset? But why the bloody hell should he be? She'd been the one to live at the orphanage, not him.

When he spoke, it was tight and controlled. "What happened with your dragon?"

She let out a breath. For a second, she thought he'd ask about her own personal punishments, and that wasn't something she ever wanted to bring up.

Talking about her dragon and their brief time together was nearly as painful, though. Still, there was a point to it—Bronx might be able to give her a better game plan for taming her beast and reuniting with her.

So even though she'd never, ever talked about this event in her past with anyone, she made an exception. *I'd do almost anything to get my dragon back.* She replied, as if from a distance and not the person in the memory, "She came out later, around age ten. I don't know why then, so don't ask." *Wrong.* She'd been malnourished, afraid, and miserable all the time, and she hadn't blamed her dragon for wanting to hide from all that. "At first, I kept her a secret. I knew some kids disappeared shortly after their dragons talked with them, even some of the good kids. And even if the orphanage was a fucking hellhole, better the devil you know, and all that."

She paused, trying to think of the best unemotional way to go forward. Bronx merely waited, not pushing her, his eyes kind and encouraging, which was weird and new. It made her uneasy.

Once she had her thoughts together, she continued, "I'd memorized every bit of information I could find about inner dragons. There wasn't a lot—we had maybe one book that was actually written for dragon-shifters—but I was determined to keep her in line. That was the only way I wouldn't show flashing dragon eyes and alert the orphanage staff to her appearance."

She'd wanted to keep that one thing for herself. She'd failed, though.

After clearing her throat, she said, "When she first emerged and talked with me, I nearly screamed. Only because my former roommates had left a few weeks before, meaning I temporarily had my own room, did no one find out my dragon had shown up. But she wasn't out of control or bossy or any of those things." Percy almost smiled but remembered Bronx was watching her. "She was curious and chatty and nice to me."

Nicer than anyone had ever been to Percy in her life.

No, don't think about that, or you'll start bawling like a baby. She somehow kept her voice strong. "And it became a matter of keeping her entertained so she wouldn't throw a tantrum. I was alone a lot, so that was easy." *Fuck, did I really say that?* Desperate for Bronx not to notice, she blurted, "When I needed to join the others for a meal or go to class, I thought of games and mazes for my dragon to play with. And it worked for a while."

Then she'd grown so dependent on her dragon, needing that friendship to keep her from trying to run away or worse, and grown reckless.

Even now, she mentally kicked herself for losing control. True, she'd been eleven when she let the truth slip, but even at that age, she'd lost her innocence and naïvety years before.

If only she'd been more controlled, more disciplined, she might never have been sold to the facility. At sixteen, she could've left the orphanage to see if a dragon clan would take pity on her and let her live with them.

Bronx's voice jolted her out of her head. "How did you lose her?"

Her gaze shot to his. The gray eyes weren't full of pity, only curiosity, almost as if he wanted to know as much as possible so that he could help her.

It was probably bullshit, and he got off on power plays or something, but his reasons didn't matter. All she wanted was vital information. "I let my pupils flash during class, and the teacher noticed. I was taken to the headmistress—administrator, maybe, but we called her headmistress—and was told that since I hadn't reported my dragon waking up, which was one of the rules, I'd lose her for at least a week, maybe more, depending on my behavior."

They'd used the inner dragons as methods of control. And to someone as lonely and isolated as Percy, it'd been the worst kind of punishment.

Her throat closed up at remembering how they'd tied her down and given her a shot, and her dragon had vanished within minutes. She'd even been weak, crying and sobbing to let her come back, but to no avail. She'd broken the rules, and they said she deserved the punishment.

Despite all her safeguards, something wet slid down her cheek. She quickly brushed away the tear and acted as if it hadn't happened.

She wouldn't—couldn't—allow Bronx to think her

soft. She wouldn't be exploited ever again, if she could help it.

After clearing her throat, she said coolly, "She never came back, my dragon. They always found reasons to keep giving me shots and make her silent. In retrospect, I see it was to keep me in line and make me do their bidding. Shortly after I turned thirteen, they sold me to the facility. And, well, they made the orphanage look like a walk in the park by comparison. Needless to say, they never allowed my dragon back either."

She should have held Bronx's gaze and remained strong on the outside, but she was too tired. Reliving this, plus trying to retell it without all the emotions it triggered, was exhausting.

Looking down, she plucked at the blanket on the bed, which helped to channel some of her pent-up emotion. She had no bloody idea how Bronx would react to her story, but all she could do was wait and see before she could figure out what to do next.

Not for the first time, she hated how little experience she had with interacting with others. That was another thing she needed to work on, to learn how to navigate, or she wouldn't last long in the outside world.

But concrete tasks, such as learning to socialize, were good. As long as she had distractions, she wouldn't dive too deeply into her past and possibly fall apart.

Chapter Ten

Bronx wished for a concrete target, some person who'd fucked over Percy in the past, someone he could punish for what they'd done to her. His late mate's life hadn't been easy, but even from what little he'd learned so far, Percy's had been far, far worse.

His dragon danced at the edges of his mind, wanting to say something, but had remained silent since Percy had started discussing her memories. For all he knew, flashing dragon eyes might be too much for her right here and now.

And watching her pluck at the blanket, avoiding eye contact, made her look so bloody young, much younger than ever before.

Bronx wanted to hug her close and murmur that there were plenty of good people in the world—such as inside Stonefire—and that he would show her they existed, if she gave him the chance.

Which was bloody ridiculous, of course. She was

his student, a damaged one, and even if she wanted to lean on him, to rely on him, and allow him to care for her, Bronx had fucked that up before. When the time came, she'd have to find someone else to do that for her long-term. His job was to help her heal, keep it together, and learn how to work with her dragon, if possible. Nothing more.

He said softly, "Well, your dragon will be wild and try to take control when she comes out again. She was when I found you last night, and we need to prepare for that. However, it's been a very busy few days for you, and I don't want to push you too far." He stood—a bit awkwardly as always, since his prosthetic was good but not his actual leg—and added, "The doctors said the sedative should remain in effect and calm your dragon until tomorrow evening. So I'm going to allow you some time to thumb through these books, write out some questions, and then we'll start lessons tomorrow."

"Can't I just ask my questions instead of writing them out?"

He frowned. "I suppose, although giving me a list will give me more time to prepare. I don't claim to know everything."

Her lips twitched, and the sight made his heart swell. "You're the first male I've met who's ever admitted that."

Recognizing that Percy needed to steer the conversation away from her past, he shrugged. "Well, there are a lot of arseholes in the world. I have faults, of course." He lifted his trouser leg, exposing his missing lower limb. "When you lose a part of your body, you learn really fucking quickly that admitting the truth is a hell of a lot easier than always pretending everything is fine or that nothing has changed."

He quickly dropped the material, wondering why the hell he'd done that. Her life had been bloody horrible, and him losing his leg didn't begin to compare.

Percy finally raised her gaze from his leg to his eyes. "How did that happen?"

Bronx didn't like talking about it. Only his brother, Hudson, had managed to get the story and some of his struggles out of him. "You don't need any other burdens to worry about."

She drew her legs up and wrapped her arms around them. The action made her look so tiny; the first time he'd met her, he hadn't believed she was a dragon-shifter because of her short stature.

Of course now he knew they'd starved her as one of her punishments, stunting her growth.

Percy said, "If you don't want to talk about it, just say so. I've had a lifetime of bullshit and excuses and the like. I'd like honesty for once. I'm not saying I'll instantly trust you, because that's bloody stupid, but it might help us both to be at least a little honest. Then we can skip all the dancing around and awkwardness. Because if you keep treating me like a doll you can break, how am I supposed to handle a wild inner dragon?"

He blinked. This female was fucking astute. "I think there's a middle ground. Anything related to inner dragons, we're completely honest about it. When it comes to anything else? Either one of us has to earn that. Sound fair?"

She shrugged one shoulder. "It's not like I have any leverage in this situation. I may have helped Ava and Joey, but that will only get me so far."

He wanted to shout that sometimes people wanted to help others and not demand repayment for every little thing. Yes, he'd been paid for his search-and-rescue job. But it wasn't a lot, and he'd loved the thrill of helping someone, of saving them, and doing what he hadn't been able to do for his mate. It hadn't been completely altruistic, but a sort of middle ground.

Still, bartering or trading information was probably all she knew. So Bronx risked putting out a hand. "Honesty when it comes to anything related to an inner dragon. Shake on it and make a vow?"

She frowned. "Why?"

Fuck. Did she not know that people made deals or vows and would honor them?

Maybe not everyone, but Bronx certainly did. "Most dragon-shifters take vows rather seriously. It's a type of honor, a way to prove we aren't the monsters many humans have made us out to be."

Her brows scrunched more together. "Monster? You?" She shook her head. "I was always told that I was one of the worst kinds, the ones dragon-shifters wanted nothing to do with. How can pure-blooded dragons be monsters when those like me exist?"

Bloody hell. This poor female really had been fed a bunch of lies and bullshit over the years. "Violet is the same as you. Has anyone treated her like a monster?"

"Well, not yet."

"And they won't. She's part of the clan, and under Bram, we do whatever it takes to protect and help one another. It was us against the world for a long, long time, although now we have other clans as allies, and things are changing." He paused, seeing his words meant nothing. No wonder, given how she'd been manipulated and treated over the years. "How about this? You can meet some of the humans living on Stonefire. While you've met Melanie, there are loads more. You can judge for yourself if any of their half-human children are viewed as monsters. Oh, and maybe you can meet Nikki too. Her mother was human, same as you and Violet. And she's second-in-command of clan security."

Percy frowned harder. "People trust a half-dragon-shifter to protect the clan?"

He nodded. "With zero hesitation. I'll see about Nikki stopping by." He noticed the circles under the female's eyes and how she tried to bite back a yawn. He lowered his hand and stepped back a few paces. "For now, I'll leave you alone. If you need anything, anything at all, just shout or come find me and Violet. Okay?"

She nodded, and Bronx took one last look at Percy, looking all alone, exhausted, and sad, and forced himself to leave the room and close the door.

He leaned against it, closed his eyes, and sighed. His dragon spoke up. *We need to do whatever we can to help her.*

I agree.

That includes making her smile or laugh or not look as if the world is crushing her.

It was unusual for his dragon to worry so much about a stranger. *Don't get too attached, dragon.*

His beast huffed. *I like her. And she needs people who will protect her, stand up for her, and convince her she's both strong and brilliant for surviving this long. Many wouldn't have.*

To lose one's inner dragon after meeting them was hard on any dragon-shifter. In fact, some even went insane after losing their beast for an extended period of time. *I know. But as soon as she's trained and ready to tackle the clan on her own, we step back.*

Maybe.

He didn't like his beast's tone. And yet, Bronx wouldn't even think about what his dragon's attitude could mean.

If Percy's inner dragon were out and present, his beast would know if she was their true mate.

And for a beat, he didn't want to help her. His late mate had died birthing Violet, something she never should've attempted. Edith hadn't been his true mate, which had made her chances as a human having a dragon's baby less favorable. He should've stayed firm and said no children.

But he hadn't.

Even if he'd fucked up his choice about having a child with Edith, he wouldn't have the same options if he found his true mate. He'd have to never, ever kiss her. Because if he did, it'd send his dragon into a mate-claim frenzy, taking away both his and Percy's choices since his dragon would keep fucking her until she carried their child.

Not that Percy was his true mate.

His daughter's voice was nearby and soft as she asked, "Are you okay, Dad?"

Opening his eyes, he looked at his daughter, who

wasn't that much shorter than him these days. She was growing up too bloody fast.

And Bronx couldn't fathom how he'd been able to keep her at a distance for several months after Edith's death.

He reached out and pulled her into a hug. Her presence was always calming and a balm to his soul. Violet was his life, his everything. He most definitely didn't have room for anyone else in his heart or life.

"Just a little tired." He pulled back and met her brown-eyed gaze, so like her mother's. "How about we make some pizza for dinner? I think we have everything."

Her eyes lit up. "We do, and I even have the dough recipe memorized. Plus, maybe Percy can help make it and then finally try some."

He smoothed some stray hair strands back from Violet's face; her hair never stayed in the braid she always wore. "Percy needs some time alone, love. But maybe we can practice tonight and get it just right so next time she can have a perfect example of pizza."

As soon as the words left his mouth, he regretted them. Why was he planning any sort of future with Percy? For all he knew, Bram could replace him as her teacher, or Dr. Rossi could return early and decide Percy was better off without him.

However, Violet tugged his arm, intruding on his thoughts. "Come on, Dad. The dough will need a little time to rise, and I want to finish before my show starts."

He bit back a smile. Violet loved the human soap operas on TV, and she watched at least one of them every day, without fail. "All right, Vi. Although you do know you can stream it on the computer later. I've seen you do it before."

She rolled her eyes. "I only do that if I have to, but it's not the same, Dad. When I watch it live, I know everyone else is watching it and probably shouting at the latest ridiculous thing to happen. I mean, how many of the characters can go to prison, have surprise babies with like four different dads, or mysteriously return from the dead?"

As they walked into the kitchen, he couldn't resist teasing her. "Then why watch it?"

"Because I can't help it! It's addicting."

He laughed, and Violet joined in. And as he made pizza with his daughter, he temporarily forgot about Percy, how both man and beast wanted to make her happy, or what the future might hold for any of them. Right here, right now, he made a memory with his daughter, one he'd always treasure. It wouldn't be long before she was all grown up and moved into her own place, and she might never want to spend a night at home making dinner with her dad again.

Chapter Eleven

Percy had fallen asleep soon after Bronx left—although she'd heard the exchange with his daughter, which she still had trouble believing was real life—and woke up early to tackle the books he'd left her.

She'd understood almost all the words in the children's ones and could guess from context the ones she couldn't read or sound out. The adult one, though, made her want to throw it across the room.

And while she was staring at the blank notebook, pen in hand, debating if she even wanted to try writing out questions—Bronx might ridicule her spelling or handwriting—a knock sounded on the door.

Violet's voice came through. "Percy, can I come in?"

Closing the notebook quickly to hide the blank pages, she answered, "Yes."

Violet walked in, a plate of something in her hands. A savory smell greeted her, one of ham and other scents she couldn't identify. Because all her meals had been plain to date, except for maybe salt, she didn't really know what spices smelled like.

Violet placed the plate on the table. Steam rose from some sort of flattened bread with little toasted marks on it in lines. She could see ham and cheese oozing out.

Percy's mouth watered, and her stomach rumbled.

Violet tore off a small piece and popped it into her mouth. Once she swallowed, she pushed the plate toward her. "It's a panini. Basically a fancy toasted sandwich, although I added some basil this time to the ham, cheese, tomatoes, and onions. Hopefully you like it."

Since the teenaged girl didn't start gasping or turning blue, Percy picked up the bread and bit into it. The crunchy outside surprised her. As all the flavors melted together in her mouth, she chewed slowly, wanting to savor something other than plain potatoes, peas, or boiled, cheap meat of the day like she'd always eaten in the past.

Violet picked up one of the books as she waited for Percy to finish eating. "This one was mine. I'm sure you noticed all the drawings around the edges. I know I shouldn't have done it—I love books and wouldn't do it now—but back then, I was bored. I learned to read really early, and the teachers didn't know what to do with me." She placed it back onto the stack on the table. "It gave me a lot of time to think of my mum, which often got me into trouble. I just wanted to know more about her, you know? And I love my dad to pieces, but he rarely talks about her." She sighed. "And

I'm rambling. I tend to do that, so tell me to shut it whenever you like."

Percy smiled at the girl. She was so much more open than anyone Percy had ever met before. "No, I like it. I spent most of my life alone, often in silence, so a friendly voice is a nice change."

Violet's eyes widened. "That's awful. And you know, I have some ideas of how to fix that. Dad's getting you a radio today, and maybe you can watch one of my soap operas with me later. I don't know if you'll like *Coronation Street* or *EastEnders* better, so we could try both. The people on *Corrie* sound more like us, if accents are hard for you to follow. Although the other one has had loads of drama lately, so it's never boring."

Even if Percy had never had a TV of her own, they'd been on sometimes when she'd been taken for a test, experiment, or checkup.

She'd never really watched it beyond the first time, because seeing people laugh or smile on the screen had seemed mocking. No doubt, the facility staff had done that on purpose.

But she couldn't keep avoiding everything related to her imprisonment. And certainly, watching make-believe people on a screen who couldn't see her, belittle her, or manipulate her wouldn't hurt her. "Okay, I'll try your shows."

Violet grinned. "Brilliant. We can make dinner beforehand too. Although there was another reason I came in here. My dad wants to start giving you lessons about dragon-shifters. I wanted to help, but he said maybe later." She sighed dramatically. "I have loads of schoolwork to do first."

Before she could stop herself, Percy blurted, "Be grateful you can go to school."

The younger dragonwoman blinked. "You didn't go to school?"

Fuck. Now what? She didn't want to reveal how she'd barely received any education in the orphanage and then none after leaving it. While Percy didn't think of herself as stupid when it came to life and dealing with bloody awful situations, she lacked maths and language skills, for certain.

Although, why she cared about what Bronx and Violet thought of her, she had no idea.

Violet stared at her, as if trying to figure her out, and her pupils flashed.

That stab of jealousy flared again.

Something flickered in the back of her mind, a few bursts of purple light. She dared to ask, *Dragon, are you there?*

Nothing.

She was about to growl her frustration—what if the doctors here had given her something that had completely silenced her beast?—when Violet's voice interrupted her thoughts. "I know me saying you should be honest with my dad means nothing, but he wants to help you, Percy. He won't ridicule or talk down to you. He never does that. One of my cousins is dyslexic, and over the last year, my dad has been helping him with his reading since Dad's had more free time."

She frowned. "Why does he have more free time?"

Violet glanced at the door and lowered her voice. "My dad lost his leg over a year ago during a rescue mission. He was kind of a firefighter and wilderness rescue officer. If people were trapped in a burning building or lost on a mountain, he helped save them. Well, there was a massive warehouse fire on Lochguard —the Scottish dragon clan—because of a bomb. My dad flew with others from Stonefire to help. And when he was doing a last check for people inside the building, part of the roof collapsed and trapped his leg. They had to cut off the bottom part to save his life."

Violet paused, wiping away tears, before continuing. "He's struggled to find a new purpose since he can't do his old job, especially in his dragon form. But ever since you've shown up, he's more like his old self—confident, happier, and making plans. All things he didn't do for months." She reached out and squeezed Percy's shoulder, and Percy didn't even flinch because she was too wrapped up in Violet's words. The teenager said, "Just give him a chance and let him help you. With him on your side, he'll move heaven and earth to try and make things happen. It's just who he is."

Percy searched Violet's gaze, looking for any signs of deceit or manipulation. Early in her life, some of the doctors had used sob stories to get her to help with new prisoners.

Those had ended badly for her, especially as she got older and they decided to try fertility experiments.

That flickering light appeared again, but nothing else. Was it her dragon?

She bit her bottom lip and looked at her hands,

studying her fingers. Just reading the children's books had revealed how lost she was in this world of dragon-shifters. At twenty years old, Percy probably knew only a fraction more than most humans. Until she could bolster her reading skills, she would have to lean on someone to get her up to speed.

Could she try to give Bronx the benefit of the doubt and risk being deceived all over again?

Unwinding her fingers, she rubbed her temples. Over all the years she'd held on to the dream of being able to shift into a dragon and fly, she'd never imagined she would have to trust anyone to get her there.

As naïve as she was, she'd thought if her dragon just came out, she could talk to her beast and they would pick up where they left off.

However, as she lightly touched the nearly healed scab where she'd clawed her face, she knew it wouldn't be that bloody simple.

Lowering her hands, she looked at Violet again. Maybe it was the female's youth, her innocence, or her pure zest for life, but Percy didn't hold back when she said, "I can't handle someone else betraying or hurting me, Violet. I'm just... tired."

As the truth escaped her lips, heaviness settled over Percy. She sometimes felt old, quite old, as if she were fifty instead of her true age. Only her dream of being reunited with the only friend she'd ever had and flying in her dragon form had given her the strength to keep going.

The thought of never being at peace with her dragon again was too much. She had to do all she could to talk with her, work with her, and learn to be the dragon-shifter she always should've been.

But she was still afraid, so very afraid, of being betrayed yet again.

Violet leaned down until their eyes were level. "My dad is an amazing male. He saved my mum's life, you know. She found a safe space here on Stonefire and, by all accounts, was happy for the short time she lived here." Violet tucked some hair behind her ear before adding, "Just give him a chance is all I'm asking. You have me to rely on too. And before long, I'm sure half of Stonefire will be clamoring to help you. Well, provided you're not a spy." She raised her brows. "Are you?"

Percy blinked at the abrupt change in conversation. "Pardon?"

"You know, a spy. Trying to be nice to us so we give you information to pass on to the people who held you captive because you learned to like them. What's it called? Oh, that's right—Stockholm Syndrome. I learned about that recently, and you might've formed attachments to your guards."

She spit out, "No fucking way. I hated those bastards and what they did to me."

At the venom in Percy's voice, Violet took a few steps back. "Right, well, I believe you."

Realizing she'd just shouted at a teenager, she scrambled for what to say next. "I'm sorry, Violet. The doctors said I'll probably suffer withdrawals, and my moods might get strange. I didn't mean to raise my voice."

Violet shrugged. "No worries. For a few days a

month, I'm an absolute bear." She walked closer and put out a hand. "Let's be friends, Percy. I know maybe it's weird being friends with someone my age, but I think you need as many as you can get. So you're stuck with me."

Percy stared at Violet's outstretched hand. It should have been easy to shake it, and yet, doing so would be a monumental step for her. It'd mean letting down her guard, even just a little, with someone else.

The flickering light in her head flashed even more this time before dimming. It had to be her dragon. And maybe being someone's friend, even if she mostly maintained her distance, might be a step closer to her ultimate goal of being reunited with her inner beast.

She gingerly took Violet's hand and shook. As soon as she released it, Violet grinned. "Brilliant. Now maybe we can take sides against my dad sometimes."

She frowned. "Why?"

"Just because. I have loads of male cousins—even more now that Uncle Hudson is with Sarah and her two sons—and it'll be nice to have another female to even the numbers. Especially since there are *always* more male dragons than female ones, and I know we'll never outnumber them."

Percy had never heard that before. "Really? Is that true?"

Violet nodded. "Yes. But it's not the most important thing to know. Well, as long as you're not thinking of having kids anytime soon, because knowing you'll probably have a male over a female might help you prepare better."

She blinked. "Um, no. No children for me."

"Right, well, I'm sure my dad is waiting for you. He said to find him after lunch, although he must know I'd stick around to chat a bit with you." Violet went to the door. "But don't forget about dinner and telly later. It'll be loads of fun, just wait and see."

With that, Violet left Percy alone. It took her a second to process what had just happened.

Had she really one, agreed to be Violet's friend, and two, decided to not view every move she and Bronx made with extreme skepticism?

She brushed her hair back and touched the scab again, a reminder that she might not be able to do this completely alone.

So yes, yes she had agreed to those two things.

Panic crept over her, and Percy's first impulse was to find Violet and maybe tell her to fucking mind her own business. That way, she could reinforce all those walls around her heart and emotions.

But then she remembered all the purple light flashes inside her head, which were probably related to her dragon. Being around people seemed to make them happen more often.

In other words, she needed to do more than sit alone in her room and tell the world to fuck off.

With a sigh, she washed her hands, picked up her books and the plate, and exited her safe space to look for Bronx. Now that she'd decided to ask for help, she was impatient to get started.

Chapter Twelve

Bronx was sitting at the kitchen table, going over the latest notes from Dr. Rossi about both Percy and his training in general, when Violet walked in, wearing a grin.

Since that always spelled some kind of trouble, he asked, "What did you do?"

Her smile broadened. "Oh, nothing. I'm going to work on my schoolwork in my room, although I'll keep the door open, and Percy can call for me anytime."

He eyed his daughter suspiciously as she whistled. She was most definitely up to something.

His dragon laughed. *When isn't she? But she seems genuinely interested in helping Percy, so I doubt she'll run off.*

Great, it's come to me being happy she won't try to sneak onto a train to visit a human city.

Violet waved at him. "Percy will be out soon, Dad. Try to be nice to her, okay?"

His daughter's words pricked his pride. "Of course I'll be nice to her."

She studied him a second, nodded to herself, and said, "I'll come back out when it's time to make dinner."

And then she was gone.

He said to his beast, *She acts more and more like an adult every day. I'm both proud and terrified.*

Don't worry, she'll probably have a rebellious phase like our brother Brooklyn and then settle down.

He snorted. *Only because he found Letitia. That female is a saint.*

Bronx's sister-in-law, Letitia, was one of the few who could tame Brooklyn when needed.

Percy's voice prevented his dragon from replying. "What were you laughing at?"

He looked up and blinked. She'd showered. Her hair now fell in soft waves about her shoulders, and she wore jeans and a T-shirt that revealed both how small she was for a dragon-shifter but also how soft she was in all the right places.

What the fuck? No, just no. This female had been traumatized, abused, and mistreated, and she'd lived through hell. He wouldn't be the bastard who stared at her body, no matter how much he might want to.

And no, he really didn't want to. He was never taking a mate again, after all.

His dragon said softly, *You don't have to want a mate to woo a female.*

Ignoring his dragon, he cleared his throat and remembered her question. "Just my dragon. He's an arsehole sometimes and likes to tease me."

Since it was true and they teased each other, his dragon merely gave a toothy grin inside his mind.

Percy placed the empty plate in the sink, set down some books on the counter, and leaned forward. He trained his eyes only on her face as she said, "I-I kind of remember that. I never laughed before my dragon, and…" Her voice trailed off as she stared at the counter, tracing a design with her fingers.

She looked so fucking young and lost.

"Well, I guarantee if you spend much more time with Violet, she'll make you laugh. She's good at that."

Percy gave a barely there smile, and it made his heart skip a beat. She replied, "I like your daughter. She's, er, nice."

He laughed. "That's a very diplomatic answer. But Violet is my world. I love her more than anything, and she has a light about her, one that glows without her even trying."

Percy nodded but didn't say anything else.

Bronx stood, keeping distance between them. Even though Violet wasn't far away, he didn't know how Percy would react to him being near. He gestured toward the books. "I take it those mean you're ready for some lessons?"

She traced the edge of one of the books. "Yes."

He resisted frowning. Percy from earlier had been bold, unafraid to say what she wanted, and would've told him to sod off if she felt like it.

Something had changed, although he didn't know what.

Regardless, he was determined to bring back some of her fire. "You don't have to be so polite with me, Percy. Just honest. I don't know what the hell they did to you, and you don't have to talk about any of it until you're ready—if you ever are—but I vow not to hurt you intentionally. I'm not perfect—no one is—so I may get grumpy or blurt something I shouldn't. But all I want to do is help you learn and to work with your dragon, and to help you reach any goal you set."

She met his gaze again. And as her pupils remained round, he vowed he would do whatever it took so she could talk with her dragon, provided she wasn't rogue. That was one thing he couldn't control.

Percy nodded. "Okay. I don't trust anyone, and I don't know if I ever will, but I believe you won't hurt me intentionally. I know that's bloody ridiculous, considering I don't know you. And yet, my gut says I can. And despite everything, my gut has gotten rather good at these things over the years. Well, once my naïvety and innocence were shattered, at any rate."

He itched to ask her how but knew she wasn't ready. She might never be ready with him. "Right, well, then let's get started. Open the book titled *Department of Dragon Affairs: Rules and Regulations* to the first chapter and read the first paragraph out loud."

Percy froze a beat and then picked it up. She opened it, stared at the page…. and kept staring.

Thinking about her life thus far, Bronx realized he was a bloody idiot. They probably hadn't taught her while she was in the facility. And who the fuck knew if an orphanage who sold children would even bother educating them. Maybe she couldn't read.

But then she read the first sentence. "This book lists all the rules and… re-regulations for dragon-shifters to follow. Breaking them results in in-inca…"

"Incarceration."

Heat filled her cheeks as she stared at the book some more.

Since this had to be fucking mortifying for her, he debated how to handle it. He settled on "You didn't attend school until age sixteen or eighteen like everyone else does, did you?"

While school was mandatory for dragon-shifters until sixteen, when they received their dragon tattoo, most continued until age eighteen.

She shook her head, still refusing to look at him. "No." She paused and whispered, "Only until I was twelve."

Fucking bastards. If Bram hadn't already found the orphanage who'd screwed up Percy's life—they'd been closed for a few years now, after a DDA inspection revealed the rot—Bronx would've done it himself and found a way to make the staff pay for what they'd done. "Well, we'll add some extra lessons to your curriculum that deal with reading and writing, and maybe maths too. Tristan might be able to help us, or his fellow teacher, a female dragon named Ella Lawson, can."

He didn't reveal how the pair taught the younger students. He didn't want to embarrass Percy or let her think he thought less of her.

But she continued to stare at the book, as if willing herself to instantly be able to read it.

He took a step toward her. Since she didn't flinch or move away, he stayed put. "School is important, but it's not everything, Percy. You've learned more about life than most, I'd gather. With a little work, you can level up your book-learning too, to become a truly kick-ass female."

She glanced up at him, frowning. "Why would you say that?"

"Because you survived what most people couldn't. That tells me you have a core of steel. Lean on it, use it to prop yourself up when you feel as if you're about to crumple, and you'll be able to accomplish so bloody much. I just know it."

She remained silent. Bronx's dragon danced at the edges of his mind, but he knew not to interrupt. It felt as if Percy were on the cusp of something, of taking her first real step toward her new future, and he didn't want to spook or distract her.

When she finally severed eye contact, she whispered, "I just want my dragon back. Nothing else matters."

The heartbreak and longing in her voice shot straight to his heart. He'd wanted to help her before, but now? Bronx would fucking move mountains to do it.

Not wanting to think of why, he replied, "And we'll try everything we can. But I'll be honest, as I'll always try to be with you—things could be complicated or bloody difficult. Are you strong enough to endure more hardship? Because it could come to that, with your dragon, if she ends up rogue."

She looked at him again, her gaze more confident than earlier. "Yes. Where my dragon is concerned, I'll do anything."

He nodded and gestured toward the book in her hands. "Right, then let's go over some of the basic rules you need to know from the start, and then we'll see if you still have enough energy to tackle some reading lessons. I can help with those. I do them with my nephew. But the rest of your education will have to wait for the dragon teachers."

She readjusted her grip on the DDA book. "That's fine. My dragon is my main priority, and the rest is secondary." She bit her bottom lip and then asked, "Will the clan leader approve of all of this? And what do I need to do in return for more lessons?"

He didn't hesitate. "Bram has already approved helping you until you can live on your own, either here or with another dragon clan."

"Another clan?"

"All dragon-shifters have to live with a clan, Percy. Violet mentioned it before, but I don't know if you remember her words. Basically, there are a few rogue dragons on the lam, hiding in the forests or mountains. But if they're caught by the DDA, they'll go to jail. Since I know you don't want to go back to any sort of prison, it means you'll have to live with a dragon clan. However, for now, Stonefire is your home. You can decide later if it's your permanent choice."

She murmured, "Home."

Something she'd never had.

His dragon spoke up. *She can stay with us as long as she wants, maybe even forever.*

Don't go there, dragon. We're just helping her until she can survive on her own. That's it.

That's what you said about Edith.

Well, I won't do that again.

His beast sniffed. *We'll see.*

He didn't like his dragon's words. But Percy walked

toward him, book against her chest, and he focused solely on her.

He sat down at the table, in his usual awkward way, and then gestured to a chair farthest away from him, as well as to the sofa on the other side of the room. "Sit wherever you feel most comfortable."

She hesitated but then sat at the table, across from him.

And the fact she hadn't opted for the sofa sent a rush of approval through him.

Although as she handed him the book, he realized something. "Do you even like being called Percy? If you want me to use something else, just let me know."

She shrugged. "Percy is all I know. And since my dragon liked the name, I want to keep it. That might help her recognize me."

It was unusual for a dragon half to comment on the human half's name, but considering what Percy had endured, nothing should surprise him. "Right, then, Percy, let's start with the first chapter. We'll read it together, and as we go, write down the words you don't know. It'll probably be overwhelming at first, but it'll better help me understand what to do next. Does that sound okay?"

She bobbed her head. "Just don't make fun of my handwriting."

"Considering mine looks like chicken scratch, I'm not one to judge." She eyed him skeptically, so he opened the notebook on the table and wrote out, "My name is Bronx Wells, and I hate writing by hand."

He turned it toward her, and she scrunched up her nose. "What the hell does that even say?"

Laughing, he told her, and she added, "I can do better than that."

He wanted to praise her but held back. For all he knew, praise had been a manipulation tactic. "Right, then time to stop messing about and get to work. Tell me to stop when you need to write down a word, and don't dare hold back, okay?"

She bobbed her head. He read the first chapter, stopping whenever Percy needed to jot down something on her list, which was often. He noticed how she relaxed more and more the longer she heard his voice. Add in how she kept making quips about unnecessary words—"Why not just say *bad behavior* instead of *disorderly conduct?*"—and he grew hopeful.

Not too much, though, as it was early days. Although when he explained a lengthy word, saying some people needed to feel important and act as if they were smarter than everyone else, Percy smiled, and both man and beast nearly hummed.

Yes, he needed to give her dragon-shifter and reading lessons. But he was also determined to make her laugh, learn to trust, and understand not everyone in the world was as fucking selfish and cold-hearted as her former captors.

All of which his dragon wholeheartedly approved of, maybe with a little too much enthusiasm.

Chapter Thirteen

At the end of her lessons, Percy was completely exhausted and took a nap before Violet came to get her.

Making dinner was, well, nice. Bronx hovered, always at a respectable distance, and kept a notebook ready for when she found another word she didn't know.

She'd half-expected Violet to make fun of her, but the young dragonwoman barely batted an eyelash. No, the female was extremely determined to make the best curry of all time, albeit not too spicy for Percy, and took it all rather seriously—to the point that when she added a wrong spice, she wanted to throw out the whole batch and start again.

Luckily, Bronx convinced Violet it would be fine because they could salvage it. And so they finished making it, and everyone sat in front of the TV, food in hand.

Violet was next to Percy on the couch. She turned

to her and asked, "Aren't you going to try it? The show will start soon, and it's going to take some work to get you up to speed on all the characters and relationships. And I want to see your reaction when you taste the curry. There's no potatoes in it, so you can't use that excuse."

Percy brought the dish closer and inhaled. She replied, "I'm just memorizing the smell, is all. I've never eaten anything like it."

Violet ate a big spoonful of her curry and rice, and once she swallowed, she nodded. "It turned out okay after all. Although next time, I can do better."

At the determination in Violet's tone, she smiled. When Violet wanted to do something, little could stop her, or so Percy was discovering.

Bronx stopped eating long enough to say, "Told you so."

Violet stuck out her tongue. "You're my dad. Aren't you supposed to be all supportive and uplifting?"

Bronx raised his brows. "I am supportive. However, you need to pull back sometimes, Vi, or you're going to burn yourself out one day. I do it because I love you."

Violet huffed but then laughed. "Maybe."

Watching the father-daughter pair was fascinating. Percy had never witnessed such a relationship before and didn't know if a TV show could even compare to the real thing. They were so at ease around one another and didn't hold back teasing or gently pointing out faults. It seemed almost as if nothing was off limits between Bronx and Violet.

Well, almost. Anytime Violet had tried to bring up

her mother when cooking dinner, Bronx had quickly changed the subject.

Not that it was any of Percy's concern. Worrying about a crack in their family didn't help her with getting her dragon back, let alone get her closer to shifting.

She finally took a spoonful of the orange-red curry and put it in her mouth. An explosion of flavor hit her, but she didn't have words to describe it beyond savory and a little hot, given how her mouth tingled.

Once Percy swallowed, Violet leaned forward. "Well? What do you think?"

She thought about it and then said, "It's different."

Violet frowned, and Bronx chuckled. He said, "That's not bad, Vi. But just imagine if you've never had spices before, except for salt, and then have curry. It's bound to be a bit confusing."

"I suppose," the teenager grumbled.

Percy took another bite before saying, "It's better than what I had as a kid, and that's the truth. But I think I liked the panini better."

Violet nodded. "Well, we'll have that for lunch again tomorrow. But I'll have to think of what else I can make without potatoes. Maybe stir-fry? Or pizza? Tacos? I guess there are a lot of options." She waved a hand. "Look, the show's starting. I'll try to fill you in as much as I can, but sometimes even I don't know every character and their past. Some of them leave for years and years before returning. And Dad wouldn't let me watch it until I was thirteen."

For a second, she wanted to ask why. But the show started, and she did her best to follow who was related to whom, who had married or dated whom, and what was the current storyline.

The whole thing was confusing, and yet it was interesting to watch these fictional people's lives. Most of them had a lot of problems, and often, it was relationships with friends or family that helped them survive it.

That only reinforced her drive to be friends with her dragon again. Her inner beast was the only friend she needed, and with her, Percy could keep fighting and surviving, no matter what.

Chapter Fourteen

Over the next two days, Percy worked with Bronx and Violet on her lessons, met with the female doctors a few times a day, and even watched dragons fly overhead, coming and going from Stonefire.

The first time she'd seen the magnificent beasts, she almost cried. She'd kept it together only because Violet could see her through the kitchen window.

A real-life dragon didn't compare to what she'd seen inside her head as a child. They were big, powerful, and beautiful. She loved how their scales glinted, even on a cloudy day.

Her beast had been purple, and one of those overhead had been the same color. Later, when she asked about it, Bronx had said it was Nikki, the half-human dragon-shifter who helped protect the clan. He kept saying she would meet Nikki, but Percy didn't dare hope he'd follow through. Bronx had been patient with her reading, had answered all of her questions without complaint, and never yelled or belittled her.

It all felt too good to be true.

And as she stared at the sky, hoping to see yet another dragon flying, Bronx's voice came from the back door. "Someone's here to see you, Percy."

She turned from the empty sky and walked toward him.

He moved aside to let her through and shut the door behind her.

"Who? Dr. Sid? Or is it Layla again?"

A female voice came from the hall. "I'm afraid not. You'll just have to settle for me."

A woman who was older than her, but probably not by much, walked into the room. From the tattoo on her bicep, Percy knew she was a dragon-shifter. Her stature was shorter than the other adult females Percy had met, though. Her skin was more tan than pale, and she had thick black hair pulled back into a ponytail.

The female smiled. "I'm Nikki Hartley-Gray. I've heard about the crap they told you about dragon-shifters with human mothers, and I'm telling you they're all lying wankers."

Percy blinked, unsure what to say. Bronx stepped closer, and she almost closed the distance to be at his side. Somehow, some way, he felt safe to her already.

What the fuck? No, she wasn't going to think he was safe. Males always betrayed her—everyone had, really—and just because he was patient and nice didn't mean anything. Once he'd finished his assignment, he would leave her and move on to the next thing.

No attachments—that was her motto. Only her dragon mattered.

Nikki stood her ground, not moving closer as she watched her.

Her pupils flashed a few times before she smiled. "Sorry, I should be nicer and make a better first impression. I'm used to battling it out with my mate and sometimes forget that not everyone acts like him. Rafe may be human, but he's as stubborn as a dragon-shifter." She placed a hand on her lower belly. "And carrying any of his children makes me cranky. I'm pretty sure they do it on purpose."

Her eyes zeroed in on Nikki's lower belly. Mixed feelings crashed over her. For the last few years, the facility had been trying to get her pregnant, using various methods and settings, documenting everything, trying to figure out what would work. Every time she'd been forced to sleep with one or more males, she'd hoped to finally be pregnant, if only to make it all stop.

But it'd never happened. And so she'd been put through it again and again, in a hellish loop.

Maybe with distance, she'd be glad not to have birthed a baby inside that fucking place. However, she'd always equated getting pregnant with the road to an easier time and less attention from the facility guards.

Tears pricked her eyes, and she willed them to stay put. "Sorry," she mumbled and exited into the hallway. Once she was inside her bedroom, she leaned against the door, closed her eyes, and took a few deep breaths.

Remember, you're no longer in that place. For now, no one will force you to do those things again. To these people, babies are normal and even wanted. They won't become yet another experimental test subject. That was something she still had trouble believing. Watching the TV show, seeing the lengths the parents had gone to have a child to love, had confused her.

A soft knock on the door made her jump. Bronx's voice came through the door. "Are you okay, Percy? Do you need to talk with one of the doctors?"

His voice was the final pull needed to get out of her head. She stared at the books, the radio, and even the little potted plant Violet had given her. She wasn't in *that* place. And so far, the odds were they wouldn't keep her in a room with a male, starving them both until they had sex enough times to meet their demands.

"Percy?" His gentle voice made her eyes water a little. It almost, almost, sounded like he cared about her.

For a split second, she wished it might be true. Not as anything more than friends, but just to have someone other than her dragon care for her would be nice.

The now-familiar little purple flashes of light flickered inside her mind, brighter this time. *Dragon? Is that you? Please, please come out. We can be friends again, talk, and you don't have to stay away. But I need you to be more than flashes of light.*

The purple lights burned a beat longer before disappearing.

She slid down the door until her arse hit the floor. Even if Bronx didn't say anything, she could hear him breathing on the other side of the door.

He was patient, always so patient with her. Before she could think better of it, she blurted, "Why are you nice to me?"

For a second, she thought he might not answer. However, his voice was nearer, as if he'd sat on the ground on the other side too, when he replied, "It's what I do, Percy. I was a firefighter and emergency rescue responder. I'm also a dad, a brother, and an uncle. I like to help and protect and try to see what others are struggling with instead of instantly judging them." He paused then added, "I've always been this way, ever since I was a kid. I used to help stray animals and even had a little recovery shed out back to nurse them to health." He chuckled. "My brothers always made fun of me, but I was the oldest, and so a scowl usually chased them away. Even if it hadn't, I wouldn't have stopped or given up. Sometimes there's a part of you that just has to shine, no matter what others think. Maybe one day you'll discover that part of yourself as well."

Percy stared at her hands, threading her fingers together and then apart and back together again. "All I know how to do is be stubborn. There's not much else to me. Compared to everyone else, I'm boring."

For a second, she froze. Had she really just said that out loud?

Bronx replied, "Just because you don't have twenty hobbies doesn't mean you're boring, Percy. You're a fighter, a survivor, and when many people might've given up, you didn't. That makes you brilliant and amazing and more interesting than you think."

She laughed derisively. "That's you just being nice. I only thought of myself and didn't help anyone else when maybe I could have." She paused, thinking of the new inmates over the years and the ones she'd never seen again. "I'm not amazing, Bronx. So stop saying it."

Silence fell a few seconds before his voice came through the door again. "Sometimes, we can't save everyone, even if we want to. I've dealt with several situations over the years where we could only rescue one person and had to make the bloody awful decision about who we had to leave behind." He cleared his throat. "It's something you never forget, either. Sometimes it goes away for a while, and then it hits you when you least expect it, maybe even if you're merely doing the shopping."

She turned around and laid her forehead on the door. Closing her eyes, she tried to imagine Bronx making a tough choice about who lived or died and then living with it forever. He might not have been a prisoner like her, but his life wasn't as perfect as she'd originally thought.

Placing a hand on the door, she whispered, "Nikki's pregnancy reminded me of the time… before."

He cursed. "I'm so sorry, Percy. I didn't even think of that. If you want to meet anyone else in the future, I'll be more careful about who. Can you forgive me?"

She opened her eyes, leaned back, and frowned at the door. "Why does my forgiveness matter?"

"Because it does. My goal is to never intentionally hurt you, but I also don't want to inadvertently do it, either."

Even a few days ago, she would've called him a liar, scoffed, or merely dismissed his words.

But Bronx had always asked her permission for everything, asked what she wanted, and listened to her.

No one had ever done that before, apart from her dragon.

As she stared at her hand on the door, the one with scars on the back from when she'd fought one of the guards in the early days inside the facility, she quickly pushed away any hope of Bronx being different.

In the end, all males wanted to control her, overpower her, or use her for their own pleasure. He might be nicer and put on a show of asking her things, but it'd all melt away at some point, revealing his true colors.

It always did.

Standing, she said, "I just need to be alone. Please leave me alone."

She heard him also get off the floor and then nothing. Eventually, he said, "As you wish, Percy. Although I hope to see you for our lessons tomorrow. I had planned a surprise, but I can cancel it, if you want."

"I hate surprises." They'd always been new trials, experiments, or a new guard wanting to use her.

He said, "I was going to take you to the children's outdoor dragon lessons. If you want to go, then be ready tomorrow morning by nine a.m. If you're not, then I'll cancel it. Oh, and Violet will bring you some dinner later. I'll leave you alone, as you asked, but I won't allow you to go hungry ever again."

With that, she heard his footsteps grow fainter until they were gone.

She sat on her bed, put her head into her hands, and said, *Dragon, are you there? Please, are you there?*

Nothing.

Confused, overwhelmed, and all-around unsure about anything, Percy let her tears fall.

She was so fucked up, and just when she thought she was doing better, she went backward.

Maybe her dream had been naïve.

Maybe it was time to give up.

But then that flicker of purple in her head was there again. It glowed but never went out like before. While it was still quiet inside her head, the light was comforting and almost felt familiar.

Even though she had no proof, she thought it was her dragon.

And with the comforting light still there, she curled up on the bed. Emotionally exhausted, she fell asleep instantly.

Chapter Fifteen

The next morning, Bronx paced inside the living room. Violet sat at the kitchen island, watching him, but said nothing. That, in and of itself, was fucking weird.

His dragon spoke up. *She's concerned, is all. I don't know if it's about us, Percy, or both. But Violet only gets quiet when she's worried.*

Or plotting.

Yes, but I don't think she's doing that right now.

Bronx eyed his daughter and met her gaze. He grunted. "What?"

She shrugged. "It's been a while since I've seen you so worked up."

"I'm not worked up."

She raised her brows. "Liar."

Since she was, indeed, correct, he merely scowled and paced some more. Yes, he was concerned—mostly about Percy and whether she would come out of her room today. But he was also worried about himself.

Why had he told her about his tough choices when it came to past rescue missions? She didn't need anyone else's burdens on her shoulders.

His dragon spoke up. *I still don't see it that way.*

Ignoring his beast, he ran a hand through his hair and glanced at the clock. It was 9:01 a.m. Percy was late.

He was about to sigh and call Tristan to let him know they wouldn't be coming when Percy's door opened. Going still, he watched the entryway until she was there, standing at the doorway without entering. He asked, "You want to go see the children? Or are you telling me you want to cancel?"

She plucked at the jeans she'd been given, as if still unsure about her decision.

He waited, noticing the circles under her eyes as well as how they were slightly puffy, probably from crying.

The thought of her crying twisted his heart.

She finally replied, "I want to go. I might not be able to stay long, but I want to at least try."

He nodded, itching to go over to her, erase her doubtful looks, and make her smile.

But he didn't move. After yesterday, he didn't want to spook her.

While he knew she was usually strong—bloody hell, look at what she'd survived—he also knew that sometimes remembering a traumatic event could make someone jumpy or nervous. It'd been that way with his late mate, and no doubt, Percy was the same.

Violet spoke up, thankfully. "Brilliant, then we can

go together. I need to turn in my schoolwork and chat to the teachers a little."

His daughter hopped off the stool and walked over to Percy. After Violet threaded her arm through Percy's, she tugged lightly. "Come on. Dad likes to be on time, and he'll start scowling if we don't get a move on."

Bronx scowled. "I'm not that bad."

Violet grinned. "You can be. But even grumpy, I still love you." She turned back toward Percy. "It's cute watching the children trying to understand their dragons. It will be a display in what *not* to do, for the most part. Threatening your inner dragon doesn't work so well. Yes, we can contain them, if needed, with mental mazes or inside mental boxes. But only when you start talking *with* them and not *at* them do they let down their guard. Once they're fully open to you and vice versa, meaning you completely trust each other, then you should be able to start shifting."

As they left the cabin and headed down the path toward Stonefire—Bram had cleared Percy to visit, saying nothing had come up to say she was an enemy, at least not yet—Violet chatted about school, lessons, and even the show from the night before.

He watched Percy smile with his daughter, and Bronx smiled himself. Seeing Percy outside, in the faint sunlight, enjoying herself, made him happy.

Not to mention the sun highlighted the lighter streaks of her hair, made the blue of her eyes glow brighter, and more fully revealed the pinkish birthmark on her neck.

In the past, she'd always tried to turn away from him or Violet to hide it. He wasn't sure why. Yes, it was visible and covered one side of her neck, disappearing underneath the collar of her shirt. But it was a part of her, and if he tilted his head just right, it looked like a dragon's head roaring.

And for a second, he wanted to kiss where her pale skin met the pink, to see what she tasted like and what she smelled like and to maybe brush aside her hair to feel how soft it was before teasing her earlobe.

He stopped walking for a beat. What the fuck was he thinking? The last thing she needed was a male's attention.

Not to mention he was the last male who should ever notice her. Not only because of her past, but also because she was so bloody young. Definitely too young for him.

His dragon spoke up. *She's not like most twenty-year-olds, though. And a young male, out to prove himself or strut around, as if he had the biggest dick in the world, is the opposite of what she needs.*

As if you know what she needs.

A more mature, patient male who is confident enough to support her instead of always trying to impress her.

Why the bloody hell are you even talking about this? If she's our true mate, you'd better tell me, dragon.

I still don't know. Without her dragon, she's only half a person.

I'm working on it. Then realizing how his beast might interpret that, he added, *To help her become independent. Not for any other reason.*

His beast snorted. *Sure. I'll remind you of that the next time you think of kissing her neck.*

At his dragon's words, he glanced up at Percy again.

She faced away from him, and he could only see her from the back. His gaze traveled down her slight form, stopping at her arse.

Fuck. He glanced away, picked up his speed, and kept even with both Violet and Percy, ensuring Violet was also between him and Percy.

The sooner they could get to the school, the better. Surrounded by kids, including his nephews, he wouldn't be tempted to think of Percy inappropriately. She'd be another student, and he'd fall back into his role as a teacher. That was what they were and all they would ever be.

PERCY WAS both excited and anxious as they approached the walls surrounding the main grounds of Stonefire. A metal gate was up ahead, and the words *Clan Stonefire* were entwined within the bars.

She was finally setting foot inside of a dragon clan for the first time in her life.

As she went past the gate, she expected something to happen. Maybe for someone to throw something at her, call her names, and tell her to get lost. Or maybe a group would shout that half-dragon-shifters weren't welcome and she needed to leave.

But nothing happened. Violet waved to the tall male near the entrance, the blond one Percy remembered seeing right before she'd blacked out inside the facility.

Violet shouted, "Hi ya, Kai. There's no need to

scowl. We won't cause any trouble. Well, Percy won't.
We'll see what I get up to."

The dragonman grunted. Bronx, on the other side
of Violet, sighed and said, "You're going to be the
death of me one day, Vi. I just know it."

Violet winked at her dad. "I wouldn't do that. I'd
miss you too much. But I'm definitely up for giving you
a few more gray hairs."

Bronx brushed his temples, which had a smattering
of gray. "All from you, love. All from you."

Violet laughed, and Bronx grinned. He did that a
lot around his daughter. And every time, Percy couldn't
stop staring at the one dimple he had, on his left cheek.

This time was no different. But once she realized
what she was doing, she looked at Bronx's eyes. His
pupils flashed rapidly.

Fuck. Had he caught her staring at him?

Facing forward, she willed her cheeks not to flush.
She didn't want him to get the wrong idea. But she'd
never seen many people smile in her lifetime—at least
in a non-menacing way, like the guards back inside the
facility—and never with dimples.

And apparently, she rather liked dimples.

For a beat, she wondered what it'd be like to touch
Bronx's and then feel his usual late-day stubble against
her fingers.

Percy quickly banished that image, one she would
never act upon. Bronx had been a fairly good teacher
so far, and she wouldn't ruin that and risk ending up
with someone else who would try to rush her.

If she wanted her dragon, then she would most

definitely stop staring at Bronx's dimple. He was a means to an end and nothing else.

As they walked farther inside the clan, Percy easily distracted herself by taking in the buildings. There had been a large one not far from the gate—the security office, Violet had pointed out—and then it'd been a pathway with a few plants and shrubs for a few minutes. Then the plants cleared, revealing a few streets and several groups of buildings. Most were stone cottages, but there were also some two-story brick buildings that were shops ranging from food to clothing and even a jewelry place, judging by the sign with rings and bigger bands with engravings.

Violet must've caught her staring because she waved toward the jewelry shop. "That's the silversmith. Well, one half of it is, anyway, and the other part is where you can paint pottery. It's run by Dylan. He makes all the mating cuffs for couples, plus he also designs everyone's dragon tattoos."

She glanced at the younger dragonwoman. "So you can just pick one out from a book or something?"

Violet shook her head. "No. Your tattoo design is given to you as a gift from your family, soon after you're born. And not literally on your skin, but as a framed print. Then when you turn sixteen, you get your tattoo permanently inked onto your upper arm." Violet paused to tap hers. "I can't wait to finally get mine in less than a year. My design is kind of like my dad's, but not really. Maybe Dad can show you his?"

She glanced at Bronx, and he grunted. "Maybe later."

For a split second, disappointment rushed through

Percy. She'd only had brief glances of them since arriving, but she'd never studied one for any length of time.

But she pushed aside the feeling. Seeing a dragon tattoo had nothing to do with her goals.

As they continued walking, Violet pointed out the various stores, explained who ran them, and even gestured down a street to where she lived. "We're closer to the high street than most people. But it's useful for my dad, so he can get to the Protector building quickly."

Bronx grunted. "Not anymore."

Percy leaned forward a little and asked, "Why not?"

He shrugged. "I can't do rescue missions any longer."

Violet waved a hand in dismissal. "But he still helps out with advising and helping to coordinate missions sometimes. Regardless, it's been my home my whole life, and I like it."

She wondered what it would feel like to have a place of your own, to be in control of how things were arranged or decorated, or to even just control who could enter. The idea was so bloody foreign to her.

A female voice shouted, "Bronx, Percy, wait up!"

They stopped, and Percy turned, spotting a dragonwoman with dark skin, black hair pulled back into a bun, and dark-brown eyes.

When the woman finally reached them, she held out some tins to Bronx. "My boys forgot their lunches. Brooklyn said you're visiting the school, so could you give it to them? I'd do it myself, but I have that human event to cater, and I never have enough hands."

Before she could ask, Bronx gestured toward Percy. "This is Percy. And, Percy, this is my sister-in-law, Letitia. And of course I'll take their lunches. For all we know, Jayden could launch some mission to sneak away to go home and get his."

Letitia nodded at Percy and then sighed at Bronx. "Don't remind me. That boy is going to be the death of me." She looked back at Percy, both her smile and her eyes warm. "Thank you for helping Joey. He's my newest nephew, and I can't imagine not having him around."

Percy shifted her feet. "Sure."

The dragonwoman studied her a beat before saying, "Well, once I'm done with this event, maybe you could come over, and I'll make your favorite meal. Especially if you're having to eat what this pair make, as more often than not, it's a little burnt, unless it's a baked good. Violet has a knack with desserts, to the point I keep asking her to help me bake for events."

Before she could stop herself, Percy blurted, "Violet is a good cook, full stop."

Letitia blinked. "Oh?" She smiled, glanced at Violet, and said, "Sorry, Vi. I didn't know you'd been practicing."

Violet shrugged. "It's mostly easy stuff, and it's nothing like yours, Auntie Letitia. Percy just hasn't had a lot of choices when it comes to food. Oh, and if you know of any good dinners without potatoes, then send the recipes to me. Please?"

Percy's cheeks burned at Violet's words about lack of choices. She wondered how much or how little the people of Stonefire knew about her.

Bronx jumped in. "We need to keep going. I'll give the boys their lunches, Letitia. And we'll see about the dinner."

Once Letitia made her goodbyes, smiling yet again at Percy, they walked out of the crowded center of the clan and toward a larger building in the distance. Children's voices drifted from the area.

Needing a distraction from wondering what everyone thought of her here, she asked, "Is that the school?"

Bronx answered, "Yes. All the students go there, from the youngest to those who're eighteen. Although given all of the mates and the children born over the last several years, I've started to wonder if we'll need to build an addition soon to accommodate them all."

Violet nodded. "There have been a lot, haven't there? But I think welcoming and having more humans live here is a big part of it. Maybe at some point, humans and dragons could interact freely without all the restrictions and rules and the like. That would be even better for the clan. Don't you think so, Dad?"

Bronx nodded. "Probably. But today's not a history lesson, Vi. And as soon as we get to the school, go visit your teachers and don't get distracted."

Violet sighed. "I know, I know." She turned toward Percy. "And don't worry, Percy. All the teachers are brilliant, even grumpy Mr. MacLeod. If you have questions, just ask them. Or the children. No matter what you were told growing up, they don't care if your mother was human. You're a dragon-shifter and nothing else."

The certainty in Violet's words made her throat

tighten. Everyone kept saying that, although she still thought it too good to be true.

Thankfully, they'd reached the gate of the school, so she didn't have to think of a reply. The dragonman who'd been playing games when she'd first woken up days ago, Tristan, walked up to them. He grunted. "Good. You're here. The students are already out back, in the smaller practice area. This way."

Violet waved goodbye and headed inside the building, leaving Percy alone with Bronx and Tristan.

Neither male crowded her or walked too close. She did slowly gravitate toward Bronx's side, though, craving the familiar over the unknown. "Why do they practice outside?"

Tristan answered, "Because young dragons are unpredictable. And if they accidentally shift into their full dragon form instead of just a talon or two, they could do serious damage to the classroom and maybe even structural damage to the building."

She glanced at Bronx and bit her lip. He smiled at her in encouragement, and she found the courage to ask Tristan another question. "You can change just a part of you?"

Tristan nodded. "Yes. It's easier to start with only a small section. The exercise gives the children a chance to work with their dragon, not allow them to take over, and it teaches patience, which is essential for a dragon-shifter. After all, you might not always agree with what your inner beast says. However, you can't ignore them or walk away. You're with them for life, and you have to make it work."

"But what if it doesn't?"

Tristan's brows came together. "It's rare, but if it happens, then it usually doesn't end well." He looked at Percy a beat, his pupils flashing, before adding, "If you lose complete control of your inner dragon, we call it 'going rogue.' And without the human half to help restrain some of their animalistic urges to fuck, fight, and eat, things can go south quickly."

Bronx said, "But that can usually be avoided if a student starts slow, building up to a full shift. By the time they can change into their dragon form, the pair has become a sort of team and has learned to share control."

The kids were closer now. Before Percy could change her mind, she blurted, "What happens if my dragon turns rogue?"

Tristan glanced at Bronx, who nodded, before the dragonman answered, "If that happens, the DDA will hunt you down. They'll try to capture you alive, but if it's impossible and you're a major threat, they'll shoot to kill."

Bronx said softly, "Which is why we're moving slowly with you, Percy. But you must absolutely tell us if your dragon starts talking to you. She might be unpredictable and may require some creative thinking or problem-solving to keep her in line."

"And if that doesn't work?"

Bronx stated, "Then we'll have no choice but to keep her silent."

At the thought of finally being reunited with her beast and then losing her all over again, Percy's heart squeezed. There was no bloody way she would let that happen. For as long as she could manage her beast, she'd keep it a secret, like she had at the orphanage.

Unlike back then, she was older and was learning more about what to do and how to handle an inner dragon. So she would do like always—sort things out herself.

For a second, she didn't like the idea of keeping something from Bronx and Violet. They'd done so much for her.

And yet, her dragon was everything. Percy would rather die than lose her again.

The two males watched her as she walked quietly, lost in her thoughts. However, as soon as they reached the outdoor class, a familiar little dark-haired boy rushed up to her—Joey.

He stopped a few inches away from her, took her hand, and blurted, "Thank you, Percy, for helping me get out of that place. My mum explained why you had to lie to me, and it's okay. She said sometimes, once in a while, lying might be better. But in general, we need to tell the truth."

Guilt crept over Percy at her recently made plans to hide any dragon-related activity from Bronx and Violet. But then she dismissed it. As nice as people were being to her, they could turn in an instant, and Percy had to protect herself.

She murmured, "No worries."

Tristan said to Joey, "Go back to your class, Joey."

"Yes, Mr. MacLeod." He dashed off to the group of younger children.

Not wanting to think of her deceptive plans, she asked, "Why is he here? Isn't he human?"

Tristan nodded. "Yes. But when Daisy, the first human child, moved to Stonefire, we decided it was best for the human kids to also come to these lessons. Even if they don't have inner dragons, it's important to understand how it all works, especially if they plan on eventually staying with a dragon clan and mating a dragon-shifter."

She blinked. "Wait. How many other human children live here?"

"Three so far." Bronx gestured toward the slightly older kids nearer to them. "Joey's brother, Mark, is in the class we're going to watch today. Daisy's on holiday with her family, but she's in a class above Mark." He waved toward a man in the distance, one who had the same dark hair and gray eyes as Bronx. "And my younger brother, Hudson, is stepfather to the two human boys. This is their first day back after the ordeal." He glanced at Tristan. "Is it okay if I quickly introduce Percy to my brother? Once we're done, we'll sneak to the back of the class and try not to be disruptive."

Tristan grunted. "Let me know if Percy wants to be introduced."

They both looked at her, and she shook her head. "No, I don't want the attention."

Tristan bobbed his head, waved goodbye, and went to the group of children waiting for him.

Bronx looked at her and searched her face. "If you want to meet my brother, that is. He just wants to thank you properly for saving his new stepson. But if it's too much, just tell me, and it can wait."

Percy felt eyes on her—way too many eyes—but she

focused on Bronx's face. Otherwise, she might get overwhelmed. She hadn't been around this many people at once since she was at the orphanage, taking meals, all those years ago.

Looking into Bronx's familiar gray eyes and flashing pupils, she noticed an almost eagerness to his gaze, as if her meeting his brother would make him happy. That might make him smile again and show his dimple.

Not that it should matter. Pleasing Bronx wasn't her job.

And yet, before she could convince herself otherwise, she nodded. "Okay."

He smiled, that dimple on full display, and her belly flipped. Not like when she'd felt dread back in the facility, but in a sort of nice way.

What the fuck is happening to me?

Bronx waved for his brother to come over, and Percy forced herself to look away. She most definitely didn't want to have flushed cheeks when his brother walked up.

As she took a few deep breaths, Percy watched the slightly younger dragonman head toward them. They did look a lot alike—obviously, they were related—but Bronx's nose was a little bigger than his brother's. Plus, the brother had a slightly smoother walk, probably because he hadn't lost part of a limb.

When the brother stopped a few feet away, Percy also noted how he was a little shorter than Bronx.

Bronx clapped his brother on the shoulder and then gestured toward Percy. "Hudson, this is Percy Smith. Percy, this is my youngest brother, Hudson. He's mated to Sarah, the mother of the two human boys, one of whom is Joey."

Hudson smiled at her, but he didn't have a dimple. And while he seemed nice enough, she didn't feel as safe around him as Bronx.

She took a step closer to her dragonman.

If Hudson noticed, he didn't comment. "Nice to meet you, Percy." He glanced between Bronx and Percy. "I heard how my brother was assigned to be your teacher. He's probably doing a fantastic job, but if you need anything, anything at all, from me and my family, just say the word. Because we can never repay you for protecting Joey like you did."

Her cheeks heated from the praise. "It was nothing. I used them as a way to escape."

Hudson raised his brows. "Joey said you made them food, and even put them in a room while you stood guard outside. I think you did more than use them as pawns, Percy."

Unsure of what to say—he might be right, but she refused to admit being soft toward the two kids—she shrugged. After a beat of silence, Hudson looked at his older brother. "In a day or two, Sarah might come visit you and Violet. She's calming down and finally accepting that her boys are safe, and she wants to ask you something about a picnic."

Bronx replied, "Sure, have her stop by. I'll be staying in one of the cabins for the foreseeable future."

Because of Percy was left unsaid.

For a beat, she felt guilty. Because of her, Bronx currently lived away from his family, who, for some reason, all seemed to care for him and Violet. Not only that, they wanted to spend time with them and acted like it'd be a treat to do so.

After the brothers shared a few parting details, Hudson said goodbye, and Bronx gestured toward the area where Tristan walked among a small group of children. "Come on. I'll explain as we watch."

And once he started explaining what the scrunched faces meant or pointed out a child successfully turning a finger into a talon, Percy drank it all in, trying to memorize everything. Maybe clues from watching how the students changed body parts would help her to do the same.

As more and more children whooped and completed their task, the familiar purple light was back inside her mind. No matter what Percy said, though, there was no response.

It never extinguished, though. And so even when they went back toward the cabin, the familiar light always hovered in the background, as if standing watch.

Chapter Sixteen

Once Percy was finally alone again in her room, she sat on the bed, leaned against the wall, and closed her eyes. The purple light was larger than ever before, and she swore it was stronger.

Bracing herself for disappointment, she said, *Are you there, dragon? Are you finally coming out? Please come out. I just want to talk with you.*

The light flickered but then burned even brighter.

Heart racing, she gripped the bed cover with her fingers. *Did you like watching the students today? That's what we should've done, back then. Sorry, dragon. I didn't know what to do.*

The light turned almost blinding.

She barely avoided begging as she said, *If you come out now, we can start trying some stuff. There's loads more to learn, but I already know more now than everything combined from the last twenty years. I think we have a better shot this time at success.*

The light changed shape, growing into something more than round. But just as she swore a dragon form took place, someone knocked on the door.

Without thinking, she blurted, "What the fuck do you want? Leave me alone."

The light inside her head turned back into a circle, sphere, or whatever it was, and Violet's voice drifted into the room. "Sorry, Percy. I won't bother you again."

At the hurt in the girl's tone, she opened her eyes. *Fuck.* Violet didn't deserve to be yelled at.

Still, Percy couldn't help but say inside her mind, *Please, come back. Are you there?*

The light remained unchanging.

Sighing, she stared at the door. Violet's footsteps faded until the only sound was the wind blowing outside and the nearby plants brushing against her window.

Part of her wanted to scream over being interrupted when she'd been so bloody close. And yet, Violet hadn't known what she was doing. Not to mention the girl usually only knocked when she had information or resources related to helping Percy in some way.

For the first time in a long, long while, she felt true remorse. Not since her early days in the facility, when she'd been punished for trying to help the other prisoners, had she felt the emotion.

And it fucking sucked.

Her conscience prickled. Maybe she should find Violet and apologize.

But wouldn't that show weakness? Not to mention

if she let one piece of her inner wall fall, would the rest come tumbling down soon after?

Her eyes landed on the collection of children's books Violet had slowly been bringing her. At first, she'd been embarrassed and thought it was to mock her reading skills.

But Violet had asked her to read them, and it was a series centering on dragon-shifters who didn't quite fit in and how they learned to be better people to both others and their inner dragons. The stories were mostly about embracing differences instead of hiding them.

It was almost as if Violet knew Percy struggled with being the outsider and was trying to show her that she didn't have to be.

Bloody hell, realizing that made her feel two inches tall.

Sighing, she got off the bed and went to the door. She opened it slowly, making sure no one was out there, and her eyes landed on a book on the ground.

She picked it up and thumbed through it, going back inside her room. As she read the story, she felt even more like an arsehole for yelling at Violet.

The story was about a dragon-shifter student, and her inner dragon was the only one who hadn't emerged yet, no matter how much she wanted it to. The female would cry and try to hide from the students who all had flashing dragon eyes, even her friends. She sometimes hid from her family too, hating how people pitied her.

However, one of her friends eventually found her and said to have faith it would happen one day. Until then, the friend said she could ask her dragon questions anytime she wanted, until they got their own, so the female dragon-shifter wouldn't feel so lonely.

By the end of the story, the late bloomer had her inner beast. And because she'd taken her friend up on the offer and asked a ton of questions, she'd been better prepared to work with her dragon than if she'd stayed hidden away.

Closing the book, Percy traced the picture on the cover. Even if Violet's knocking had stalled her dragon coming out, the girl had only been trying to help her.

The middle of her chest hurt. As she rubbed the spot, her eyes heated with tears. For the first time in her life, she thought someone might be trying to help her without wanting anything in return.

And how had she reacted? By treating Violet like crap.

Wiping the back of her hand across her eyes, she took a few deep breaths and went searching for Violet. She could try again with her dragon later. But for now, she needed to make things right. As weird as it was, the fifteen-year-old might be her first-ever friend who wasn't her dragon.

It was scary as fuck to think she wanted to apologize and care about someone else's feelings. But to not do it, to just brush it off, seemed so very, very wrong.

And so Percy went looking for Violet.

BRONX FINISHED his call with Bram and headed back inside the cabin, only to find Violet madly stirring some sort of dough or batter. That meant something had upset her.

He went over to the kitchen and leaned against the counter. "What happened?"

She mixed the contents of her bowl more briskly. "Nothing."

"Then why are you about to start flinging dough or batter, or whatever the hell is in there, all over the kitchen?"

She huffed, stopped mixing, and set down the bowl. She turned toward him, her cheeks flushed and her pupils flashing rapidly. "Why would someone try to push everyone away? And shut them out? Even if all you want to do is help them?"

He had a sense something had happened with Percy, but he wouldn't jump to conclusions. "Everyone's past is unique, Vi. And many people go through trials and tribulations, which make them the way they are. No two people are ever exactly the same, and that actually makes life more interesting."

She grunted. "And bloody difficult."

He resisted smiling at her tone—which he knew wasn't funny, but she was rarely gruff—and replied, "Yes. Want to talk about what happened?"

She sighed. "I don't want to complain about something that seems trivial when compared to so many other things."

"Just because you think your situation is arguably better than someone else's doesn't mean your feelings are less important."

She smiled. "You sound like a dad right now."

He shrugged. "That's what I'm mostly good at, I think. Well, most of the time."

Violet came closer to him and looked into his eyes. Yet again, her height made him realize how grown-up she was. "You're a brilliant dad." She grinned. "Most of the time."

He chuckled. "We all have our faults." He gently kicked his good foot against hers. "So, tell me what happened."

Sighing, she turned to lean next to him, against the counter. "I think I made Percy mad. But I wasn't trying to do it. I just wanted to help her, and she shouted at me." She bit her lip and then added, "Part of me thinks I should leave her alone. And yet, she always looks so sad and lonely and in need of a friend. I don't know what to do, Dad."

He studied his daughter's profile a second, and his dragon spoke up. *Tell her some more about her mum. It might help her understand.*

Bronx had always said Violet was too young, that someday she could handle the truth. But Violet was only a few years younger than Edith had been when Bronx found her. Only five years younger than Percy.

And yes, both of those females had suffered a lot more and grown up fast. However, if he continued to think of his daughter as a little girl and treat her as such, it would most likely drive her away at some point.

Sighing, he looked forward again. Not looking into her eyes made it easier to talk. "It was the same with your mother, in the early days." He heard Violet suck in a breath, but he didn't look at her. If he wanted to finish, he couldn't be distracted. "You know she was hurt when I found her hiding in an abandoned boat shed, not far from Stonefire. However, what I never shared was that she'd been badly beaten by her bastard former boyfriend."

Violet gasped. "What?"

He crossed his arms over his chest and gripped his arms. "Yes. She hadn't made dinner the way he wanted, and he hit her repeatedly until she passed out." He gripped his arms tighter. "As soon as he left for work the next day, she fled with little more than the clothes on her back. Since he kept most of the money tightly in his control, she could only afford a train ticket as far as Keswick in the Lake District. Then she walked and walked, until she couldn't manage it any longer."

When his late mate had eventually shared her story, he couldn't believe she'd made it as far as the lake near Stonefire. But Edith had said that wanting to live had given her strength she hadn't known she had.

Violet asked quietly, "How did you finally convince her to trust and like you?"

"I was patient. She recovered under my mum's care, in a different cottage. Eventually, she was well enough to receive visitors. I went every day, talked to her about anything and everything, even if she didn't say much. But then one day, well, I got her to laugh. And the rest is history."

He smiled at the memory of when he'd shared the latest argument with his inner dragon. It'd been silly, about trying to pluck up one of his younger brothers in his dragon form before tossing him into the lake as payback for a prank. But Edith had never thought about brotherly dragon antics and had found it hilarious.

Her smile had caught his eye, and he'd worked every day after to make her do it again and again.

His daughter said, "I'm glad you told me, Dad. I'm sorry she was hurt, but at least in the end, she found you, didn't she?"

He looked at his daughter, who looked so like her mother, and he felt a flicker of sadness. "Your mum would've been so proud of how you've grown up, Vi. I mean it. Despite her rough past, once she felt safe and came out of her shell, she always wanted to help others, if she could—volunteering, watching some of the clan children when needed, or even just helping to stock the underground rooms we use in case of emergencies." He smiled. "You remind me a lot of her at times."

"Will you tell me more?"

At the eagerness in her eyes, he suddenly wondered why he'd put this off for so long. Violet, of all people, deserved to hear about Edith, rough past and all.

As he debated what to say next, he heard something drop and crash onto the floor in the hallway. He turned and said, "Who's there?"

Percy poked her head from around the doorway. "I'm sorry. I can come back later." She hesitated and then looked at Violet. "I just wanted to say I'm sorry."

Violet waved for Percy to come into the room. Once she did, Violet said, "It's okay. I know sometimes you need time alone after spending so many years like that. I guess I was just really eager to give you the latest book I found."

Percy smiled shyly. "I read it and loved it. Thank

you for bringing it to my room." She shifted her feet. "I can leave you two alone again."

As she turned, Bronx said, "No, stay, if you want. I'm sure Violet could use our help in the kitchen."

Violet nodded. "Yes. I need to get these biscuits into the oven, and then we can chop stuff up for dinner."

For a second, Bronx thought Percy would leave. But she turned slowly around and nodded. "Okay."

And soon Violet put them both to work.

As she chopped vegetables, Percy kept stealing glances at both Bronx and Violet. She hadn't meant to eavesdrop on their conversation. She'd just been waiting for an opening to apologize to Violet.

True, she could've come back later. However, she'd been afraid that if she didn't apologize as soon as possible, she might lose her nerve, ruining her relationship with Violet. Funny how a week ago she wouldn't have given a shit about what someone felt or thought. And now? She wanted to mend fences with a teenager.

Hearing about how Violet's mother had been beaten made her understand Bronx a little better. Not to mention it reinforced his words about liking to help people. After all, he'd mated a desperately broken and hurt female, making her laugh, and eventually had a daughter with her.

In a way, it gave Percy some hope.

Oh, his late mate had been human and didn't have the same dragon troubles as her. And yet, if someone else who'd been so damaged and abused could find happiness, maybe she could too.

Wait. Why does happiness matter? She wanted it with her dragon, yes. But she didn't need it with anyone else.

Once she finished chopping the onion, rather enthusiastically, Violet sent her to help Bronx with the kale and sweet potatoes for the soup. Apparently, sweet potatoes didn't taste like regular potatoes, and Violet was going to make Percy try them.

She approached Bronx but stayed about two feet away. "What do I need to do?"

He glanced at her. "Well, that depends—are you going to accidentally chuck the sweet potatoes out the window for having the word *potatoes* in their name or not? Because if so, I'm going to have to protect them. With my life."

He grinned, and she laughed. The sound was rusty, and she took a second to recover.

Percy couldn't remember the last time she'd done that.

Bronx raised his brows. "Well? Because if you hold the name against them, I *will* huddle over them and protect them until they go into the soup. I rather like sweet potatoes."

She smiled and shook her head. "You're being ridiculous. But, no, I won't throw them away. I'm willing to try them at least once."

He offered the knife to her, handle out. "Then you can chop them into cubes. Violet says I always make them too big."

His daughter chimed in. "You do! And then it takes forever to cook, making everything else soggy."

Percy took the knife from Bronx, her fingers brushing his in the process. A small tendril of heat rushed through her. And since she was staring into his eyes, she noticed how they flashed rapidly.

He cleared his throat and turned back to peeling the sweet potatoes. "Right, well, I'm hungry. So let's get this done."

She finally forced her gaze away from Bronx and went to work with the knife. And yet, as she cut the sweet potatoes into cubes, her heart still raced a little faster than normal from Bronx's touch.

What the fuck was wrong with her? She'd never felt anything like that before.

Her gut said it would be better to ignore it. So she spent the remainder of the prep time doing what Violet asked, ensuring she didn't touch Bronx again, and counted down the minutes until she could be alone so she could try coaxing out her dragon once more.

Chapter Seventeen

Violet had made a new recipe with Italian sausage, sweet potatoes, kale, and onions, and Bronx had devoured it. Once Bronx finished eating his soup, he left his daughter and Percy alone on the couch to clean up in the kitchen.

As he filled the sink with hot water, his dragon grunted. *Why are you running away from her?*

I'm not running.

You are.

Maybe he was. But seeing Percy laugh for the first time, where all her burdens evaporated for a few seconds, had turned her into a bloody beautiful young female. He still remembered the crinkles at the corners of her eyes, the way her open mouth had highlighted her plump lower lip, and even just the way she'd sounded—like even the laughter had surprised her. Add in the brush of her fingers against his, shooting straight to his cock, and he'd done everything possible to keep from touching her again.

His dragon sighed. *Why? I liked feeling her skin against ours.*

You know why, dragon. She needs time to heal.

I'm not saying we fuck her tomorrow. But woo her a bit. I'd like to see what happens.

Alarm bells blared inside his head. *You would tell me if she's our true mate, wouldn't you?*

Yes. Because then you wouldn't be able to ignore her.

But she's not?

I still can't tell. Until she gets her dragon, I don't know if I ever can.

That meant not kissing her on the lips and taking her bottom lip between his teeth.

Wait, no. He most definitely wouldn't do either of those things.

Bronx finished washing the dishes, and he turned to look at the two females sitting on the couch. Violet was explaining some complicated relationship web between the characters on the show, and Percy drank it all in. She probably didn't realize it, but the guarded look was gone, replaced with curiosity and a little annoyance.

When Violet finally stopped, Percy asked, "Why the fuck would she come back home if she knows that guy's going to kill her?"

Violet snorted. "They almost always come back. It just means some sort of major thing is going to happen soon—either a showdown, someone gets hurt, or they kill off the character."

Bronx smiled. He'd always avoided watching the soap operas in the past. But when Violet had learned that her mother had watched them, she'd pestered him constantly. Eventually, he'd caved and had no choice but to sit through them to make sure she was old enough.

And he'd secretly become hooked himself. Sometimes a person just wanted to escape into the ridiculous.

Percy grunted. "Well, I won't feel bad if she dies. I don't care if she has like four kids and a three-legged dog. If she's an idiot, she deserves it."

Bronx couldn't hold back his laughter. Percy turned around and narrowed her eyes. "What? You support the idiot?"

He put up his hands. "No, no, I agree. But sometimes it's fun to root for characters to be killed off. One female on that show, in particular, deserves it. And yet, she always seems to be the one who survives."

Violet shrugged. "If a character can stir your emotions, Dad, then it's a good thing."

He rolled his eyes. "Sometimes I wish I could go back to the day I'd never seen that show."

Violet pointed at him. "Liar."

He grinned. "Okay, maybe. But only because watching them helps me know you better, Vi."

Violet gestured toward Percy. "And now Percy. I mean, her comments are classic and make me laugh half the time."

He met Percy's gaze. "Yes, I'll admit her biting quips make it more enjoyable."

Percy's cheeks flushed. "I don't really have a filter— as Violet calls it—yet. And since I don't think I'll be punished here, I speak my mind."

And just like that, Bronx's amusement faded, replaced with anger.

He burned to ask about her punishments, more of what she suffered.

However, Percy turned back toward the TV and went back to asking Violet questions about the show.

His dragon said, *She's not ready yet.*

I know, dragon. Although it's getting harder and harder to be patient.

Because you want Percy to find her place on Stonefire, to be able to start over. And to do that, she will have to confront some of her past.

Start over, yes. But it's her choice of where.

His beast grunted, and Bronx braced himself for a fight.

But thankfully his dragon remained silent, and he went back to tidying up the kitchen.

Once the show was over, he watched Percy hurry from the room and lock herself inside her bedroom.

He itched to go talk to her some more but tamped it down. He had plenty of work to do—going through both more information about the facility and notes from Dr. Rossi—and Percy obviously wanted to be alone.

Maybe if he were more than her teacher, he'd say fuck it and knock on her door.

But he wasn't. And so Bronx busied himself with work, doing his best to forget Percy's laughter and the light brush of her fingers against his.

Chapter Eighteen

Over the next few days, Percy was extremely careful to A, avoid Bronx as much as possible, and B, focus on getting her dragon to come out.

She couldn't avoid her lessons, of course, and she saw Bronx then. But thankfully, she didn't have to avoid the nightly TV shows with Violet, because the dragonman mainly worked at the kitchen island during the programs and always ignored her. Oh, he was attentive and patient for any of her reading lessons, or dragon lessons, or anything a teacher would do for any of their students.

But any sort of ease or sense of familiarity between them had cooled. And Percy did her best to ignore how she didn't like it. That was why she now sat with her legs crossed atop the bed, her eyes closed, and tried once more to coax out her inner beast.

The purple light in her head was always there, but it hadn't changed in its size or intensity since the day

Violet had interrupted her. She was convinced the purple light was her long-lost friend, and even if her dragon hadn't responded again, she wasn't giving up.

So Percy concentrated on the light. *Dragon, are you there? Don't you want to come out and play? Or chat? Or anything you like?*

Nothing. She growled and searched her brain for something she hadn't tried before. Then it hit her— she'd made up a song with her dragon way back when. Maybe that would entice her beast out, especially if she left a line unfinished.

She went through the song about a young dragon-shifter being able to fly to the moon and came to the final line: *As she soared through the stars, the light making her scales almost glow, she knew that…*

One beat, then another. And soon, the light flickered. Percy repeated the line, dropping off at the same point. And this time, the light began to morph into a shape. Bit by bit, it turned into a fuzzy outline of a dragon.

She held her breath, afraid she would mess it up.

But when a purple dragon much larger than she'd ever seen in her head before finally appeared in her mind, she blurted, *Dragon? Is that you?*

The shape said nothing, just stood there a second. So Percy said, *It's me, Percy. Remember?*

Percy? The voice was rusty, unsure, and barely audible.

Yes, it's me. We can be together again. Please don't go away.

The dragon form said nothing. And in the next second, it morphed back into a glowing sphere.

Percy cried out. *No, no, don't go! Please don't go!*

But the dragon didn't come back, no matter how much she called out to her.

After trying for about ten minutes, Percy finally just sat on her bed, staring at the floor, disappointment crushing her.

She'd always thought that if her dragon would come out, then everything would be perfect. They'd be instant friends, they'd learn how to shift together, and then they could fly away and be happy.

And most importantly, they would be free.

But her inner beast had spooked so easily, treating Percy as a stranger, running as if she would hurt her or something else awful.

Would Percy ever have her only friend back again? Or had her beast been silenced for too long? Maybe because Percy had received too many drugs to mess with her system?

Maybe she wasn't really a dragon-shifter any longer?

Not quite human, but not a dragon either. She was even more a freak than she'd been as a child. But this time, her dragon wouldn't appear and make everything better.

Tears trickled down her cheeks, followed by more, and soon, Percy was sobbing. The only friend she'd ever had didn't want to talk with her—her dragon was too afraid to stick around.

And if she couldn't convince her beast it was safe to come out again?

Then she'd always be alone, so very alone.

The thought of all her years of surviving, finding ways to cope, all so she could be reunited with her beast only made her sob harder. Had she really done it all for nothing?

At some point, someone came into the room, but she didn't dare open her eyes. If her dragon wouldn't stick around, then what did it matter if someone came to hurt her, kidnap her, or who the fuck knew what?

Weaknesses didn't matter, either. Let them pounce and maybe stop the pain.

So Percy cried and wailed, letting out years of sadness, frustration, and loneliness, along with a multitude of other emotions.

Because at this rate, she'd be alone forever.

BRONX HEARD the first sob coming from Percy's room and walked slowly to her door. As he placed his ear against the door, her cries grew louder and more intense, until she was gasping for air.

He placed his hand on the doorknob and hesitated. She deserved her privacy. He needed to prove Stonefire was different from her former prison and that she had control over who could enter her room.

And yet, as her sobs turned heart-wrenching, almost as if she were dying, he made the decision to check on her.

He knocked, but nothing. "Percy?"

Still nothing.

Each of her cries shot straight to his heart. If she kept it up, she'd make herself sick.

His dragon said, *If her health is in danger or there's a risk of her dragon coming out and going rogue, we need to check on her.*

We are nothing like the bastards who imprisoned her. We care about her.

Bolstered by his dragon's words, he entered the room. Instantly, his gaze latched on to Percy sitting on the bed, tears streaming down her face and her arms wrapped around her torso, as if she were clinging for dear life.

She was in pain, so much pain, and he couldn't leave her alone without trying to ease it.

Bronx walked slowly toward the bed, ready to back away if needed. But Percy didn't notice him. Eventually, he sat next to her, and she still didn't so much as flinch or raise her head.

She just kept saying, "I'm alone," over and over again.

Percy looked so lost, sad, and broken. All he wanted to do was hug her close, stroke her hair, and murmur he was there and he'd help her in any way he could. All she had to do was ask.

And yet, he stayed in place. She'd been fragile even before this breakdown. Would him touching her send her into a panic or bring back all those memories and make the situation a hell of a lot worse?

His dragon spoke up. *She's hurting and sobbing about being alone. I say try. Even if she grew up more like a human, dragon-shifters like touch and affection. And even if she balks, we'll need to get her calmed down and call the doctor.*

His dragon was right. However, he would try talking to her first. "Percy? It's me, Bronx. Tell me what's wrong, love."

She didn't seem to hear him, only hugged herself tighter and hiccupped as she continued to cry.

The picture wrenched his heart nearly in two. "You're not alone, Percy. I'm here, and Violet will return soon, and the both of us can help you."

More crying.

He took a deep breath. "I'm going to touch you now, Percy, okay? If you don't calm down soon, love, you might make yourself sick. And I can't bear it."

She was still lost in her grief, anger, or whatever was making her fall apart.

He gingerly placed a hand on her shoulder. When she didn't react at all, he squeezed her gently. "Percy, oh, Percy, tell me what's wrong."

He moved his hand down to her upper arm, where her dragon-shifter tattoo should've been, and rubbed up and down. "I'm here when you're ready, Percy. I won't go until you tell me how I can help."

For a few seconds, he merely rubbed her arm in a soothing motion. Then suddenly, she turned toward him and buried herself against his side.

He blinked and then slowly, oh-so-slowly, wrapped his arms around her. Instead of tensing, she melted more against him.

Murmuring soothing words, he rubbed circles on her back. He didn't know how long he did that, but slowly, her sobs lessened, and eventually, she was quiet.

He tried to unwrap his arms to let her up, but she whispered, "No. Don't."

As she hugged his torso, he held her slight form tighter against him.

They sat that way for a long while, and the longer they did, the more it felt right to embrace her, to support her, and to let her know she didn't have to be strong all the time. It was okay to show weakness, to break down and release the emotions she'd kept bottled up for so long.

He even tightened his hold a little more, laid his cheek atop her head, and tried not to think about how he wanted to ensure Percy was never alone again.

AT SOME POINT, Percy realized she was being held. But when that finally registered through her meltdown, she didn't panic. No, because the male scent filling her nose was familiar.

She was in Bronx's arms.

And maybe because she was emotionally exhausted or because she was so lonely after her dragon's appearance and disappearance, but for whatever reason, she wanted to be held, to feel the warmth of another person, and to know someone else was there.

She listened to his heart under her ear; the steady rhythm was soothing. When he held her even tighter and put his head atop hers, she sighed. Percy had never been hugged in her life before. And the reality was so much better than any of her dreams.

Later, much later, once she'd calmed down and her turbulent emotions had mostly receded, she would realize how letting Bronx hold her was a fucking mistake. If she started relying on anyone emotionally, she would be in big trouble. She'd done that with her dragon all those years ago, and look at what had happened today, when her beast ran away again.

She needed to pull back. She really did. But despite

her determination to be strong and independent, she didn't budge. It was too bloody nice to be held, to pretend she was normal and not an emotional wreck with a bloody awful past.

For a few seconds, she could pretend to be someone else besides Persephone Smith.

Closing her eyes, she hugged Bronx tighter and reveled in his familiar scent, his warm body against hers, and the solidness of his muscles, as if they signaled he could shoulder anything.

Bloody hell, he already had, given what she'd heard about his late mate and then later losing part of his leg.

But the moment ended when Bronx asked, "Can I do anything to help, Percy?"

The words snapped her back to reality, to all those memories she'd tried to push away of people manipulating or taking advantage of her, and she slowly pulled away from Bronx. Only when she sat two feet away from him, staring straight ahead, did she answer, "No, nothing."

"Are you sure?"

He reached out a hand as if to touch her. For a split second, she wanted to grab his hand and go back to leaning against him.

But she quickly pushed it aside and inched farther away from him. Wiping her cheeks, she focused on the one thing that she still needed to do, despite the setback: coax her dragon out.

She'd been weak to cry about one botched encounter. Maybe now she would have a clear head, wouldn't have all these pent-up emotions to muddle things, and could accomplish her goal.

Despite today, her beast was still her main focus—her only focus. She'd shift into a dragon and finally fly, obtaining her freedom, even if it killed her. And forming no attachments meant she could leave whenever she wanted, with no complications.

That meant she needed to anger Bronx again. Then he would go back to his teacher role and put that distance between them. "I said I didn't fucking need anything." Taking a deep breath, she forced herself to meet his gaze. For a beat, the concern there was like ambrosia to her soul. But only for a beat. "Get the fuck out of my room, Bronx. You said Stonefire was different, and yet you entered my room without permission. Now that I know it's just like my old prison, I'll have to be more careful."

His pupils flashed to slits and back as he frowned. She expected him to growl, shout that he wasn't like those fuckers, or try to make more promises he'd break.

But after a beat, he stood and walked to the door. "You're right. I shouldn't have entered. But if this happens again, I will call Dr. Sid or Dr. McFarland. Because you might not care about yourself or your health, but I won't let you make yourself sick if I can help it."

With that, he exited the room, slamming the door on his way out, and the room fell silent again.

She stared at the door, wondering if maybe she should've done something differently, such as not trying to piss him off on purpose. His checking on her was nothing like the guards who'd come to rape her or the doctors who'd come to pump her full of new drugs. Their motivations had been selfish.

Bronx had only thought of her well-being.

But as the purple light in her head flickered, she knew she'd done the right thing. She couldn't afford distractions or attachments. And if she had to be an arsehole to keep it that way, she'd bloody well do it.

Chapter Nineteen

Over the next week, Percy only emerged from her room to either conduct her lessons or to eat her meals in the back garden. Bronx was as cool to her as she was to him. Percy was certain Violet noticed, but the female's behavior was the same gentle, funny, and enthusiastic one as before.

The only time Violet pushed her was when Percy declined watching TV together in the evenings. And yet, Percy had let herself get distracted with the outrageous storylines, using it as a chance to get to know Violet, which was another thing she needed to stop wasting time on.

So Percy spent the evenings alone in her room. Every time she wanted to catch up on what was happening on the TV—especially to see if the idiot character had been killed off like she deserved—she focused on the purple light in her head instead.

While it'd never morphed into a dragon form

again, the light had flickered, changed shape a few times, and showed her that not all was lost.

She was just about to try a new tactic with her beast when someone knocked. Violet's voice drifted through the door. "Percy, can I come in?"

Sighing, she rubbed her face. "Why?"

Violet paused and finally replied, "Because you have new visitors. And Bram wants you to meet with them."

Percy had been lucky—ever since Nikki's visit and how it'd sent her scurrying, no one apart from the doctors or nurses had stopped by.

She wanted to tell them to fuck off. And yet, Bram had provided all sorts of textbooks, clothing, and even a tablet preloaded with books and movies. She didn't have internet privileges yet—they were probably still trying to figure out if she was a threat—but she didn't care about that.

Since she owed the clan leader everything, she said, "Okay. I'm coming."

After quickly rearranging her hair to cover the side of her neck and hide her birthmark, she tugged her long sleeves down out of habit and opened the door.

Violet smiled at her. "I think you'll like the visitors today. One of them has loads in common with you."

She froze. "It's not one of the other prisoners, is it?"

Because she didn't want to see them. One, in particular, she had been forced to treat badly. And to stay alive, she'd done as she was told. Although, given how the dragonman had been catatonic from some sort of drug concoction for nearly a year, she doubted it'd be him.

Violet shook her head. "No, one of them isn't even from Stonefire. Come on."

The teenager walked down the hall, and Percy followed, taking a few steadying breaths. This would be good practice for her, after all, for when she finally could fly away and meet other dragon-shifters.

She reinforced her mental walls during the walk, so by the time she entered the living room, she could keep the surprise from her face.

A tall dragonman with dark hair stood with his arms crossed, leaning against the mantel. Next to him was an olive-skinned dragonwoman not much older than Percy, with short brown hair and flashing dragon eyes.

The female smiled at her. "Hello, you must be Percy."

She bobbed her head.

The dragonwoman placed a hand on the dragonman's upper arm, rubbing it as she said, "This is Killian O'Shea, my mate. And I'm Brenna."

"Okay," Percy said slowly, wondering if that was supposed to mean anything.

Killian watched her closely, his pupils flashing a few times. The corner of his mouth ticked up at one point, but then he went back to his stony face.

Brenna patted Killian's arm lightly before stepping away. "Since my mate is being his usual silent self in public, let me explain."

Killian reached out to swat her arse lightly, and Brenna stuck out her tongue. He grunted. "I'm trying not to be intimidating, lass. There's a difference."

His accent was different, one Percy didn't think she'd ever heard before.

And as the two teased each other, the sight made her heart squeeze. Wanting to avoid yet another happy couple—Stonefire seemed full of them, for some reason—she blurted, "Why are you here, exactly? I'm very busy."

After one last light shove of her mate, Brenna faced her and answered, "Well, we heard you've had problems with your dragon. And before you get upset, there's a reason Dr. Sid reached out to us." She gestured at Killian. "Killian's dragon went silent at one point. In fact, he even lost his memory for a while. And when his beast did come back, there was a surprise as a result of the drugs they'd given him. Dr. Sid thought it might be helpful for you to ask Killian some questions, since he understands better than most of us what you're experiencing right now."

Percy studied the dragonman, and he studied her right back. "What kind of surprise?"

He stood up from the mantel. "I have a two-headed dragon, maybe one of the only ones to ever exist."

Her mouth dropped a second. "Two-headed?"

Killian shrugged. "It's bloody noisy in my head sometimes, aye. But now, it's just my new normal. And that might not happen to you, but there might be some things that I experienced that could help you. If you want to chat or ask me anything, then go ahead."

Part of her wanted to just fire away questions, and yet, she didn't know the dragonman at all.

Looking around the room, she noticed Violet

nearby but not Bronx. Before she could think of it, she blurted, "Where's Bronx?"

Violet answered, "He's outside. This room isn't that big, and he wanted to give you some space."

Guilt pricked her conscience at how she'd acted toward him. However, she ignored it. She couldn't be reliant on anyone. That was a lesson she'd learned even as a child.

Although if Bronx were here, she'd probably have the courage to ask Killian questions. After all, Bronx had always protected her and given her everything she'd ever asked for since the night of her breakdown, without ever pushing her.

No one else had ever done that before.

Stop it, Percy. You don't need him. Rely on yourself, like always.

She kept her spot on the far side of the room and hugged her upper torso. She finally said, "I don't even know what to ask."

Killian tapped his hands against his thighs. "Well, I had amnesia from all the drugs and couldn't remember anything beyond waking up with the silent dragon. Has that ever happened to you?"

She shook her head. "No. I always remembered who and where I was." She bit her bottom lip and then asked, "How did you get your dragon back?"

The corners of his mouth kicked up. "Dragons. The first one was a baby, or young one, as he preferred to be called. I'd had dreams about him, and then I kissed a female everyone thought to be my true mate. I fell unconscious and woke up with him there."

She darted a glance to Brenna. "Her?"

Brenna snorted. "If only it'd been that easy. He did eventually trigger a mate-claim frenzy with me, but not until later. Except, once his second dragon emerged, it faded away. My dragon said he was a different person." She laughed. "Our past history is complicated."

Killian nodded. "And the second dragon came after Brenna's dragon recognized me as her true mate, once I'd started to remember my old life. Between my memories rushing back and two dragons, it was overwhelming." He moved to put an arm around Brenna's shoulders and hugged her close. "Although I have my mate and son now. And I've learned to live with two dragons in my head."

Brenna spoke up. "His situation is unique. I know that. But more than that, he knows what it's like to be held prisoner and given drugs against his will. They even removed Killian's tattoo, as if to signal he wasn't a dragon-shifter any longer." She pointed to the barely there pink outline on Killian's opposite arm. Then she pushed up the sleeve of the other arm to his shoulder, revealing an intricate black one. "But him picking out a new one helped him feel more himself."

Killian added, "And I know just spilling your secrets to a stranger isn't easy. But Brenna and I will be here for a few weeks, if you want to chat. I can't compare to being imprisoned as long as you, lass, but I do understand a little about trying to fit into the world again, especially when you're a dragon-shifter without a dragon."

She wanted to shout that she had a light in her head, which had become a dragon, and ask Killian's advice. However, that meant revealing what had happened with her beast. And she didn't want to share that with anyone, not until she could talk freely and control her.

The light flashed in head, as if trying to say something, but she ignored it. "Thank you. But it's more important for me to learn about being a dragon-shifter than to talk about the past."

Killian's gaze bored into hers, as if trying to determine what—if any—progress she'd made with her beast. Then he shrugged. "We'll be on Stonefire for a while, visiting Brenna's family, so the offer stands."

Percy moved from the doorway and to the opposite wall from Killian and Brenna. "Thank you. But I really need to get back to my studies."

Brenna smiled at her. "Of course. And if you ever want a dragon-shifter female to chat to, one who's maybe a bit older than Violet, I'm here."

Violet sighed. "I'm not that young."

Bronx's voice filled the room. "But not yet an adult." He walked in partway but kept his distance from Percy. "Brenna, it's been too long. And, Killian, nice to see you outside of video conferences about rescues."

Killian shook Bronx's hand. The whole thing was so… *normal.* No hesitations. No shuffling away from each other. Just two males making small talk and being friendly.

Brenna slipped away from her mate and approached Percy, although she stopped a few feet away. She said, "Some of us females are having a girls' night in a few days. You're welcome to join us, if you like. It'll be at Kai and Jane's house, although Kai won't be around. Jane's kicking him out for the evening. I know being around people can be overwhelming, but you can say as little or as much as you want and can leave at any time. It just might be nice to get out of this cabin."

She blurted, "Will Bram allow it?"

Brenna bobbed her head. "Yes, I wouldn't have asked otherwise. And any of us can come fetch you and then bring you back, when you're ready." She paused and then whispered, "It might be nice to get away from any males or kids for a bit."

She should say no. She didn't need to go. And yet the thought of being invited to anything, to actually having fun—did she even know what that was?—was bloody tempting.

The light in her head blared brightly for a few beats before returning to its normal glow, almost as if her dragon wanted her to go.

Well, she did need practice at being around people. Before she could change her mind, she murmured, "Okay. But I don't know how long I'll stay."

Brenna clapped her hands. "Brilliant! We'll work out who'll fetch you. And I'll make sure you get any sort of clothing you want, to treat yourself. It's going to be fun. Just wait and see, Percy."

She eyed Brenna cautiously. "Why are you so excited? I'm a stranger. You don't know me."

Brenna made as if to reach for Percy's hand but then pulled back. "I didn't mention that I'm a Protector, did I? And a mum. Together, those things make me want to take care of anyone who needs it. And not out of pity, either, so don't try that line with

me. It's just who I am." She glanced at Bronx and back
at Percy. "And I'm not the only one like that."

Percy's gaze moved to Bronx, who was laughing at
his daughter waggling a finger at Killian. The
dragonman merely blinked, as if surprised to have a
teenager scolding him. She smiled at the sight.

Brenna said, "Right, well, Killian and I need to be
off. My mother-in-law and her mate are here, as well,
helping to look after our son, and I promised we
wouldn't be too long. I'll send you information about
the girls' night via Bronx, okay? See you soon!"

Brenna collected her mate, said something that
made him smile, and then left.

Percy nearly ran after them to cancel. However, as
the light in her head flickered again, she didn't. If
meeting others helped her dragon, she'd do it. If
nothing happened, she'd add it to her list of things to
avoid.

Then Bronx approached her, and Percy didn't
know if she should run or stay in place. But with each
step he drew nearer, the sense of calmness and
rightness settled over her. So she waited to see what he
said. As long as she avoided being weak, she could
handle one meeting with him, surely.

Chapter Twenty

Once Brenna and Killian left, Bronx resisted the urge to rush over to Percy and ask if she was okay. He'd agreed with Bram and Dr. Sid that meeting Killian was a good idea, if only to show yet another person who'd suffered a silent dragon at some point, to reinforce she wasn't alone. But she'd clearly kept her distance from everyone in the room.

Ever since he'd gone into her room without permission, he'd retreated from her a little. She needed privacy and the ability to make choices. While he wouldn't allow her to hide in her room forever, he'd given her some time to study and learn what she wished.

Today, however, he was going to give her some choices before she could flee.

Instead of closing the gap, he merely took a few steps toward Percy so he wouldn't be shouting. "Before you go back into your room, I wanted to ask you something."

She raised her brows. "What?"

He hesitated a beat, but his dragon said, *Just ask her. Showing our vulnerability might help her with hers.*

His dragon was right, so he pushed on. "When you're ready, I'd like to show you my dragon form."

Violet gasped, but he focused solely on Percy. Yes, he'd barely shifted since the incident that had taken his leg. However, if shifting and trying out the hind leg attachment Dylan Turner and Will Bailey had come up with—Will was one of Stonefire's engineers—helped Percy even a little, he'd do it.

He might not be able to hug her whenever she needed it, but he could do this.

She plucked at her top. "I-I don't know."

Violet spoke up. "I'd be there too, Percy. We could leave whenever you wanted and get some tea and scones afterward, if you need a little reward."

Percy's eyes flashed. "I'm not a child."

Violet flinched, and Bronx put a hand on his daughter's shoulder, knowing she needed it. Violet murmured, "I'm fine, Dad."

Before he could say anything, Percy said, "I'm sorry, Violet. I really am."

Violet smiled. "Apology accepted. But just know even I still ask for scones sometimes—or even ice cream—when my dad makes me do something I don't want. I'm too old for rewards like that, either, but eating scones or ice cream with my dad is a kind of tradition. One where no matter what else happens, I know we'll always do it and laugh as we eat."

She smiled at Bronx, and his heart warmed. "Even

if I'm eighty, I'll still take you out for ice cream or scones, Vi. It's our father-daughter thing." He finally tore his gaze from his daughter and looked at Percy.

She shuffled her feet and twisted her hands, clearly uncomfortable.

He said softly, "Percy." She met his gaze, and he continued, "It's okay. Even I snap at Violet sometimes, without meaning to. No one's perfect and a saint all the time."

Percy replied, "I know. I just, well, I don't have a lot of practice in being nice to people."

The admission was fucking huge, but Bronx knew better than to make a big deal about it. She'd probably toss her walls back up and rush out of the room if he did.

So he decided to keep it light. "Come see my dragon and go for scones afterward, and I'm sure all will be forgotten."

His dragon snorted. *Smooth. You just want her to see us in our dragon form, be the first one she's ever seen up close.*

Shut it, dragon.

Of course, his beast was correct. At some point during her lessons, Percy had admitted she'd never seen a dragon up close. Ever since, Bronx had been thinking of ways to show her his and allow her to touch him anywhere, to fulfill her curiosity.

Percy dropped her hands. "Okay. When?"

"We could go now, if you want. If later is better, just tell me."

"Now, before I lose my nerve."

He didn't miss how she hadn't frowned or paused at

him asking her a question, allowing her a choice. His dragonwoman was closer and closer to being who she was meant to be.

Not that Percy was his; she never would be. He was her teacher, and he'd be proud of her, no matter what. That's it.

His dragon laughed, but Bronx ignored it. "Right, we'll walk to Stonefire together, and then I'll go on ahead to shift while you hang out with Violet. I'll roar when I'm ready."

She might be willing to see his dragon, but he didn't know if she could handle watching anyone shift forms, let alone be okay with his nudity. Dragon-shifters didn't really care about nakedness, but Percy was a special case.

She nodded. "Okay. Let me just change."

Once she left the room, Violet asked him, "Do you still want me to walk by the tattoo design place while we wait for you to shift?"

He faced his daughter. "Yes. Although don't force her to go in there. I just want her to warm up to the idea."

So when he offered to let Percy take that important step, to get a tattoo of her own, she'd be ready for it.

PERCY'S NERVE faltered as they passed through the main gates and walked onto the clan lands proper. Yes, she'd stared at the dragons flying overhead every chance she had. But for some reason, she hadn't thought about asking to see one up close, probably because she was so far from doing it herself and didn't want to get discouraged.

But seeing a dragon form in person might help make some of her studies easier to understand. Her memories of her inner dragon were hazy, and maybe knowing more details could help her imagine her dragon, share memories, and get her to come out again.

Once they passed the main security building for Stonefire—Protector building, she reminded herself to use the dragon term—Bronx said, "I'll dash off ahead. I'll let you know when I'm ready. Okay?"

Percy nodded, and Bronx half-jogged down the path. Before she could stop herself, she stated, "How can he run with missing part of his leg?"

Violet threaded her arm through hers. Percy barely noticed at this point since the female did it so often. "Oh, the things they can do these days are brilliant. He has different prosthetics for different activities. He's even going to try one out for the first time today in his dragon form."

For some reason, Percy hadn't put it together that he'd have the same missing part in his dragon form. "Oh. Can he fly?"

"I don't know, really." She lowered her voice. "He hasn't shifted much since the incident. I was surprised he suggested it, but I'm definitely happy he did."

She frowned. "Why would he do it for me, then?"

Violet replied, "I have my theories, but I'm keeping them to myself."

Before Percy could probe further, Violet waved at someone in the distance. "There's Melanie and Tristan."

Percy looked up, and sure enough, the human female waved at them. Percy tentatively raised a hand in greeting. Melanie elbowed her mate. He rolled his eyes and then also waved. The interaction made her smile. They were clearly comfortable with each other, and their personalities also seemed to complement one another.

What, what the fuck? Why would I waste time on noticing such things?

Not wanting to think too closely on that, she took in the shops as they passed. Seeing so much food, clothing, or miscellaneous goods laid out for sale was still strange for her.

After all, she'd never purchased anything in her life to date.

Then they passed the silversmith shop. The case in the window displayed some rings, cuffs, and even necklaces. But in the upper half of the glass were various designs drawn in black ink, with notes such as "Celebrate a birthday" or "Give your new baby their welcoming present."

Most of the ink drawings had thicker lines, although there were a few with thinner, daintier-looking ones.

Percy nearly touched her arm where hers should've been but wasn't.

Violet stopped in place, and Percy had to do the same. "My birthday is in a few months, and I can't wait to finally get my tattoo. It's sort of the line between childhood and adulthood for a dragon-shifter."

Since it hadn't been in her books, she asked, "Have you picked yours out?"

"No, my dad did, soon after I was born." She paused and added, "A little later than most babies, but he was still grieving my mum at the time."

Percy's gaze moved from the window to Violet's face. At the sadness there, she nearly hugged the girl.

Nearly.

Violet continued, "But later, my dad told me how my mother mostly designed it. That's another reason I can't wait. Then I'll always have a little piece of my mum with me, always."

For some reason, at the wistfulness in Violet's voice, tears prickled Percy's eyes. After clearing her throat, she replied, "I'd like to see yours later, if you'll show me."

Violet smiled again. "Of course I will! Maybe it'll give you ideas about your own someday."

She was about to say that she'd probably never have one, even if she could get her dragon to come out, but Nikki emerged from the shop with a tall dark-haired human male at her side.

For a beat, Nikki blinked but then blurted, "I'm so sorry about last time, Percy. I didn't even think. I promise I wasn't trying to be mean or cruel to you."

The true regret in Nikki's voice—or, at least, that was what Percy suspected it was—made her uncomfortable.

As the dragonwoman's gaze grew more frantic and worried, Percy said, "It's okay."

"Really?"

Not trusting her voice, she grunted.

Nikki made as if to touch her but then stopped herself. And for some reason, Percy wished people would stop doing that around her.

The purple light in her head grew brighter and brighter for five seconds before returning to normal.

Nikki spoke again. "Oh, and this sexy male is my mate, Rafe. He's human, if you couldn't tell."

The human sighed. "I'm sure she can, Nikki. Dragon-shifters love to say how we smell 'really human' to tease us."

She grinned at her mate. "Well, it *is* a distinctive scent." She leaned in and took a deep inhalation. "But I'm partial to yours."

Rafe laughed, and Percy couldn't drag her gaze away from the pair. Here were yet more people comfortable with each other, teasing each other, and all without guarded looks, or barriers, or hesitation.

For a brief second, she wondered what that would feel like.

A dragon roared in the distance, and Violet tugged at Percy's arm, snapping her back to reality. "That's my dad, signaling he's ready for us. We need to go. Bye, you two!"

They murmured goodbyes, and Violet half-dragged Percy down the footpath.

Soon, the raised rock walls of the landing area came into view—they'd been pointed out to her during her walk to the school before—and she forgot all about the couples she'd seen.

Her heart raced the closer she drew to the landing area. Percy was about to see her first dragon up close.

She was both nervous and excited but knew that she needed to take this step. Even if it wasn't easy, she'd do anything that might bring her closer to her dragon. And seeing another one might finally help bring her beast out.

Chapter Twenty-One

Bronx stood naked in the middle of the landing area, balancing on a cane he'd kept here. He had to stow his prosthetic while shifting to avoid damaging it.

He took a few deep breaths. He'd practiced changing forms more in recent months, before Percy's arrival, but he hadn't yet worked up the courage to show his dragon to anyone except his daughter, the designers of his fake dragon leg, and the Stonefire doctors.

His dragon spoke up. *But it's just Percy. You want her to see us this way.*

No, you *want her to.*

We both do. The situation may allow her to further realize she's not back inside that prison. I doubt she ever saw a dragon up close there.

He doubted it too. In fact, the longer he stayed in that cabin with Percy, the more he understood how horrible her time inside had been.

Even if Percy had been on Stonefire for nearly two weeks now, she sometimes woke up in the middle of the night, screaming. He and Violet had agreed that if Percy had a bad dream, Violet would be the one to check on her. If Bronx did it, he'd want to hold Percy close again, soothe her fears, and merely revel in her heat against him.

That made him a bastard on so many levels. No matter how hard he tried to remember her imprisonment or what she'd been made to do on the inside, his attraction kept popping up when he least expected it—noticing her eyes or how the sun hit her cheek or even just breathing in the scent that was pure Percy.

Fuck. He needed to think of anything else, and quickly. So he went through preparation checklists for a rescue mission, like he'd done a million times before, back when he'd led them.

Soon enough, his body cooled. Time to shift. The sooner he completed this outing, the sooner he could go back to the cabin and the familiar role of being only a teacher.

His dragon huffed. *Then get on with it.*

Bronx closed his eyes and imagined wings sprouting from his back, his nose elongating into a snout, and his entire body growing and stretching until he had to balance on one hind foot and put his wings tips into the ground, using the talon-like points to steady himself.

He opened his eyes and looked down at his rear legs. Seeing one ending in a stump still made his heart squeeze.

His dragon spoke up. *Forget about it, already. It's gone.*

We have to adapt. Just imagine being able to fly with Percy one day.

I want her to fly, but she'll do it with one of the teachers, Protectors, or both. Not us. Soon enough, our job will be over.

Tell yourself that.

Not wanting to argue, Bronx roared and then again, to let Violet know he was ready.

He heard the pair before they arrived. A few seconds later, Violet and Percy walked into the landing area side by side, and Percy's gaze latched on to him. Even from a distance, he saw her eyes widen before going blank. And for some reason, he wanted to wipe away the neutral expression she used to hide herself.

His dragon spoke up. *Then make this time special for her. I'm sure she'll be awestruck by how big we are or how shiny our scales are.*

He mentally snorted. *You and the shiny scales. Why does it matter? It's not a contest.*

I want to impress her.

An uneasy feeling rushed through him. *Do you know?*

He was asking about Percy being their true mate.

His dragon growled. *Of course not. If I did, I'd tell you. But you never let me impress anyone anymore.*

Because we're not eighteen. We're forty-two. We're too old to get cocky and impress females just to bloat our ego.

Before his beast could reply, Violet came up to him and raised a hand. Bronx lowered his head, and she rubbed his snout. "Hey, Dad, are you ready to try the fake hind leg? I'd say peg leg, but you told me I couldn't call it that."

He lightly butted his nose against her shoulder.

His daughter laughed and hugged his snout. "Okay,

okay. But let's get you stable before anything else."
Violet released him and turned toward Percy. "Want to
help me?"

Percy jerked, as if she'd been snapped out of some
deep thought or memory. "What?"

Violet walked over to her. "My dad is trying a new
type of hind leg prosthetic. It's still sort of basic.
Numerous people are working on the design. It's tricky
to make one that will stay on for flight, landing, and
takeoff, but it'll allow Dad to use his wings freely. And
showing them off, with the light behind them, is usually
the best part."

Percy blinked. "Sure."

He watched the pair walk toward the large
container that held his dragon peg leg, as Violet called
it. And Bronx did his best not to anticipate when Percy
would finally touch his scales or maybe scratch behind
his ears.

As VIOLET OPENED the storage box and undid some
straps inside it, Percy kept glancing over her shoulder at
Bronx's dragon form. He was massive, much bigger
than she thought he would be, and so much more regal.

Her only memories had been of her dragon inside
her mind, and she'd been small. They'd never seen a
full-grown dragon at the orphanage—most of the
teachers and staff were afraid of them—and she most
definitely had never seen one in the flesh inside the
facility.

More than how tall, or muscled, he was, she noticed

the elegant lines of his snout, the points of his ears, the small horns right next to them, and even how his eyes reminded her a lot of Bronx's. In both forms, they were patient, steady, and calm.

Pretty much the opposite of her, most of the time.

Violet said, "Percy? Could you help me?"

She tore her gaze from the blue dragon and helped the female take out the large dragon foot. It was crude, only made of some kind of metal and fake-leather-looking materials. But even without lifting it, Percy guessed the thing was too heavy for Violet to carry by herself. "It looks heavy. Are you sure your dad can jump off the ground with this?"

"Dragon-shifters are fairly strong in their dragon forms. Dad had to carry all kinds of gear—including baskets to carry those he rescued, with the people inside them—so this shouldn't be too bad."

They approached Bronx, now sitting on his rear with his wings still helping him to stay upright, and she could see the slightly lighter color of his belly. *Are dragons ticklish?*

She must've said it out loud, because Violet chuckled and said, "Some are. But you have to find the right spot. Although I'll give you one tip—if you scratch the small, exposed patch of skin right behind the ear, a dragon will hum and love you forever."

Smiling, she eyed Bronx and tried to imagine him purring and turning to mush like the mouser cat back in the orphanage. She hadn't seen the cat often, but whenever she had, it'd walked right up to her and let her pet it.

They reached Bronx and put the foot down.

Violet said, "Okay, we need your leg, Dad."

For a second, the dragonman hesitated. But then he raised the damaged one, and she could see where his leg had been cut off right below the knee. Looking back at his gaze, she saw uncertainty, almost like he was worried she'd find it disgusting and say something cruel.

Before she could think too much on it, she stepped forward and lightly ran her hand over his damaged leg, over the bottom, up to the knee, and back again. She said, "Your scales are so smooth."

Bronx nudged her shoulder lightly with his snout, and she met his gaze. For a second, everything melted away but the two of them, almost like they were having a conversation without words.

Gratitude, relief, and even warmth radiated from his gaze.

She whispered, "This just shows you were strong and willing to risk your life to save others. It's nothing to be embarrassed about." She stroked his leg again. "You survived."

And for a few beats, as they stared at one another, Percy sensed that he was trying to tell her she'd done the same.

Not only that, but he would gladly go to such lengths to lose another leg to help her, if it came to it, which was fucking ridiculous. He barely knew her, and she'd experienced firsthand how people were selfish at the core.

Bronx may have helped a few people before, but it'd been his job, and he'd been paid for it. If he had to rescue her, it'd only be because it was his job, nothing else.

She needed to remember that.

Dropping her hands, Percy took a few steps back, putting distance between them. Violet looked at her then at her dad and back at her.

Needing to change the subject and be distracted by anything else, Percy cleared her throat and asked, "How do we put it on?"

Violet said nothing for a beat, but then she shrugged and replied, "I'll put it in place, and you just need to fasten the straps. The long ones will have to be secured at the top of his leg. It'll be tricky, but I think we can manage it."

And so they went to work fastening the fake foot to Bronx's dragon form. If she happened to caress his scales or leaned against them occasionally to absorb some of his warmth, it was all by accident.

Yes, by accident. Not because she liked touching him, not at all.

As soon as Percy touched his leg and then told him he'd survived, Bronx had wanted to shift back into his human form, pull her close, and kiss her.

She'd said the words without thinking, probably, and didn't know how much they meant to him. So he'd resisted and merely let her know with his eyes that he would keep protecting her, no matter what, and she would be safe with him.

Even if it meant protecting her from himself.

Then she'd backed away, and he'd nearly motioned for her to come back. But he didn't. Instead, he'd let Violet distract her, although he didn't like the looks his daughter kept throwing at him, as if she were plotting.

His dragon spoke up. *She knows how stubborn you can be and probably wants to help you with Percy.*

I don't need help with Percy, because there's nothing there beyond the student-teacher relationship. And ours is fine.

So do all teachers want to kiss their pupils?

He mentally growled. *Don't start.*

Fine. But if she gives any sign, any at all, that she's interested in us like that, then I'll harass you nonstop. She's probably never been treasured or kissed like she's the most special person in the world. We could do that.

He growled, *Dragon.*

His beast sniffed. *Fine. Let's focus on trying to stand and maybe even jump into the air with this new foot.*

However, as Percy and Violet attached the contraption, Percy kept touching him and leaning against him, and at one point, she'd even brushed her cheek against his belly, which made him want to be in his human form all the more.

About the only good thing from having to suffer all her caresses and not react was it showed him she was less afraid of him this way. That was probably because she'd never suffered pain, fear, or humiliation at the hands of an actual dragon. He would definitely have to use that knowledge later, if she suffered a relapse.

After what seemed like an eternity, the two females finished and stepped away.

Violet placed her hands on her hips and nodded.

"Right, that should do it. Are you going to try and jump into the air, Dad?"

He grunted and shook his head. First, he needed to see if he could even stand with the bloody thing.

Tentatively, he shifted his weight to his legs and raised his wings. He had to flap a bit to steady himself, but despite the creaking of the metal, he sat balancing using his rear, his tail, and hind legs without needing his wings.

Bronx tested rising onto just his legs, which he'd need to do for jumping into the air, and managed to stay upright.

His dragon said, *I think this will work.*

Maybe. But I don't really want to leave Percy here with only Violet to watch over her.

This is the heart of Stonefire. No one will hurt her here.

He knew that, of course. However, she'd been put into his charge, and he took his duty seriously.

Violet snapped him back to the present. "Well, it seems to work so far. I still say you should try getting into the air." He shook his head, and his daughter rolled her eyes. "I'll be here with Percy, so don't worry about her. Besides, I'm sure she wants to see a dragon take off." She turned toward the other female. "Don't you, Percy?"

She bit her bottom lip and then nodded. "Yes."

Great, now the pair were working together against him.

His beast laughed. *You knew that would happen. Now, stop making excuses and let's impress them.*

Always you and the impressing. You'd think we were twenty instead of more than double that.

Age doesn't matter. Percy is twenty and most definitely more mature than others her age.

The words sobered Bronx, and he looked back at the female in question. The eagerness and anticipation in her eyes wiped away his hesitation. If it would make her maybe smile, he'd try it, even if it meant falling back onto his arse in the process.

He motioned a wing, and Violet took them back a few more steps. He felt Percy's eyes the whole time, and he willed himself not to mess this up.

Crouching, he made sure his weight was even. The false dragon foot felt sturdy, and the straps were tight. Then he used his hind legs to jump into the air.

While it was a little clumsy, he got high enough to beat his wings and ascend slowly into the sky. The wind against his scales felt so bloody good, and he couldn't resist diving down near the females and then rising again.

In the air, his leg didn't matter. Neither his wings nor his tail had been damaged, and both were important for flying. He circled around, not wanting to go too far, and even hovered in place for a moment to look down at Percy.

Her mouth hung open, her eyes were wide, and she had her hands clasped in front of her.

She looked so bloody young, but he suspected if any dragon-shifter had waited twenty-plus years to see their first dragon up close and watch them take off, they would act the same way. It was always like that with Percy—so young and yet so old at the same time.

He did a few more twirls and dives before descending slowly, until he was about five feet from the ground. Taking off had been difficult, but landing was just as much so.

Slowly, oh so slowly, he lowered himself until his good leg touched the ground first. Then he awkwardly placed his fake foot down. For a second, he thought he'd have a good landing. But once he put all his weight on his legs, something snapped, and he tumbled to the side.

PERCY KNEW she probably looked like an idiot with her mouth open, making all kinds of excited sounds, but she didn't bloody care. Watching a dragon takeoff was surreal. The power it took, the coordination, and the pure strength, amazed her.

And to think, maybe one day, she could do the same.

She watched Bronx's every move, loving how quickly he could turn, twirl, or pull up from the ground. It was clear he was skilled, and it made sense— if he'd had to rescue someone from a forest fire or a high ridge, he would need to make tight turns and the like.

Violet's voice finally brought her back down to earth. "This is the first time he's flown in over a year. And look at him—it's as if he never stopped." She wiped her eyes. "I'm so bloody happy right now. Because for a while there, I worried he'd never try flying again."

"Why?"

"He never gave specifics, just that no one wanted to see a crippled dragon trying to stay in the air."

The words stoked a lick of anger inside her. "I think he's beautiful, just the way he is."

Violet stared at her, but Percy kept her gaze on Bronx. Eventually, the teenager whispered, "I know my dad's supposed to be helping you, but I think you two are helping each other."

Her cheeks heated. "Don't be bloody ridiculous. I'm the burden, end of story."

Before Violet could reply, Bronx lowered himself slowly to the ground, until he was a few feet above it. Percy barely paid attention to the glowing light inside her head. Instead, she held her breath as his good foot touched the ground, followed by the other one.

For a beat, she thought everything would be fine. Then Bronx toppled over, somehow gracefully tumbling to his back, his wings outstretched to the side.

Without missing a beat, she rushed over to him and stopped near his head. His eyes were closed, and a fission of fear raced through her.

Then she watched his chest rise, and then again, before opening his eyes. His large slitted pupil fixed on her.

She touched a hand to his snout. "Are you okay?"

He bobbed his head, still staring at her. As she stroked his smooth, slightly warm scales, she said, "Maybe we should get the doctor anyway, just to make sure."

Violet shouted, "I already called! Dr. Sid will be here soon."

Bronx grunted and rolled to his side. Slowly, he tried to right himself but couldn't.

It was then she noticed the small tear in his wing membrane. She growled, "Stop being so bloody stubborn. If I can tell you're injured, then who the fuck knows what you're hiding."

If dragons could roll their eyes, she was pretty sure Bronx had just given her the equivalent.

She grabbed his snout and patted the sides lightly. "You don't have to pretend with me. Honesty, remember? We both agreed to that."

He stared at her, and she wished he could talk. Or maybe she didn't. All she knew was that she couldn't take her gaze from his.

Only when Dr. Sid cleared her throat and spoke did she jump back. "I need to check him over, Percy."

Percy put her hands behind her back and retreated to where Violet stood with another doctor she'd seen a few times—Dr. Gregor Innes, who was Dr. Sid's mate.

Percy crossed her arms over her chest and asked, "Shouldn't you be helping Dr. Sid?"

Dr. Innes raised his brows. "Should I, lass?"

Waving a hand toward Bronx, she replied, "He has a cut on his wing. And since he's massive, it'll probably take more than one person to fix it."

The doctor's lips twitched before he replied, "Aye, well, I'll see what I can do."

He went over to help the other doctor, and Violet laughed. Percy glared at her. "What?"

"My dad merely tumbled, Percy. It happens to us all, especially when we're learning. He doesn't need two doctors for something so small."

She grunted. "Well, they're both here, so I don't see the point of one standing around. For all we know, the bloody male broke a wing bone and is hiding it."

Violet moved her head closer, studying Percy as if she were an insect under a glass. "I like this side of you."

"What side? The bossy side?"

The younger female grinned. "I prefer to call it commanding, but yes. Dad can be stubborn sometimes, and he needs someone who can handle it."

She froze. "What do you mean he needs someone?"

Violet retreated. "Oh, nothing. Just a friend. Yes, a friend."

Given how mischief danced in Violet's eyes, Percy didn't believe her.

The two doctors waved them over, and as soon as they were close, Dr. Sid said, "He'll be fine and doesn't have any serious injuries. Bronx just needs to stay in his dragon form for an hour or so to heal that wing, eat a proper meal after that, and he'll be as good as new."

Percy frowned. "Only an hour? That seems really fast."

Dr. Sid nodded. "Dragon-shifters heal fast, and it's just a minor cut. But can I leave you two in charge, making sure he obeys his doctor's orders? I have a few patients I need to visit."

Even though the doctor didn't say it, Percy knew it had to do with the other inmates. She blurted, "Are they okay?"

Dr. Sid studied her. "Are you sure you can handle it?" She nodded, and the doctor continued, "Most of them will recover fully, at least physically. There's only one who hasn't woken up yet."

She had a feeling she knew who. "Kit Ashworth."

"Yes. If it's too much to ask, I'll understand. But if there's anything you can tell me about him, anything at all about what they did to him, then it might help."

Her gaze trailed over until it met Bronx's. Drawing from the strength she saw there, she whispered, "We all had our different coping mechanisms. Mine was to lock away all emotions. Kit couldn't handle what was done to him, and he became catatonic, or so the doctors said."

And I hurt him, too, at one point, when they forced me to have sex with him for an experiment. Not that she said that out loud.

An almost soothing warmth emanated from the light inside her head. It gave her the strength to add, "The only time I ever saw a flicker of awareness in his gaze was when they played some sort of upbeat music. I don't know if it was a coincidence, but that's all I know."

Dr. Sid bobbed her head. "That's a brilliant start, Percy. Thank you."

The female doctor smiled at her, and Percy noticed how the other doctor moved to her side, drawn like a moth to a flame. It almost made Percy smile too. Here was yet another couple who cared for each other, supported each other, and affected each other in a good way.

Not that she should care. She would never be part of a happy couple herself—that would interfere with her dream of freedom.

Dr. Sid stated, "If you have any questions or concerns, call me or Gregor. But my official diagnosis is he'll be fine." She leaned over and whispered for her ears only, "Although his bruised pride may need some propping up."

Frowning, Percy was about to ask why the doctor would say that to her when Dr. Sid and her mate both strode off.

Resisting a sigh, she went to Bronx's head. "Don't even think of shifting until the hour is up, okay?" He playfully butted her shoulder with his head, and she smiled. "Yes, even if I'm only a tiny person in human form, I'll think of a way to keep you here. I'm sure I can call the Protectors or your brother or someone."

Bronx huffed in what she thought was a dragon laugh.

She sat near him, stroking his scales and chatting to Violet, until the hour passed.

And as the teenager hurried her out of the area, she almost wished she could stay to see him shift back. Only for information, of course. Not because she was curious to see what he looked like naked or to judge if he was just as muscled in his human form as his dragon one.

Or to see his leg in that form, too, and let him know she didn't find it gross, weird, or any of those things; it was still a mark of survival.

Although, why she cared so much about telling Bronx that tidbit, she had no bloody idea.

Chapter Twenty-Two

Bronx slowly shifted back into his human form and did his best to maintain his balance until he could retrieve the cane Violet had left for him.

As he dressed, he replayed not only Percy ordering Gregor to help him, but also how she'd sat with him as his wing healed. She hadn't chatted nearly as much as Violet, but together, they had made up a story about a dragon rescuing a cat from a tree, using his deft skills to do it, and proving to a princess he was the most skilled of all the dragons in the area. And he accomplished it despite having a slightly crooked wing.

They hadn't been subtle. But watching Percy come up with the story at times, laughing with Violet, had made the time fly.

If she kept up her progress, Percy wouldn't need him around much longer.

His dragon grunted. *She'll eventually heal, at least*

enough to be on her own. Of course she will. However, that doesn't mean we won't ever see her again.

Stop it, dragon. Just because she let her guard down for one afternoon doesn't mean anything.

If you say so. Although if her dragon does finally come out long enough, I can tell if she's meant to be ours.

He paused while buttoning his shirt. *What do you mean if her dragon comes out long enough?*

How did you miss it? Her pupils flashed to slits once, while she was telling the story with Violet.

What?

His beast sniffed. *Yes, it happened. But that wasn't enough for me to determine anything. I wonder if Percy even noticed.*

Bronx ran a hand through his hair. *Bloody hell, how did I not see that?*

You were too busy mooning over her.

Shut it, dragon. I was not mooning.

His beast laughed a second before sobering. *Regardless, you need to ask her about it.*

I'll ask, but I won't force her. I'll never force her to do anything, unless her safety is at stake.

His dragon didn't argue, which meant he agreed.

He hurriedly attached his prosthetic, dressed, and went to find Violet and Percy at the local café. He spotted them sitting outside, both having tea and scones. Percy bit into hers and closed her eyes, bliss written across her face. When she swallowed, she opened her eyes, and her tongue darted out to the corner of her mouth to lick away a blob of jam.

The sight shot straight to his cock.

Shaking his head, he quickly thought of something boring, such as how he needed to clean the shed behind his house. Soon enough, his blood cooled, and he willed himself to stop thinking about Percy that way. His attraction to her was bloody inconvenient.

He approached the pair, and Percy smiled at him. Another bolt of heat shot through him, but he was careful not to let it show on his face.

She gestured to the remaining chair. "I had to keep shooing Violet's fingers away, but I saved you a scone."

He settled in the chair and quickly plucked the baked good off the plate. He took a bite and made an overly appreciative noise, knowing it would irritate his daughter.

Violet huffed. "That's just mean, Dad."

He made a show of swallowing, sipping the tea Percy had poured for him, and winked. "Flying works up an appetite. You wouldn't starve your dear old dad, would you?"

She rolled her eyes. "You're not going to starve anytime soon. Besides, I'm a growing dragonwoman. I need the extra food."

"You could order some more, Vi."

His daughter's eyes widened. "May I?"

"Yes, go ahead. After all your help lately, you deserve some treats."

Despite how Violet liked to state she was basically an adult now, at the promise of scones, she whooped and raced inside.

He chuckled and met Percy's eyes. Amusement danced there, and it took every bit of control he had not to act surprised at it.

She asked, "Are you sure you're okay? Do you need to eat something more substantial than scones?"

He licked some clotted cream from his thumb. "I'll be fine." He looked at Percy again, only to find her staring at his mouth.

Yet another bolt of lust rushed through him.

Needing a distraction, any distraction, he cleared his throat and changed the subject. "Thanks for helping Violet with attaching the dragon foot. Putting it on is the biggest hurdle since I can't do it myself in my dragon form."

Her gaze snapped back to his. If her cheeks were pinker than usual, Bronx did his best not to notice. She replied, "It was nothing." She bit her bottom lip, but again Bronx had the fortitude to maintain eye contact. She added, "Thank you for showing me your dragon. You're beautiful. Or, wait, Violet said to use words like *fierce* and *rugged* and *muscled*."

His dragon grunted, but Bronx laughed aloud. "My dragon appreciates the latter descriptions." He tilted his head and said, "Was that the first time you've ever seen a dragon up close?"

He'd been afraid to ask that earlier, not wanting to spook her and risk postponing this outing.

Percy shrugged, looked at the table, and played with the cutlery. "I've only ever seen them from afar. No one was allowed to shift inside the orphanage, and none of us could do it inside the facility."

Violet's voice cut in, from the door leading to the outside seating area. "Dad, is it okay if I eat with Scarlett and Valerie inside? I haven't seen them in ages."

He replied, "Of course. Just make sure to come home by dinner."

After saying she would, Violet disappeared into the café.

Percy still played with the knife in front of her. Hoping he could bring her back to the topic, he asked, "You never tried to change a small part of yourself, like a finger, when you were younger?"

He held his breath, hoping his question wouldn't make her regress or send her running. He'd sensed something had shifted between them earlier, that things were a little less distant, and he hoped he was right.

She finally whispered, "No. I was too afraid of being discovered."

Moving his hand, he nearly covered hers but instead made a fist with his fingers and kept it in front of him. "Well, if you're up for it, we can try other techniques to entice your dragon out."

Her gaze rose to his. "There are some? Why didn't you mention it before?"

"It's like anything—you have to lay the foundation before you can construct the house. It was more important for you to learn the basics of being a dragon-shifter before going over suggestions for how to communicate with your inner beast."

She frowned. "More like you wanted to wait and see if my dragon was rogue."

Bronx wouldn't lie to her. "Partly."

Crossing her arms across her chest, she asked, "Then when can we start? Can we do it here? Or do we need to head home?"

He didn't point out her use of *home*, although it was the first time he'd heard it. "Maybe not at the café, but we could stop by the school before heading back to the cabin. Even though the younger students will soon be dismissed for the day, we can use the practice area and maybe even get some extra help from the teachers."

"I suppose." He could tell something else was on her mind. So he waited until she asked, "There's something Killian told me that I wanted to ask about first. Is that okay?"

"Ask me anything, Percy. Any time."

She looked dubious but still replied, "Killian mentioned a kiss had brought his dragon out—at least for one of them—and I was curious about how that worked. I've read about true mates." She stopped, looked to the side, and added, "Do you think I'll have to find mine and kiss him to get my dragon back?"

He blinked at her question but recovered quickly. "I don't know the particulars of Killian's case. But with Dr. Sid, finding her true mate helped with her dragon troubles. I doubt it's the only way, though."

She still didn't look at him. "How does someone know another person is their true mate?"

He cleared his throat. "Well, a male dragon-shifter can usually recognize their true mate after they turn twenty—that's the age dragons are considered mature —and if they're not an arsehole, they let the other person know."

"And female dragon-shifters?"

He shook his head. "They don't know until they kiss their true mate, which kicks off the mate-claim frenzy."

"That seems bloody unfair."

He shrugged. "I didn't make the rules."

She looked at him finally. "Well, it's bloody ridiculous. I should be able to know just as easily."

So I can stay away was left unsaid.

Bronx grunted. "I agree. If—and it's a big if since sometimes dragon-shifters go their whole lives without finding their true mate—your male recognizes you as theirs, let's hope they tell you and not just kiss you."

She wrapped her arms around her torso, as if to protect herself. "Wait. Wouldn't that force the frenzy?"

What he wouldn't give to take one of her hands, kiss the back, and try to dispel her anxiety. But he couldn't. "Yes. There are some who want nothing more than to continue their line, to have their snippet of immortality through creating a child, and don't care about what someone else wants. Although on Stonefire, forcing a frenzy hasn't happened in decades. Accidental kisses, yes, which has required separating a pair and talking to each of them about what they wanted. However, Bram would never allow someone to force a frenzy on another, if he can help it."

Bronx waited to see if she'd retreat, shut down, or ask to go back to the cabin. Some might have coddled her or sugar-coated the truth. But he'd vowed to be honest, and he'd keep to it.

Besides, if she learned later that he'd kept secrets, any and all trust between them would shatter.

And for some reason, the thought of that happening made both man and beast want to growl.

～

Percy was grateful the conversation had turned toward something serious. Worrying about frenzies, true mates, and being forced into a pregnancy all helped her to forget about how she'd stared at Bronx's mouth. In that brief moment, she'd wondered what it would be like for him to kiss her.

She'd never been kissed. All of the guards and the males she'd been forced to have sex with for the fertility experiments had been intent on fucking her until they came, and then they'd left. In the early days, she'd cried and tried to fight them. But as time went on, she'd learned that it was easier to just lie there and distance herself until it was over.

Not once had she ever *wanted* to be held, or kissed, or caressed by a male. At least, not until Bronx. And that was bloody irritating because she couldn't have sex with him once and go back to normal. He was a male who still thought fondly of his late mate. He probably grew attached easily and would want more of her, and to protect herself, Percy would have to run away from him. And she really didn't want to have a different teacher assigned to her.

So Percy just needed to be strong and stop thinking about Bronx, kisses, touches, and other things like that. Talk of frenzies helped, especially when it came to the arseholes who forced it. And she still couldn't believe a female dragon couldn't identify their true mate but a male one could.

Her dragon had come out for a second earlier, back at the landing area. She only said, "I like him," before disappearing again.

So now Percy was torn—if her dragon liked Bronx,

she would have to spend more time with him to appease her beast. But if she spent more time with the dragonman, she might stare at his mouth again and dream of his kisses.

Bronx said, "Percy."

She looked at him, and his brows were drawn down. "What?"

"You've been quiet for a few minutes now. Was it your dragon?"

Sighing, she shook her head. "No."

He topped up her tea. "Well, let's finish here, and we can practice. Who knows, maybe it'll help."

Meeting his gaze, she couldn't look away. His gray eyes were so warm, concerned, and almost tender.

Fuck no. She was imagining things. No one looked at her like that. And no one had ever cared about her before, and she doubted it would start now.

After draining her teacup, she stood, nearly tipping her chair in the process. "Let's go."

She rushed out of the café. Thankfully, she knew the way to the school. It wasn't long until Bronx caught up to her. Even with his leg, he was so much taller than her, and his strides were long.

He asked, "Is there anything else you can tell me about your dragon since coming to Stonefire? The more information we have, the more I can confer with the teachers and maybe form a strategy."

Her heart warmed at how he wanted to help her. And yet, she wasn't ready to share even the two appearances of her dragon. Percy was greedy for her beast, not to mention that a few weeks hadn't cured her lifelong cynicism. "No."

She'd never even mentioned the light. And for a second, guilt crashed down over her. Of all the people she'd met, Bronx was the one person who might actually help her without wanting something in return.

But, no. She'd been naïve as a child, and she wouldn't fucking be it again.

She touched her birthmark on her neck but quickly lowered her hand.

Bronx must've seen it, though, judging by what he said next. "Has anyone ever told you it looks like a roaring dragon head?"

She frowned. "No."

He said nothing, merely keeping pace with her strides.

She and silence were good friends. And yet, with Bronx, she didn't like it. She blurted, "It's been called a mark of evil, or of being a freak, but that's it."

Bronx stopped and turned toward her. His flashing pupils made her step back. He growled, "Who the fuck said that?"

Instinctively, she knew his anger wasn't directed at her. "The other orphans. Even at the facility." She swallowed, and her voice was barely audible when she added, "Even the orphanage headmistress said it was why my mother abandoned me."

Tears pricked her eyes as she remembered all the times that bitch had used Percy's birthmark to put her down, make her feel small about herself, and to almost believe she deserved to be abandoned.

It was all rubbish, of course. But not even she could be completely rational when it came to her abandonment issues, as the doctors inside the facility had called them.

"Hey, Percy."

She wiped her cheeks, mortified to discover they were wet with tears, and met Bronx's gaze. The tenderness had returned, which only made her heart ache even more, for something she could never—would never—have.

He put out a hand as if to touch her but retreated. Before she could think better of it, she stated, "Stop doing that."

He blinked. "Pardon?"

Her cheeks burned, but in for a penny, in for a pound. "I hate when people move as if to touch me and then retreat. I survived seven years of hell, Bronx. A touch won't toss me into hysterics."

Slowly, oh so slowly, he put a hand on her upper arm. The feel of his strong, warm fingers against her thin top made her body tingle in places she didn't want to think about. When he rubbed up and down, the friction made her suck in a breath.

His voice was deep and even when he said, "I only hesitated because I wanted you to have the choice, Percy. For too long, people took what they wanted. Now I want you to have the ability to receive only what you wish."

He put his other hand on her other arm, and the combination of his caresses made her take a step toward him. But her throat was tight, and her eyes stung, and she was completely lost for what to say.

Not just because Bronx kept giving her choices. No, because she wanted to close the distance between them and revel in the heat of his chest and arms and to hear his heartbeat under her ear once more.

He moved one hand to her face and wiped away the wetness there. "But now that you've given me permission to touch you—at least for now—I might do it too much."

She wanted to tell him yes, to please touch her. To hold her, kiss her, and make her feel wanted, if only for a few minutes.

But the light inside her head shifted slowly into the shape of a dragon. Her beast stayed a few beats, tilting her head at Percy. This time, her dragon was clearly defined, complete with her beautiful purple scales, and her wings stretched out behind her.

Her dragon said, *I like him.*

Then she morphed back into the sphere, and Percy cried out.

She must've done it aloud, because Bronx asked, "What's wrong? What happened?"

Stepping backward, he released her, and Percy closed her eyes. *Are you there? Please, dragon, won't you come out again? I have so much to ask you and tell you and plan with you. Please.*

Silence.

"Percy? What's wrong?"

The appearance of her dragon had snapped Percy from the moment, which was a good thing. She had one goal to accomplish: embrace her dragon and shift. Bronx was nice, and yes, she liked his touches. But he wasn't part of her plan.

After a few deep breaths, she opened her eyes and

turned down the path, back toward the main gates of Stonefire. "I want to go home."

Bronx said nothing but merely walked beside her. He greeted a few people along the way, but Percy never looked up from the ground in front of her.

She needed to stop wasting time with stuff that didn't matter. It not only gave her ideas of things that were impossible, but also meant she still didn't have her dragon back for good.

So she walked quickly, thinking of how to entice her beast out again, and slowly rebuilt the walls she'd taken down over the course of the day.

By the time she escaped into her bedroom, she was back where she needed to be—alone.

And so Percy spent the rest of the day trying to coax out her dragon. When that didn't work, she researched as much as possible, even eating dinner in her room and forgoing TV with Violet.

She was determined not to be so easily distracted again.

Chapter Twenty-Three

Bronx knew Percy's dragon had spoken to her because her pupils had flashed to slits once when he'd held her arms. But she never mentioned it, not even over the next two days of lessons. She was polite but distant again.

And he bloody hated it.

Even now, as she sat in the garden and ate her lunch, he wanted to go out there and chat to her about something other than their latest text or reading exercise. Yet any time he tried, she shut him down.

His dragon spoke up. *Something spooked her. It could even be because of her dragon.*

I know that. If she'd only talk to me, I could try to help her. But she barely says anything to Violet, let alone me.

Watching how Percy's distance hurt Violet had twisted his heart nearly in two. He'd tried to explain that Percy would need time, lots of time, to heal from everything that'd happened in her life. And Violet knew rationally that was true, but she'd grown attached to Percy already, probably because she craved female companionship.

An idea came into Bronx's head, and he went outside. Percy didn't even look at him but merely watched the dragons flying overhead. He cleared his throat and said, "My sisters-in-law Sarah and Letitia invited you to hang out with them. They want to take you shopping for clothes you actually want to wear, ones that are your choice, and do some female things I probably would find bloody boring."

Percy never looked away from the dragons overhead and remained quiet.

He almost reached for her but didn't. "Percy, did you hear me?"

"I did."

"Well? What do you want to do?"

She shook her head. "No, I want to stay here. I have too much work to do."

He did risk putting a hand on her shoulder. For a second, she relaxed at his touch. But then she tensed and moved away.

He'd given her space for two days, but he couldn't let her retreat forever, or she'd never make progress. So he asked, "What happened? Something's different, and don't say nothing. I suspect it has to do with your dragon, but I don't know for certain."

She finally met his gaze. "Why would you say that?"

He pointed to his eyes, let his own pupils flash, and said, "Because yours did the same when we stood on the footpath, after the café."

Her eyes widened. "It was nothing."

"Was it? I thought we were supposed to be honest with each other, Percy. I've answered questions that I knew might make you uncomfortable or sad, and I did it because of that vow. Are you not going to do the same?"

Her pupils flashed once. "I don't owe you anything, Bronx Wells. And you're not as honest as you say. If you were, you'd bloody well talk to your daughter about her mum. She craves to hear about her, hear about a female who wanted her, one she never really met, and you constantly dismiss her questions. Why? I bet because it's easy, and you'd rather protect yourself than help her. So until you're honest with Violet, don't act as if you're so bloody superior, because you're not."

She turned and dashed into the house, and Bronx stared after her, his mouth slightly agape.

What the fuck just happened?

His dragon said softly, *She's right, you know.*

What? Now you're taking sides?

No. But Violet has always, always wanted to know more about Edith. She's getting too old to shelter, though. If Percy noticed it, then Violet is probably more than aware of how you avoid her questions and is probably hurting.

Bronx ran a hand through his hair and blew out a breath. *Fuck, I know I've held back. What if once Violet learns of how I didn't protect her mother, all but signed her death sentence, not to mention what I did shortly after Vi was born? She'll probably want nothing to do with me, and I don't think I could handle it.*

She would never just walk away. She's fifteen going on sixteen. She's old enough to hear and judge for herself. I suspect

Violet will view things as I do, but you won't believe me. So tell her.

He tapped his fingers against his thigh. *If I do, it's for Violet's sake, not because Percy wants it. I'll make it clear that Violet may not like what she hears and give her the choice.*

At least she'll have it, which you haven't given her before.

Fuck, this all made him sound selfish. And to some degree, he might've been. He loved his daughter more than life itself, and the last thing he wanted was to hurt her or have her look at him with anger and disgust.

His dragon spoke up. *Just talk with her. It's time.*

His beast was right, but Bronx still had to work up the nerve. He cleaned the kitchen, answered some emails, and all around kept busy, waiting for Violet to come home from her school visit.

He only hoped that his daughter would still give him hugs, or ask him to take her out for tea and scones, or want him to watch the silly soap operas on TV once he'd talked with her.

PERCY SAT ON HER BED, clutching her head in her hands, and said to her dragon, *Why are you mad with me?*

Her beast didn't come out often and usually only for a few minutes at a time, but it was still amazing to her. She most definitely didn't want to upset her dragon in any way.

Her dragon paced and finally said, *You were mean to Bronx. He's nice to us.*

He is. But I can't get attached, dragon. I can't.

She waited to see if her beast would merely disappear. Every time she'd tried to have a conversation, it'd only lasted a minute or two.

But her dragon didn't morph back into a sphere. *But I like him. Why do you want to leave him?*

She laughed bitterly. *Because while you were missing, I've had a fucking awful life. I learned a long time ago to only trust myself. He might be nice now, but he'll betray us in the end, like everyone else. I'm sure of it.*

I'm not. With that, her dragon swirled and shrank back into the shape of a sphere.

Percy cried and begged for her to come back, but the light merely glowed steadily. She clutched her head harder, as if the action would somehow bring her dragon back. But if there was one constant about her beast, it was that she came out sporadically and only when she felt like it. No amount of begging, threatening, or shouting did anything.

Slowly, she lowered herself onto the bed and tucked her hands under her cheek as she stared out the open window.

For days, she'd gone back and forth about telling the doctors about her dragon's short appearances and chats. But the need to protect her beast, to ensure no one silenced her again, was strong. So strong that she still lied to them, to Violet, and to Bronx.

Although the more she did it, the heavier her heart grew. Everyone else seemed to be able to smile, make plans, and live their lives as if they didn't expect it to turn to shit in the next second.

Why couldn't she?

She couldn't because she was bloody damaged. And Percy was starting to think that if she couldn't even be nice to someone as patient and tender as Bronx, she never would.

The fact she even cared about being nice to others scared the crap out of her, though.

Percy had no idea how long she lay there, but eventually, her stomach rumbled. And after too many years of not eating enough, she couldn't ignore it.

Slowly, she sat up, rubbed her face, and went to the door. She listened, but no one was in the hallway. She walked out the door and was nearly to the living room when she heard Violet.

"Hi ya, Dad. You asked me to come home? What did you want?"

Percy knew she should retreat and give them space, and yet she couldn't seem to move. Was Bronx really sorting things out with his daughter? Had her words impacted him that much?

And if he did talk with his daughter, what excuse could she use next time to push him away?

Maybe she wouldn't want to do that. However, she barely paid attention to that thought as she listened to Bronx and Violet's conversation.

BRONX HADN'T EXPECTED Violet to come home so soon after receiving his text message. But he was done being a coward, and he greeted her once she came in with a kiss to her cheek. As soon as she asked what he wanted, he gestured toward the sofa. "I want to talk about your mother."

His daughter's pupils flashed as she gasped. "Really?"

He nodded. "You're more than old enough to hear it all. Although I warn you, it's not all rosy and perfect, Vi. Do you really want to hear it? The truth might alter your picture of me."

She frowned. "What are you talking about?"

"First, are you sure you want the truth, no matter what?"

She searched his gaze. "You're scaring me a little, Dad." She crossed her arms over her chest, her pupils flashing, then she finally bobbed her head. "But yes, no matter what, I want to hear it."

He gestured toward the sofa, and once they both sat down, he jostled his good leg.

His dragon spoke up. *Just tell her. There's no sense in delaying it now.*

Taking a deep breath, he said, "I already mentioned how I found your mother—hiding and beaten in one of the boat sheds along a nearby lake. And how making her laugh became one of my greatest joys."

Violet smiled. "Yes."

His leg thumped a bit harder against the floor. "Well, we weren't true mates. However, I loved your mother, wanted to mate her, and wooed her into saying yes. We were happy. Edith even soon found her purpose —helping with volunteer activities and especially at the school."

He remembered her coming home and sharing with him about what she'd done that day, her eyes bright. It didn't matter if it was assisting a young student with an art project or visiting one of the elderly and dropping off groceries; Edith merely loved being useful.

He'd always hated how a female with such a good heart had suffered such a shitty life.

Violet touched his arm. "I know that much, Dad. I saw pictures from some of the archives at the school."

He nodded and patted his daughter's hand. "Well, I should back up a little before explaining what came next. Before I mated your mother, I bluntly told her that it was dangerous for a human female to carry and birth a dragon-shifter's child. While there are treatments now that give human females higher chances of survival—more than ninety-three percent—it was different back then. She'd been through so much, and I couldn't bear the thought of losing her. To protect her life, we agreed not to have any children."

Initially, Edith had almost seemed relieved. Not because she wanted to avoid sex—they'd had plenty of that—but she'd had a tough childhood and teenage life, and she'd never really been given the chance to merely be herself.

And Bronx had wanted Edith as his mate more than he wanted a child.

Violet asked quietly, "What happened, Dad?"

He blew out a breath. "Over time, working with the children made her want to be a mum. She wanted to give a child a better life than hers, wanted a little one that was part her and part me to love. It was one of the few things we argued about. I loved her so much and didn't want to risk it, risk *her*. But..." His voice trailed off, and his fingers gripped the trouser material on one leg. His daughter was about to learn how weak he'd been.

"Dad, but what?"

Glancing over, he saw Violet merely looking at him with curiosity. His dragon said, *She already knows how the story ends, so stop dragging your feet.*

Even if she does, this is bloody difficult, dragon.

Still, Violet should know everything.

He found his voice again. "Your mother was so desperate to have a baby, despite knowing the risks, that she even threatened to tell the DDA we hadn't been trying. And back then, matings between humans and dragon-shifters were usually only granted to help repopulate a dragon clan. If the DDA found out, I had no bloody idea what would've happened. And so I gave in. Instead of doing what was hard by staying strong to protect her life and safeguard her future, I let her tears sway me." He swallowed. "And even from the start of her pregnancy, she had a tough time. Your mother was quite ill for most of it. She could barely get out of bed, and yet she still went on every day about how much she couldn't wait to meet you."

The memories threatened to break free, but he kept them at bay to focus on Violet. He would get through all of this if it killed him. "Even when the doctors said she'd die if she didn't terminate the pregnancy, she refused to listen. I couldn't convince her, I-I..."

He closed his eyes, remembering how he'd pleaded and begged Edith to think of their future.

She'd even put his hand on her belly, saying maybe their child would kick for him. Instead of enjoying the moment, he'd resented it. To him, her growing belly had signaled a ticking clock to her death.

"I couldn't protect her, couldn't convince her to save her own life. And if that wasn't bad enough, my inability to do so made the last few months difficult. Edith wanted only to treasure her unborn baby, and I only wanted for her to see reason, even begged her to."

He stared out the door, at the flowers in the garden. His voice sounded distant to his own ears as he continued, "And in the end, she died, and they barely managed to save your life." He swallowed but pushed past the emotion in his throat. "And for the first few months, I wanted nothing to do with you. I wouldn't hold you. I wouldn't look at you. I kept thinking Edith would be alive if not for you. When you needed me the most and I should've been protecting you, watching over you, and treasuring the life I still had, I didn't. I was selfish and hurt and not the father you deserved."

To this day, he still felt guilty about those months. Now, he couldn't imagine not loving his brilliant, bright daughter. He treasured her teasing nature, how she easily became excited, and even how she had a way with people and could charm anyone without barely trying.

He felt a hand take his, and he made himself meet Violet's gaze. Even though her eyes were wet, she wasn't crying. Yet.

She said softly, "It had to have been hard, Dad. I don't remember those days, of course. I was too young. But from my earliest memory, you were always there, always cheering me on, and always trying to make me happy." She bit her lip a beat before asking, "But do you still regret me?"

He pulled Violet into a hug and laid his cheek atop her head. "No, Violet. Never. I love you, you're my life, and I can't imagine the world without you."

Her choked voice was hard to hear. "Even though I killed Mum?"

Bronx pushed her back until he could meet her gaze. "I've had so many years to think about this, and here's what I'd say—your mother loved you so much, even before she'd held you, to the point she risked her life for you. You were wanted, Violet Wells, and still are." He kissed her forehead. "I wish I'd spent your mother's final days viewing them as she did—with anticipation and happiness. I didn't, and I can't change that. But I love you, Vi. You're the greatest gift your mother could've given me. She would be so proud of you, love. So very proud."

His daughter started crying, and he pulled her into his embrace again, allowing her to get it all out.

She might still hate him later, but right here, right now, he just wanted to hold his little girl and be there for her, especially since she was on the cusp of adulthood. Before he knew it, she'd find someone else to rely on, to love, and she wouldn't need him as much any longer.

When she finally quieted, he still kept her in his

arms. His voice cracked as he said, "I love you, Violet. I hope one day you can forgive me for not being there at the beginning, when you should've been my top priority."

She leaned back, and he released her. After she wiped her eyes, Violet said, "There's nothing to forgive, Dad. All I know is the loving, caring father I have." She took his hand again, and he squeezed hers. "Thank you for telling me this. I know you've always tried to paint a picture-perfect life for Mum, but I like learning about the real her, even if it's not always cheerful." She searched his eyes a second and then asked, "You don't still blame yourself for her death, do you?"

He sighed and rubbed a hand over his face. "Sometimes." Violet opened her mouth, and he beat her to it. "Rationally, I know that nothing I could've said or done would've changed Edith's mind. Nothing. But my heart still thinks there was something I could've found to help her, maybe even a treatment I hadn't heard of. That somehow, some way, if I'd tried harder, I could've had you both in my life." He shook his head. "The game of what-if haunts me to this day."

His dragon sniffed. *You should think more on the present, which you can actually act upon.*

Ignoring his dragon, he focused solely on his daughter and squeezed her hand. "In the future, if you still want to be around me, I'll tell you more stories of your mum, any time you wish."

She frowned. "Of course I want to be around you. You're my dad, and as far as I remember, a bloody good one."

The certainty in her tone cut through some of the

guilt swirling inside him. "I try to be, love. Being your dad is the most important thing in the world to me."

"I hope I'm not the only thing, though. I'm nearly an adult, Dad. And, you know, it's okay to think of the future beyond me." She smiled. "I want you to be happy."

He said slowly, "Okay."

She laughed and released his hand. "Don't sound so wary."

"I want to say you're up to something, but I have no idea what."

His daughter looked innocent, too bloody innocent, as she batted her eyelashes. "When have I ever been up to anything?"

He sighed but then heard something shatter in the hallway. Bronx rushed into it and saw Percy trying to pick up the pieces of the smashed vase on the ground. He was about to tell her to stop, when she flinched and said, "Ouch."

Bronx's protective instincts kicked in. He knelt, took her hand, and examined the slice on her finger. "Come with me."

She followed, him keeping her finger up and his other hand beneath it to catch any blood, and they reached the bathroom. He turned on the tap, washed her fingers, and then dried it with tissues. He quickly put on antiseptic and then a plaster. Once it was done, he released her hand, and Percy brought it to her chest.

She stared at him, but he couldn't read her expression. Had she overheard his conversation with Violet? Would she run from him now, knowing how he'd been a crappy father at first?

She simply stated, "I heard everything."

And he waited to see what she'd say.

PERCY HADN'T MEANT to keep eavesdropping in the hallway. And yet, she hadn't been able to leave. The emotions, the pure pain in Bronx's voice as he explained about his late mate and then the guilt and regret when he'd talked about struggling to be a new father through his grief, had tugged at her heartstrings.

She'd almost always known that her life had been a shitty, horrible nightmare. And yet, it'd never really occurred to her that people who weren't imprisoned or abandoned as a baby could also have pain in their lives.

After all, Violet and Bronx had seemed so happy most of the time. And even after everything, all his confessions, they clearly still loved each other and had each other's back.

Their affection had caused her loneliness to crush down on her, making it harder to breathe. That was when she'd backed into the vase and knocked it over.

Bronx taking care of her finger had helped to ease her embarrassment. Although after she admitted to hearing it all, she tried to read his expression. She'd told Bronx he needed to come clean with Violet to show his honesty, and he had, so she needed to be more honest now.

There was still pain, sadness, and even concern in his gaze. Before she could stop herself, she said, "One of many things I learned from my time inside the facility was this—you can't save everyone. Sometimes you can help or maybe give them some food or alleviate a little pain. But sometimes, you can't do anything. Either because of the person themselves or the ones around them." She reached out with her uninjured hand and took Bronx's. His strong, solid grip sent a rush of relief through her, as if she'd been yearning for his touch again.

Ignoring that, she continued, "Your late mate was her own person, it sounds like. And what she wanted the most in the world was a child of yours. I have a feeling nothing would've changed her mind. And maybe she knew you'd be a great father, even if she were gone, and that her child would have the life she never had growing up—one of love."

He searched her eyes. "Maybe."

She shrugged. "I never met her. However, I know something about having a goal, one that shapes who you are and affects all your decisions."

Fuck. As soon as she said it, Percy knew it was a mistake.

"What's yours?"

She was torn between bolting from the room and finally sharing something about herself.

In the end, she couldn't yet bring herself to share her dragon with anyone, not even Bronx. So she gave him a half-truth. "Freedom."

He stared at her, and she wondered if he could tell she was hiding something from him. But in the end, he squeezed her fingers and said, "If you want me to, I can ask Bram about you getting your own place soon, on Stonefire proper. If you're monitored closely, regarding your dragon, it might just be possible. There are some cottages at the edges of the clan that should be safe for everyone and give you some space."

Yet again, Bronx was trying to give her what she asked for and give her choices.

She desperately wanted to trust him, and yet she still couldn't bring herself to do it. She'd been abused and used, and her cynicism and distrust might never go away.

That made her heart squeeze, and she wished she could be more "normal." Maybe have a life where complaining about a boss, or not wanting to wash dishes, or worrying only about how a character would fare on a TV show were her biggest troubles.

But Percy doubted she'd ever have that kind of life.

Her voice cracked as she asked, "Why are you so nice to me?"

He raised a hand and brushed her cheek with the backs of his knuckles. She couldn't hide her shiver. It wasn't from fear, although the heat of her lower belly and her racing heart did scare her a little.

Because she might just actually want to share her body with this male, of her own choice, for the first time.

Thankfully Bronx spoke before she could run away to protect herself. "You deserve more than you were given, Percy. And if it's up to me to prove to you that the world isn't only full of monsters, I'll gladly do it."

"Oh."

He lightly placed his finger under her chin and made her look into his warm eyes. "But there's a selfish reason too."

Was it her imagination or had he leaned in a little? Should she do the same?

But just as Percy swayed toward him, Violet appeared in the doorway. "Are you all right, Percy?"

She and Bronx split apart instantly, and Percy shot past Violet to stand in the hallway. "I'm fine. I'll just make a sandwich and go to bed."

Violet asked, "So you don't want to watch telly with me tonight?"

Percy glanced at Bronx, and just one look made her skin warm and her belly flip.

Warning bells went off inside her head, and she inched back a little more. "Not tonight, Violet." She looked at the teenager and saw a flash of disappointment.

Damn it, she didn't want to hurt Violet, especially not after the truths Bronx had shared with his daughter. Despite her no-attachment rule, she said, "I'll watch with you tomorrow, okay? You'll just have to catch me up."

Violet smiled and bobbed her head. "Brilliant. I'll have to fill you in about the guy returning with amnesia and how he survived a plane crash."

Her words poked at her curiosity, but she glanced at Bronx again, her heart skipping a beat, and she knew she had to retreat to her room and sort out her head.

And her feelings.

Wait, no, she didn't have feelings for anyone. "Okay."

Percy dashed to the kitchen, made the quickest sandwich in history, and retreated to her room.

While she managed to temporarily forget about

Bronx as she read her dragon-shifter books, she couldn't control her dreams.

And the fact that she'd kissed him—and more—in them made her worry about what she was going to do about everything. Because at this rate, she'd get too attached. And Bronx or even Violet could hurt her, and she'd be even worse off than before.

Right?

Chapter Twenty-Four

Bronx should've felt like a bastard about his cock hardening for Percy when she'd swayed toward him as if to kiss him. And yet, he couldn't do it. In that moment, she'd wanted him as much as he'd wanted her—he was sure of it.

She was attracted to him, at the very least.

But to wish for anything more was bloody ridiculous.

And it didn't help that as he waited for her to come out for her morning lessons the next day, he kept remembering the softness of her cheek under his knuckles and the way her breath had hitched when he placed a finger under her chin.

He could only imagine what it'd be like to show her pleasure and tenderness, to be the first male she chose to take to her bed. *Wait, what? No, no, no. That would never happen. Ever.*

His dragon sighed. *If she's the one to kiss us, it's her choice, and she's not being forced.*

Or she thinks it's a way to repay me for being nice.

His beast grunted. *No. Stop trying to brush aside what Percy is becoming to us.*

Nothing, dragon. She's nothing.

Are you sure?

Why? Do you know if she's our true mate, and you're not telling me?

Her dragon still hasn't come out long enough for me to judge one way or the other.

Then we need to find a way to get her beast to stick around. Because if she is our true mate, we need to be reassigned.

His beast growled. *Don't be bloody ridiculous.*

I'm not. Think of it—the last thing she needs is a mate-claim frenzy.

It's not as if we'd claim her without her consent.

That was true—even if he kissed Percy and it kicked off the frenzy, his dragon would be demanding but would never force a female. It just wasn't who they were.

Regardless, neither he nor Percy needed that complication in their lives.

As he started to rethink the special outing he had planned for the day, Percy emerged in her usual T-shirt and jeans, her hair pulled back from her face. He did his best not to react to that last bit because she'd never worn her hair up around him before. Usually, she had it down and rearranged over her neck to cover her birthmark.

Don't read anything into it, he cautioned himself over and over again.

His dragon merely laughed.

Ignoring the bastard, he smiled. "Don't bother

sitting down. You'll need some shoes for what I have planned."

She frowned. "Why?"

"Because today we're taking a field trip."

She searched his gaze. "You know how I don't like surprises, Bronx."

He shrugged. "We're visiting a nearby lake, one where the young dragons have swimming lessons. And yes, they'll be in their dragon forms."

Her eyes widened. "I can go too? Bram will allow it?"

He stood and walked over to her but didn't touch her.

No matter how much he wanted to. "Yes. He wants to give you true freedom; he really does. But until we sort out your dragon, we have to be a bit cautious."

"Did you ask about a place at the edges of Stonefire for me to live?"

Bronx nodded. "Yes. He's working on it."

Surprise flared in her eyes. "I-I get to be part of the clan? Just for a short while, of course. But I can have my own place?"

For a second, irritation flashed through him at the fact she wanted to be rid of him. But Bronx quickly pushed it aside. Even if Percy had nearly kissed them, it didn't mean anything. "That's the goal. But it takes some time to put everything together, of course. Especially since Bram is dealing with the DDA about you staying here."

She tilted her head. "Do I have to stay on Stonefire?"

His heart twisted at her wanting to leave. "Once the

doctors clear you, then you can pick any dragon clan in the UK. Well, provided the clan leader approves it. But all of the leaders—the other clans are Lochguard, Snowridge, Skyhunter, and Northcastle—are brilliant people. I don't see it being a problem."

The corner of her mouth kicked up. "Trying to get rid of me?"

"Absolutely not. Violet would never forgive me if I did that." He gestured toward her room. "The sooner you get your shoes, the sooner we can go. That way, you have more time to watch or even interact with the young dragons, if you wish."

Her eyes lit up, and Bronx wished he could do that for her more often. "That would be brilliant. I never had the chance to shift into a young dragon form, so it'll help me understand things a bit more to see them for myself. Just a second."

She raced into her room, and he chuckled. He loved seeing some of her youth come out once in a while. Percy more than deserved some lighthearted moments.

Within minutes, she was ready, and they headed toward the big lake near Stonefire, the one that belonged to the clan but still sometimes had human visitors. And as they walked, he couldn't stop staring at Percy's smile as she pointed out some flower or an animal.

She looked so happy. But it also reminded him of how sheltered and deprived she'd been.

Never before had he felt so much older than her. And even if it rubbed him the wrong way to think it, he wished for her not to be his true mate. If she ever did find that person, he should be younger like her, someone able to run and jump into the air easily, a male who could give her all the things she'd missed out on.

His dragon growled. *Stop it. We're not decrepit. And a younger male would probably hurt her more easily.*

I'm not so sure.

I am. She needs steadiness, someone more sure of who they are. A young buck won't do that.

Using the phrase "young buck" only reinforces my point about being older. At any rate, it's a good thing we're trying today to bring her dragon out long enough for you to determine whether she's our true mate or not.

His hope was that seeing all the young dragons and their antics might resonate with Percy's inner beast. It wasn't a guarantee, but most dragons loved children, and it was something he hadn't yet tried with her.

And Bronx desperately hoped it would work. The sooner he knew Percy wasn't his true mate, the easier he could build a wall between them. Then he could keep it professional and let her discover who she was before being forced into such a life-changing decision.

PERCY KNEW she was acting like a child, but everything was just so *new*. Flowers she'd never seen, birds with pretty colors, and even the sight of the peaks and hills of the surrounding landscape—it was better than any views she'd had at the orphanage and far better than the handful of pictures inside her set of apartments inside the facility.

She was so absorbed in it all that she didn't even realize she'd grabbed Bronx's arm and wrapped hers around his. Every time she pointed and asked about something, he explained what it was and patiently suffered through her enthusiasm.

Although nothing compared to when they crested a hill and she saw the lake for the first time. It was long, not too wide, and a deep-blue color. The lake was filled with small dragons of every color—black, gold, red, blue, green, and purple—splashing, floating, diving, and swimming around.

That was what she should've done as a child but never had. For a second, tears filled her eyes, but she willed them away. She wasn't about to allow her past to ruin this day. It was too magical and beautiful, and she wanted to memorize everything about it.

The light inside her head pulsed a few beats but then went back to a steady glow. Maybe seeing so many dragon-shifters in their dragon forms would coax her beast out and convince her to stay around longer.

Percy didn't realize she'd stopped in place until Bronx said, "Do you want to keep going? Or do you want to head back?"

She tore her gaze from the lake and looked at him. Unlike earlier, when there had been amusement and patience, she couldn't read his expression.

And that irritated her.

Ignoring the feeling—she was getting fucking bombarded with them on a regular basis now, and she didn't know how to handle them—she answered, "I definitely want to keep going. Are they expecting us?"

He nodded and gestured for them to walk again.

"Tristan knows we might show up, and if we do, he and the other teacher, Ella, will signal the dragon children to come back to shore when you're ready. That way you can see them up close." He paused and smiled. "And the human children will be there, so you'll finally meet Daisy."

"Why are you smiling at that?"

He laughed, and the sound nearly startled her. She liked how deep and gravelly it was. Bronx most definitely needed to laugh more.

Not that it was her concern.

He replied, "Daisy is a force of nature. But in a good way. You'll see." He pointed to the shore ahead. "She's the blond one. Near her are Joey and his older brother, Mark."

She spotted the trio of children shouting things for the dragon students to try.

The sight was strange to her. Growing up, she'd been told so many times that humans hated dragon-shifters. And even inside the facility, she'd been told no one cared if she was an experimental test subject because she wasn't human and dragon-shifters were expendable.

Although she should know by now that she'd been fed lie upon lie inside that hellhole.

The light flickered inside her head again but still didn't morph into a dragon. Resisting a sigh, she focused on the other people standing on the shore. Tristan was there, plus a tall female with dark hair who was filming something, one who didn't have a tattoo on her upper arm.

"Is she human too?"

"Yes, that's Jane Hartley, Kai's mate. He's the blond dragonman who rescued you from the facility."

She frowned. "Wait. Even the head of security is allowed to have a human mate?"

He nodded. "Anyone on Stonefire is, although it wasn't always that way. However, Bram's mate used to be an employee for the Department of Dragon Affairs, and she's worked hard to change a few things around here for the better."

Percy had learned a lot about the DDA over the last few weeks, although she was still unsure about if they were good or bad for her kind. "Violet has mentioned several times that there are more male than female dragons, so I guess that makes sense to allow human mates."

"Dragon-shifter numbers tend to skew male. Well, until recently. There are theories that a male human paired with a female dragon will more often have daughters than sons."

She tapped her chin. "Really? If so, then it's almost as if humans and dragons always should've lived together, to create the right balance."

As soon as she said that, Percy felt naïve. But Bronx grunted. "That makes sense, actually. Being so strictly separated from humans pushed our numbers rather low over the last fifty years or so, to a worrying degree." He gently touched the back of her hand with his fingers. "Which should be the last proof you need that half-human dragon-shifters are most definitely wanted. Otherwise, we'd have too many males and not enough females."

"I suppose." She couldn't resist brushing her hand

against Bronx's and loved how the light touch sent a rush of happiness through her. But she wasn't bold enough to take his hand. "Thank you for today."

"It's barely started, Percy."

She smiled up at him. "Regardless, it's turning into one of the best I can remember."

He took her hand, but she didn't pull away. "Then come on. Let's see if we can make it even more memorable."

She laughed as he tugged her along and she struggled to keep up. For a man missing a part of his leg, he could be bloody fast.

Out of breath from laughing, she had to take a moment once they reached the other humans and dragon-shifters in their human forms before she could truly take in everyone.

And as Bronx made the introductions, she didn't even notice how he still held her hand.

SEEING Percy laugh so easily had done things to his heart, not to mention to his cock—both things he shouldn't have been feeling.

But she was so bloody beautiful, with little crinkles around the corners of her eyes, her ponytail swaying in the slight breeze as they jogged down the pathway toward the shore. She should always be in sunshine and free to run outdoors and given the chance to be happy.

And even though he should've put distance between them, her light brush against his fingers had made him crave more of her touch, to the point he'd taken her hand. Maybe he should've worried that his sister-in-law and his brother, Hudson, could see them. Or that all of the children would plainly see them walking hand in hand.

And yet, he hadn't wanted to let go.

They reached the bottom of the hill and slowed their pace. He debated releasing her, then she gripped his hand tighter and squeezed.

His dragon spoke up. *See? She wants us.*

I hardly think hand-holding means what you think it does.

For Percy, yes, I do.

Not wanting to think on his dragon's words, he waved to his brother and sister-in-law. However, before he could reach them, Daisy and Joey raced up to them, while Mark merely stared at him and Percy from a distance.

Bronx whispered, "If it gets to be too much, just let me know."

Percy gave him a curious look before the full force of Daisy Chadwick reached them.

"Bronx! They said you might bring the new clan member to the lake." She grinned up at Percy and held out a hand. "I'm Daisy Chadwick. And no, I'm not a dragon-shifter, which is why I'm not in the water. Although it'd be brilliant to have an inner dragon, for sure. But I can't. So I just try to talk to everyone else's when I can. If yours ever wants to say hello, I'll be here, ready to listen. I could always use another dragon bestie like Freddie, even if you are older than me. But that would just give me more stuff to learn, right?"

Bronx held his breath to see how Percy would react. But she merely smiled down at the little human female and shook her hand. "Hi, Daisy. Call me Percy. And thank you for the offer."

An older version of Daisy with blond hair—her mum, Dawn—rushed over. "Daisy, you know Mr. MacLeod said to stay near him and Miss Lawson for the outing today."

Daisy looked up at her mother. "But, Mum, I needed to say hello to Stonefire's newest member. I know everyone's name, and I needed to put a face to Percy." She turned back toward Percy. "I really do know everyone. So if you ever need help, just ask. I can introduce you to my favorites first, and then the others. Even though I know I shouldn't say I have favorites, I do. I can't help it."

The dark-haired female, Jane, had finished filming and stopped nearby, laughing. "It's okay to have favorites. I know my mate is one of mine." She smiled down at Daisy. "And I still say you'll be running the clan one day, Daisy. I've been here longer than you, and yet you still know more than me. How is that possible?"

Jane winked at Dawn, and the two women chuckled.

Daisy hadn't seen the exchange, so she replied, "I just try really hard. And don't worry, Jane. I'm still thinking up loads of ideas for your videos. I still need to write them all down, but that won't take very long."

Dawn placed her hands on Daisy's shoulders. "Hello, Percy. I'm Dawn, another one of the humans here on Stonefire, and Daisy's mum." She gave a fake-stern look at her daughter. "And if my daughter ever pesters you too much, just send her away. She likes to talk to everyone and loves people, which isn't bad, but we're still working on some boundaries."

Daisy sighed. "I know, Mum. I'm trying. I really am."

"I know, love."

The two smiled at each other, and Bronx felt Percy tense. Not because of Daisy herself, but probably at seeing a mother love her daughter so freely.

Growing up with a brilliant mother of his own, he'd never really thought much about what it'd be like to have a horrible one. Even his late mate's mother had tried to protect her until she'd died when Edith was in her teens.

Percy had never had anyone, not even a foster parent or mentor. It was yet another fucking thing he hated and wished he could change.

Bronx squeezed her hand and said, "We need to meet up with Tristan and say hello to my brother. So we'll see you later, Daisy, okay?"

She nodded and raced off back toward Mark, who looked even grumpier when Daisy started chatting about something.

Bronx said goodbye to Jane and Dawn and steered them toward Tristan. It was on the tip of his tongue to ask if Percy was okay, but a quick glance revealed her watching the young dragons again.

Since he didn't want to ruin the day, he merely kept her hand in his and guided her closer to the lake.

~

SEEING Dawn and Daisy together had made Percy jealous. Again.

Was Stonefire just a big, loving family? How could so many people be so happy?

Although as her gaze went back to the dragons swimming near the shore, she decided to embrace today and make new memories instead of focusing on old ones or on how unfair life could be to some and not others.

The sunlight glinted off the scales of the small dragons as they played. One dunked another, and yet a different dragon used their tail to splash a friend.

The light in her head slowly grew and changed into the large form of her inner dragon. Her beast said, *I want to do that.*

Careful to keep her outward expression neutral— she didn't dare risk someone interrupting her right now —she replied, *We can't until we learn how to shift into our dragon form.*

Then why not do that?

Because I need your help to shift forms.

Her beast paused, and with each passing second, Percy waited for her dragon to hide again.

But she didn't. *What do we need to do?*

Her first instinct was to tell Bronx and see what he suggested.

And yet, that would mean revealing her dragon and how she'd hidden the truth from him. That made her stomach churn because she could only imagine his reaction, and it wouldn't be good.

No, the best plan was still to keep her dragon to herself. For now.

At least until she could shift somewhat. Then maybe she'd tell Bronx. Surely if she proved she could handle her dragon enough to change even a finger into a talon, then no one would try to make her dragon silent again.

She didn't want to believe they would, but she wasn't fully trained, and Stonefire might want to be proactive in protecting their people.

She replied, *Let's get away from the others, and I can teach you what I've read so far. We need to work together to change forms. So please don't go away.*

Asking that was a risk. But she needed to be honest with her dragon, if no one else.

Her beast flapped her wings inside her mind. *I suppose. But hurry up. I'm getting sleepy, and I want a nap.*

She nearly blurted that her dragon had slept for years, but she didn't. *Just stay a few more minutes, and I'll arrange it.*

As they approached Tristan, Percy tugged her hand. Bronx released it, and she instantly felt colder. But she knew her dragon was her top priority, not Bronx.

Besides, he didn't say a word about it. He chatted with Tristan about the outing and how the students had been doing, and as soon as there was an opening, she asked, "Can I sit over there and watch the students by myself?"

Tristan frowned. "Why not just watch them from here?"

"No, no, the hill is a better place. Then I can see them all better." She paused and then added, "I was never able to shift as a child, and I want to memorize what small dragons look like playing, to draw on later."

The grumpy dragonman studied her, as if he could tell she was hiding something. But then he shrugged. "I don't see why not. I'm not your guard, Percy. And as long as you don't threaten my clan or my family, you can do what you wish."

She bobbed her head. "Then I'll go."

Bronx said, "Wait."

She stilled but didn't look back. He walked to her side and whispered for her ears only, "What's wrong? Are there too many people?"

It felt as if acid filled her mouth as she replied, "Yes, that's it. I just need a small break to recharge, and I'll come back. I don't want to go home, but this is a way I can stay."

She could feel his eyes boring into her back, and she almost apologized for lying to him.

But he finally touched her fingers with his and murmured, "I'll be here, if you need me."

For a second, she contemplated telling him everything. She'd like to think that Bronx wouldn't rush to the doctors or that they'd start poking, prodding, and asking her all kinds of questions.

Before maybe silencing her beast.

Then her dragon flapped her wings inside Percy's mind, and she knew this was a chance she couldn't risk losing, even if it meant lying to Bronx.

So Percy nodded and dashed toward the small hill alongside the lake. And when she plunked down on the ground, it took every bit of willpower she possessed not to look at Bronx.

Instead, she said to her dragon, *Okay, let's go over some things, and then we'll try to shift our finger.*

And as she went to work, the rest of the world faded away. She was getting so bloody close to her goal. Although her guilt at hiding the truth from Bronx never fully went away.

BRONX KNEW Percy was keeping something from him. Her pupils had flashed once—he thought he was the only one to see it since he couldn't keep his eyes off the female—and then she'd scurried away.

Her dragon was back, in some capacity. He said to his dragon, *I only hope she asks for help if she needs it.*

We all try to shift at first, before we're ready. No doubt all the children make her yearn to try it by herself.

He grunted. *Maybe.*

He watched her, but she merely sat on the ground, cross-legged, staring out at the lake.

Hudson's voice garnered his attention. "She's doing well, Bronx."

Forcing his gaze from Percy, he faced his brother, who wore an amused expression. "What?"

Hudson lowered his voice so only he could hear it. "I saw you holding hands, Bronx. What's going on between you two?"

If it were anyone else, he'd tell them to sod off. However, Hudson had been the one to help him after Edith's death, and then Bronx had been there to help Hudson after his first mate's death. If he would talk to anyone about Percy, it would be Hudson.

Bronx sighed. "I don't know."

Hudson raised his brows and kept his voice low. "That's more honest than I expected."

He glared. "I'm supposed to be her bloody teacher, Hudson. Not to mention she's half my age."

Hudson shrugged. "Does that really matter? You wouldn't be the first dragon-shifter to have an age gap with your mate. Dr. McFarland even went the other way, with her male being younger than her."

Of course Hudson would bring that up. "That's only a twelve-year difference, not nearly twenty-two."

His brother snorted. "Been thinking about this a lot, have you?"

Bronx debated what to say, but his beast spoke up. *This is Hudson. At least be honest with him. Maybe he'll be on my side and convince you that you're being an idiot.*

Great, as if he needed that. Although as his brother tilted his head in question, he sighed. "Yes, I have."

"Have you kissed her yet?"

He shook his head. "No. Until my dragon can tell if she's our true mate or not, I won't. Er, not that I ever will."

Hudson grinned. "I've heard that before." He glared, but Hudson paid him no mind. "But in all seriousness, don't completely push someone away if there's even a chance of it working out. I know my mate wasn't looking for a male again—and fuck, I can't blame her, given her arsehole ex—and yet Sarah took that leap of faith with me. And I like to think she's happy now."

As Hudson stared over at Sarah, who was frowning

down at Mark, Bronx noticed the adoring look that came over his brother's face.

And for a second, envy shot through him.

His dragon spoke up. *It's possible for us to have that again.*

It was then he noticed Percy jumping up and dancing in place. Narrowing his eyes, he scanned her and saw one of her fingers had turned into a talon.

Before he could debate whether to go to her or not, Percy met his gaze and grinned. Then she held the talon toward him. And he decided fuck it, she wanted to share the win with him. And so he ran up the hill as fast as he could.

And Bronx was unable to take his eyes from her flashing pupils the entire time. Had her dragon finally stuck around?

But when they had almost reached her, his dragon said softly, *She's ours.*

He stopped in place. *What?*

She's our true mate. Her dragon makes it so I can recognize her.

A mixture of emotions rushed through him—fear, excitement, dread, wanting, wariness, and joy.

Percy frowned at him, her pupils remaining round, and her finger changed back into a finger. She was close enough that he could hear her. "What's wrong, Bronx? If it's about my dragon, don't worry. She's not rogue or crazy."

He tried to put on a smiling face, tried to forget what his dragon had told him. And yet, he'd vowed not to lie to her.

So he walked a few paces closer before stopping again, which only deepened her frown.

He took a second to memorize how the sun played on her hair, highlighting the roaring dragon birthmark on her neck, and even how the blue of her eyes dazzled with a multitude of colors he might never be able to fully identify.

She was so light, beautiful, and the most carefree he'd seen her to date.

And he was about to ruin it all.

No longer a coward, he said softly, "Your dragon came out long enough for me to recognize it, Percy."

"Recognize what?"

He took a deep breath and said, "That you're my true mate."

After her eyes widened a beat, she turned and ran in the opposite direction.

Chapter Twenty-Five

No, no, no. This couldn't be happening to her. It couldn't.

Percy had been having the best day ever. She'd spent more time with her dragon than ever before and even managed to embrace her beast long enough to change her finger into a talon.

Even the look she'd shared with Bronx had made her heart race. He'd looked so proud, and excited, and happy.

For her.

In that moment, she'd decided then and there to tell him everything about her dragon, how long she'd been around, and how sorry she was for hiding it. He would surely understand her, as Bronx had a knack for that.

Him racing toward her had sent a rush of happiness through her body too. She'd never had anyone to share things with—at least since her dragon had been silenced—and she'd found a friend.

Maybe more than a friend.

Not that she was ready to tackle that.

Then he'd stopped, looked appalled, and said she was his true mate. Panic had set in first because she'd read about true mates, mate-claim frenzies, and what happened as a result. And just the idea of being used for sex, over and over again, until she became pregnant sent a mixture of fear and disappointment through her.

So she ran, and ran, and kept going, ignoring anyone who called out her name. She needed to get away, to ensure she didn't have to endure something close to what she'd had before, and then think of a plan.

At least her dragon was still there and hadn't disappeared. Although her beast remained quiet as she ran and ran, going through a small forest and up another hill, and kept going until she thought she might drop from exhaustion.

And still, she knew she needed to hide. Otherwise, they'd drag her back to Stonefire and lock her in a room with Bronx so his dragon could do whatever he wanted with her.

Percy didn't know how long she'd been running when she finally spotted an old cottage with a mostly missing roof and went inside.

There was an old chair and some bric-a-brac scattered about. But the most important thing was half the cottage was protected from any potential rain.

She moved to a corner, the farthest from the door, where she could keep an eye on the entrance and slid to the ground. After tugging out the hair tie and letting her locks tumble about her shoulders, she drew her knees close and hugged them tightly.

After everything, after all the shit she'd been through in her life, Percy had thought she'd finally turned the page and could maybe even find some sort of happiness.

But now she was alone again, needing to protect herself, without anyone else to rely on. Because no matter what bullshit they claimed about Stonefire wanting to help her, they'd always support Bronx over her. Always.

Her dragon finally spoke up. *I'm here. You're not alone.*

She wiped the tears from her cheeks and replied, *Sorry, dragon. I spent so many years without you that I haven't grown used to the fact you're there.*

Her beast paused before saying, *I'm still trying to get used to not being locked away inside your head. I could sometimes see and hear things but could never move beyond a barrier.*

So you weren't just sleeping?

Not always. Although later, I mostly slept to pass the time.

Silence fell in her mind, and Percy debated what to say.

It was just a blatant reminder of how fucked up she still was. Bloody hell, she couldn't even be at ease around a second part of herself.

Hugging her legs tighter, she watched as the rain began falling. The steady patter against the stone floor of the open half soothed her, as did watching the water run away from her, toward the far side. Anything that kept her from thinking about Bronx, Violet, or even Stonefire in general was a welcome distraction.

Eventually, her dragon said, *I don't think being a true*

mate would be a bad thing. Doesn't it mean we have a greater chance of happiness with Bronx?

She laughed derisively. *Our chances of happiness haven't been great to date, so I wouldn't count on it.*

Her beast huffed. *Then what? We constantly go on the run? We've learned how the DDA doesn't like that.*

Wait. Have you been learning along with me?

Yes. The sphere shape was to protect myself inside it.

Protect from what?

Anything. Everything. Hiding is all I've known, apart from a few months.

Then why aren't you hiding now?

Her dragon paused so long, Percy thought she wouldn't answer. But finally, her beast said, *Because you're sad, and I don't like it.*

I'm not sad. I'm afraid.

Her dragon huffed. *You can't lie to me.*

She growled but knew her beast was right. Although a few techniques and practices could keep select information private, her inner dragon could hear her thoughts and feel her feelings. She knew Percy better than anyone.

And her dragon would be honest with her too, if she asked for it.

It rained harder, and she kept an eye on the water running on the ground. She couldn't stay here forever. But where would she go?

Her dragon spoke up. *Go back to Stonefire.*

Are you mad?

No. But they're different, judging from your memories about the facility. Or even the orphanage.

Maybe on the surface, but they'll want to use me as a

broodmare just like the facility. You heard Bronx mention how the dragon-shifter population was getting low until recently.

And you think he's just going to whip out his cock and fuck us, uncaring how we feel about it?

It was hard to picture Bronx doing that, especially as memories of him giving her choices, asking permission, and all around trying to support her flashed into her mind.

But then she remembered what she'd read about true mates. *All it would take is one kiss, and he couldn't stop himself.*

Then don't kiss him until you're ready.

As if it's that easy.

Her dragon grunted. *It might be. Or just ask for a different teacher and avoid him. With time, it'll fade.*

It was a good suggestion—remove temptation, and she'd be safe.

But the thought of never seeing Bronx again, never talking with him, and never being near him and feeling safe, squeezed her heart.

Not to mention she'd miss watching TV with Violet and sharing meals with the both of them. They were her friends, or at least people who wouldn't constantly fuck her over.

Which, given her past, was a huge step up.

But to go back and merely tell Bronx she couldn't do it—would he listen? Wouldn't Stonefire's clan leader just ship her off to a different clan, where she'd have to start over?

Rumors would fly about why she was there, and people would find a new reason to look at her with disdain or pity.

She readjusted her arse on the floor—it was getting bloody cold—and tried to further sort out her thoughts.

Because she also remembered how she'd nearly kissed Bronx before, how nice it'd been to feel his heat, the firm grip of his hand holding hers, and how handsome he was when he laughed.

Without the burden of being his true mate, would she have wanted more eventually?

A resounding yes echoed inside her mind. She'd actually wanted to have sex with him, feel what it was like with someone she'd chosen, and to maybe learn what tenderness or even true desire felt like.

Her dragon spoke up again. *If you want to run, I will still be here. But if you want my opinion, I say go back to Stonefire. Talk with Bronx, with Bram, and maybe with others who've gone through the frenzy. It could help us form a plan without just running from it.*

Running, hiding, or shielding had been her survival tactics, to the point she'd never been honest with anyone, not even herself.

But if she was honest with Bronx and talked about her fears and wants, would he listen?

Or would he toss them away, take what he wanted to appease his dragon, and turn into someone she didn't recognize?

After all, Bronx had known his dragon his whole life and Percy only a few weeks.

Laying her forehead on her knees, she debated if she had enough courage to risk being hurt.

Because if she did, she might end up with a chance to get what she wanted and find some happiness.

Chapter Twenty-Six

When Percy fled, Bronx's first reaction was to dash after her. When she didn't stop, no matter how many times he called her name, he realized it was a bad idea.

After all, he was the one she'd run from.

His brother and Tristan eventually reached him. Hudson asked, "What happened?"

"My dragon recognized her as our true mate, I told her, and she ran."

Tristan grunted. "Not the best start."

Hudson glared at Tristan. "That's not helping."

Bronx stared in the direction Percy had dashed, even though she was long gone. "I think she'll just keep running if I go after her. Someone needs to find her."

Even just saying those words twisted his heart.

Hudson placed a hand on his shoulder and patted it. "I can go."

Tristan shook his head. "You're Bronx's brother, and she'll see you as trying to catch her to give to him."

Hudson frowned. "I wouldn't bloody force her to do anything."

Bronx jumped in. "No, but Tristan's right. Remember, her entire life, she's never had a choice in anything. So she probably views being a true mate as just another version of that."

His dragon grumbled. *I would never hurt her. We're nothing like those bastards in the facility or even the orphanage.*

We know that. But Percy is still recovering from a lifetime of pain, suffering, and hardship. Trust won't be easy for her.

Tristan sighed. "Fine, I'll go. But, Hudson, help Ella round up the children. Then have Jane run back to tell Kai what's happened and get more help."

Hudson nodded and dashed down the path. Tristan made to leave, but Bronx said, "Be gentle with her, Tristan. She's had a fucking hard life."

The dragonman's face softened. "I will. Arabella had difficulties, as well, and I've learned from that."

Arabella was Tristan's younger sister, who had been tortured by dragon hunters as a teen. She was doing brilliantly with her mate and children in Scotland now, which gave Bronx hope for Percy's future.

Bronx grunted. "Thank you."

Tristan nodded once and dashed off in the same direction Percy had.

His dragon spoke up. *The clan will help find her.*

I know.

But it still hurt that she'd run from him.

Hurt that she thought he'd hurt her, force her, and who the bloody hell knew what else.

His dragon spoke up. *Maybe once the initial panic wears off, she'll recognize how we're different.*

I hope so.

His sister-in-law Sarah and her two boys approached him. When she was close enough, Sarah gently touched his arm. "I heard about what happened. But don't worry, aye? I have faith someone from Stonefire will find her and bring her home."

Home. Yes, he wanted Stonefire to be Percy's home.

Even if it meant avoiding her for the rest of his life, he'd do it to give her that chance.

PERCY SHIVERED as the light faded from the sky. The rain was letting up, which meant she'd have to make a decision soon about what to do. She would either run or hope that Stonefire would prove to be a better and more understanding lot than anyone she'd known in her past.

Her dragon was still in her dragon form, curled up and asleep inside Percy's head. True to her word, her beast had stayed with her.

Percy should have been happier about it. After all, that had been her goal—to get her dragon back.

But she was starting to think that wasn't enough, not nearly enough, to truly make her happy.

Percy didn't know how long she'd been staring into nothingness when she heard a male voice shout, "Percy! Where are you?"

The voice was sort of familiar but not quite. It most definitely wasn't Bronx's.

Which sent a rush of relief through her. Well, mostly. A teeny, tiny part of her was disappointed.

Her dragon yawned. *What will you do?*

You're not going to convince me one way or the other?

No. Telling you would probably only make you dig in your heels and do the opposite.

Too tired to argue, she stretched out her legs and winced at the pins and needles.

Another voice joined the first—this one, female—and she stood slowly, using the wall to help maintain her balance as blood rushed to her limbs.

If she was going to run, she had to do it now. But no matter how many times she eyed the door, Percy stayed put.

She was so tired of hiding, of guarding herself, and of keeping her distance from everyone and everything. Over the last couple hours, she'd thought more and more about the people of Stonefire's actions versus what the arseholes inside the facility and orphanage had done.

And with time, the gap widened more and more.

Apart from the very beginning, when Dr. Sid had given her the sedative to calm her dragon so she'd stop hurting herself, everyone had always asked her what she wanted to do, or eat, or even learn.

It would've been easy for Bram to order her to do this or that—he had an entire clan of dragon-shifters at his disposal, to do as he wanted.

But he'd never demanded anything. Bloody hell, when she'd actually offered to have sex with people in exchange for help, he'd looked horrified.

Even though she had contributed nothing to the clan beyond a few blood draws for the doctors to test,

Bram had given her a place to stay, food to eat, and clothes to wear.

He'd also given her Bronx and Violet.

And just the thought of never seeing either of them again had made her cry while sitting inside this dilapidated cottage, staring at the rain, all by herself.

Alone had been her normal once, but she wasn't so sure she liked it any longer.

Her dragon asked softly, *So you'll go back?*

Time to be honest with both her beast and herself.

Percy was done with running.

Although voicing the words was hard, she still replied, *Yes. I don't know when it happened, but Stonefire is my home now.*

The voices drew nearer. Taking a deep breath, Percy made her feet work again and went to the door. She hesitated only a second before shouting, "I'm over here!"

The voices silenced a second before the female one shouted, "Say it again so we can find you!"

"I'm here!"

In less than a minute, a female dragon-shifter she'd seen once or twice—her name was Myla, a young Protector—rushed into the area. On her heels was the head of security, Kai Sutherland.

The ginger-haired female approached her as Kai stayed back. She smiled at Percy. "We've been looking for you, Percy. Are you ready to come back to Stonefire? Oh, and before you answer, just know that you'll be staying with Brenna and Killian for now."

She frowned. "Why?"

"Well, neither is related to Bronx, so hopefully you won't feel nervous or cornered."

Before she could think on it, she blurted, "I don't think Bronx would corner me."

The dragonwoman blinked. "You don't?"

She shook her head and spoke the truth she'd long been denying. "I trust him."

Kai spoke up. "Right, well, for now, you'll spend the night with Brenna and Killian. In the morning, you can chat with whoever you need to. But Bronx wanted me to pass on a message."

Her heart rate kicked up. "What is it?"

"That he wouldn't ever force a kiss or the frenzy on you. It's your choice."

Her eyes pricked with tears. Of course he would say that.

And she believed him.

Her dragon spoke up. *Good. Because I like him.*

Kai grunted. "And your dragon is back?"

Percy was tired of constantly lying to everyone. "Yes, for now."

"Good." He gestured toward the dragonwoman. "Myla will escort you back to Stonefire. I'll follow behind you two at a safe distance, just to make sure no one's following us. You never know with dragon hunter arseholes."

As they headed back toward Stonefire, they all remained quiet, probably to avoid attracting unwanted notice. However, even with words or reassurances, Percy knew in her gut that Kai would protect her, if it came to it. She felt the same about Myla at her side, who gave her warm smiles every once in a while.

And unlike even a month ago, Percy thought the woman's warmth and concern was genuine.

Her dragon stirred but then went back to sleep. That was probably for the best, because the closer they drew to Stonefire, the more exhaustion weighed her down. Not just from all the running, but also from her emotions going through the wringer, as well.

Percy was so tired that she barely murmured greetings to Brenna and Killian before she showered, ate, and fell asleep, wondering what she'd say to Bronx the next time she saw him.

Chapter Twenty-Seven

The next morning, Percy woke up, dressed, and went looking for Brenna or Killian. She found the dragonwoman in the kitchen, feeding her son. Watching Brenna make airplane noises before guiding a spoon to the baby's mouth made Percy smile.

Brenna cleaned up the mess that hadn't made it into her child's mouth before glancing at Percy. "You're up. Are you hungry?"

She nodded. "But maybe not what he's having."

Brenna chuckled. "It's not bad, just pureed fruit. But I think after the shocker of yesterday, you could do with a fry up."

She slid into one of the chairs at the small table in the kitchen. "That sounds lovely."

Brenna held out the bowl and spoon. "Do you want to feed Tiernan for me? I promise he doesn't bite."

She hesitated a second, but then the baby gnawed on his tiny fist, and Percy decided surely something so tiny couldn't be that scary. Gingerly, she took the spoon, loaded it with the fruit mush, and merely put it to the baby's lips. He took it inside his mouth and made babbling noises after he swallowed.

Before she could convince herself not to, she asked, "Is it hard being a mother?"

Brenna flipped the bacon in the pan. "Sometimes, especially since both Killian and I are both Protectors back in Ireland. But his aunt and uncle spoil him, as do his grandparents—even his step-granddad."

She fed the tiny one more food before asking, "You had a frenzy when you conceived him?"

Brenna took out the bacon, cleaned the pan a little with paper towels, and cracked some eggs into it. "Mine and Killian's story is sort of... strange. Another female was his true mate first. But then when his baby dragon came out, kissing him triggered a mate-claim frenzy with my own dragon."

Percy frowned. "But not his?"

Brenna shook her head. "No, and it gets stranger. Because once his second dragon emerged, my dragon no longer recognized him as our true mate, and the need for a frenzy faded. As I said, ours was a special case. Eventually, we did try for a baby and had our little one. And I certainly cursed Killian during the early months of my pregnancy, when I was ill all the time and vomiting nearly everything I ate. But that was only temporary."

Brenna removed the eggs from the pan and went to make the toast. Percy continued feeding Tiernan, his chubby cheeks wobbling as he ate.

She'd never thought of being a mother by choice. Yes, she'd wished to get pregnant inside the facility to make it all stop. But she'd never thought she'd be free, let alone would learn about how true mates existed.

Maybe eventually, she would give in. But not quite yet. She asked Brenna, "So with the frenzy, does the male just instantly start fucking you, regardless of what you want?"

Brenna blinked. "Er, no. Dragon-shifters, at least the non-arsehole variety, understand consent. Sometimes that means staying apart, sometimes it means drugging a dragon silent until both parties figure out what to do, or some males will stay away and wait for the opportune moment to finally woo their mates." Brenna crossed her arms over her chest and leaned her hip against the counter. "Bronx will do any of those things, Percy. As long as you don't kiss him on the lips, he'll be able to control his beast."

Given her past, she couldn't help but blurt, "Will he, though? I trust him. I really do. But I don't understand how strong a mate-claim frenzy pull could be, and that worries me."

Brenna's face softened. "Look, I can't even imagine the life you've led up until now. I truly can't. But I know Bronx. I lived on Stonefire most of my life, and he's always been a good male. He was patient with his first mate—I'm just old enough to remember her—and he'll be patient with you too."

"Because he's a nice guy."

The bread popped up, and Brenna snatched them out of the toaster. "Of course he's nice. But it's more than that. I saw him last night, before you were found, and he was a wreck." She pointed a slice of toast at her. "He cares about you, Percy. I don't know how much or how deep it goes. But it's a good start, for sure. You should just talk to him."

Brenna fell silent as she dished out beans and finished up the plates. Percy fed Tiernan the last of his fruit mush just as Brenna slid a plate in front of her.

Percy nibbled on her toast and watched as Brenna cleaned up her son and tickled his jaw.

She'd been a child never loved by a mother or father. Maybe she was too fucked up to ever be a parent. And considering a mate-claim frenzy always resulted in pregnancy, she would be a mum if she went through with it.

Could she risk it?

Her dragon spoke up. *You don't have to decide that just yet. Just talk with Bronx, see what he has to say, and make decisions from there.*

Her beast was right. She'd sort of made the decision already, when she called out to be found the night before.

But now, in the clear light of day, she still yearned to see Bronx again, hear his voice, and maybe even curl up against his chest again, where she felt safe.

She blurted, "After breakfast, I want to see Bronx."

Brenna nodded. "No worries. I'll get it set up."

As she ate her breakfast, anxiety and anticipation swirled in her stomach. Now that she'd admitted she trusted Bronx, she was eager to see him again.

BRONX PACED the small room inside the main Protector building and tapped a hand against his thigh.

He hadn't really slept. Instead, he'd spent the night worrying about Percy. He knew she needed a break from him to rest and have room to breathe. But he hadn't expected one night's absence from the cabin to make him this crazy and desperate to see her again.

He said to his dragon, *You aren't doing this to me, are you, because she's our true mate?*

His beast sniffed. *As I've said before, I recognized her and want her. But we haven't kissed her, so there's no frenzy pull or desperation. This is you realizing what I noticed a long time ago.*

What are you talking about?

You want her as our mate too.

He ran a hand through his hair. *We haven't even bloody kissed her yet.*

So? Love works in mysterious ways. There's no one way to get there.

No, I'm not bloody in love with her.

If not, you're close.

He tried to muster an argument about how ridiculous it was. Yet, the pull to always be near her, to hear her voice, to make her laugh, and to hold her in his arms—not to mention dreams of her naked and under him, on top of him, and any way he could imagine—made it hard to completely refute his beast.

He didn't want another mate, though, and especially not a frenzy. Because then he would have to wonder if he'd lose Percy in childbirth, like he had with Edith.

His dragon said softly, *Percy is a dragon-shifter. The chances are a lot better for her.*

But not foolproof.

Dr. Sid has improved survival for all females on Stonefire when it comes to childbirth. Percy will survive.

That was true. Sid worked with various dragon doctors across the globe, sharing information and looking for all kinds of ways to help her patients. Not since Catriona Belmont—a human sacrifice who'd died birthing Murray, whom Bram had adopted—had anyone else died in childbirth. And that had been years ago.

He sighed. *Even so, Percy may not want any of it.*

Well, talk to her and see. There's a lot we can do to woo her —in and out of the bedroom—without starting a frenzy. It might help to make her come with our tongue, with no cock at all, to prove she matters to us, her pleasure matters, and that we are not like the arseholes she dealt with before.

It was a good plan, and one he would happily do.

He'd woken hard after his dream of imagining her thighs spread before him, bastard that he was.

His dragon growled. *We're not a bastard. She's beautiful, is attracted to us too, and she'll like it.*

Cocky, aren't you?

Yes. It's been too long since I last tasted a female. And now I want her.

Bronx hadn't exactly been a player around Stonefire, especially not since he'd lost part of his leg.

Before he could tell his dragon to calm down and stop being so randy, someone knocked at the door. Bram walked in, followed by Percy and Brenna.

Violet had wanted to come, but he didn't exactly want to discuss maybe fucking Percy in front of his daughter.

Plus, Percy knew Brenna. That was why she was

here instead of Bram's mate, Evie. He'd wanted to give Percy some female support. How things unfolded would be up to Percy.

Percy met his gaze, and he drank in her eyes, her face, and even the birthmark on her neck. He croaked, "You're all right?"

She nodded. "Yes."

Silence stretched, and he fucking hated it. Bronx wanted to talk to her alone, but he knew Bram had some stuff to say before that would happen.

Stonefire's leader gestured for them to sit. Once they all had, he said, "I'm not going to beat around the bush. Bronx's dragon recognizes you as his true mate, Percy. Now, I can understand how that's overwhelming. But let me be clear—no one will force you into it. Ever. Do you understand?"

Percy nodded. "Yes."

Bram blinked, surprised. "Aye, well, we need to decide today if you want to remain on Stonefire, or if you wish to be transferred to another clan to stay away from Bronx."

Percy met his gaze, her expression unreadable.

Her flashing pupils made him smile. "Your dragon is still around."

She grinned, and some of the weight on his shoulders lifted. "Yes. She seems to be staying put this time."

He almost reached across the table to take her hand but caught himself.

Percy noticed, though, and stared at his hand. Slowly, oh so slowly, she reached out and covered his with hers.

A surge of hope, longing, and desire shot through him. "Percy?"

Fuck, he wasn't being overly eloquent today, was he?

She squeezed his hand, and that hope grew. "I'm not saying I want the frenzy anytime soon. But…"

Her voice trailed off, and she bit her lip. Damn, all he wanted to do was wrap his arms around her and support her.

And then maybe kiss her. A lot. "But?"

She answered, "I-I want to stay on Stonefire, I think. If you can take things slowly with me."

Joy raced through him, but his cynical side blurted, "What?"

The corner of her mouth ticked up, making her more bloody beautiful. "You were definitely more eloquent during our lessons."

Bram laughed, but Bronx ignored him. He cleared his throat. "Sorry, but after yesterday, I didn't think you'd want anything to do with me."

Percy glanced at Bram and then Brenna. "Can I talk to Bronx alone?"

Bram stood, and Brenna followed suit. "No problem, lass. Although we'll be on the other side of that door, if you need us."

Brenna gave her shoulder a squeeze before exiting with Bram.

As soon as the door clicked closed, he placed his other hand over hers. When Percy didn't pull away, his hope grew even bigger. "When you ran, it terrified me, Percy. I was so afraid you'd be hurt or killed or maybe even kidnapped." He swallowed. "And the cabin wasn't the same without you."

She placed her other hand over his, making their little hand pile complete. "It was... a lot to take in. And I needed time to think. My first instinct is to run or hide or push people away to protect myself. I've never had someone I could rely on, or even want to be around, before. So when you said I was your true mate, well, I panicked. I thought all of my choices would be taken from me again."

"Never, Percy. I would never force you into a frenzy you didn't want."

She smiled. "I realized that, with the help of my dragon. She's a fan of yours, by the way, so it's sort of unfair."

He grinned. "Welcome to the life of a dragon-shifter. Our dragon halves are our best friends, but they can also be bloody annoying at times when they disagree."

She laughed, the sound a balm to his soul.

Fuck, he wanted to hear it all the time.

But if so, he had to work on convincing her to give him a chance, because even just one night apart had shown him what he'd tried to deny—he was falling for her and wanted her as his mate in truth.

His dragon sniffed. *About time.*

Ignoring his beast, he focused on Percy. "But in all seriousness, we can take this slow, love. As long as I don't kiss you on the mouth, it won't start the frenzy." He rubbed his thumb against the side of her hand, loving how her pupils flashed. "I'd like to slowly introduce you to how good intimacy can be, if you'll let me."

Her cheeks flushed. "How, exactly?"

His gaze moved to her lips for a beat, but then lower, to her neck. "I'd like to kiss your outer dragon."

"My what?"

He met her gaze again. "Your birthmark. I mentioned it looks like a roaring dragon's head, so it's your outer dragon. It's as if it was always there, to remind you that you are a dragon-shifter, no matter what anyone else said."

She whispered, "Bronx."

"It's true. And I want to trace it with my tongue."

She sucked in a breath, and he waited. He could be even more patient, if needed. But he had to feel out Percy, determine where she was, and formulate a plan from there.

She swallowed. Her voice was husky as she said, "Then do it."

He searched her gaze. "Are you sure?"

She nodded, and he pushed his chair back from the table. Patting his leg, he said, "Then come here. Sit on my lap. That way, you can retreat if you need to."

As he watched her stand and walk toward him, he allowed himself to caress her body with his eyes. Her lovely pale neck, the slight swell of her breasts, the softness of her hips, and thighs he wanted to grip and eventually push apart, revealing her pretty pussy for him to feast on.

He waited for shame to rush over him, but when he met Percy's gaze again, the heat and wanting there made him blink.

Slowly, she eased onto his lap, narrowly missing his rapidly swelling cock, and put her arms around his neck.

He put a hand on her hip, using his other to caress her cheek. "You're so beautiful, Percy. I've wanted to tell you that before but thought it would be a bad idea." She tilted her head. "What changed?"

He cupped her cheek and brushed her warm skin with his thumb. "The thought of losing you forever scared the shit out of me, love. I want you despite the fact I'm so much older than you or that you've been through so much or that you weren't looking for a mate." He squeezed her hip gently. "I want you so fucking badly right now."

Percy wiggled on his lap, her hip brushing his dick, and he sucked in a breath. She offered her neck to him. "Then show me what it feels like to be wanted, Bronx. You're the first male I've ever wanted to kiss me."

He growled at her words and barely brushed his lips against her neck. When she growled, he smiled and then traced the outline of her birthmark with his tongue.

Bronx licked slowly, around and down, then nipped where her neck met her shoulder before trailing his tongue back upward. She gripped the back of his neck and moaned.

His cock was like steel now, but he ignored everything but worshiping Percy's neck and skin, drinking in her feminine scent mixed with some sort of flower.

He couldn't stop himself from putting his nose

against her skin and inhaling deeply. "Fuck, you smell good."

She laughed. "Okay, that's not what I expected you to say."

He wanted to keep tasting her, maybe work his way to her shoulder with kisses, but he forced his head up to meet her gaze. "Forget everything you think you know about males. I'm going to show you how a real dragonman worships his female."

She frowned. "Worships?"

He ran a hand from her hip, up her ribcage, and back down again. "Yes. I'm going to eventually work toward making you orgasm, Percy. But there is zero pressure. Tell me to stop at any time, and I will. I vow it."

As she searched his eyes, he willed for her to see the truth. Because if she didn't believe him now, he wasn't sure she'd ever believe him.

Chapter Twenty-Eight

P ercy had never thought that having a male lick her neck would be something she liked, let alone feel good, and yet, as Bronx traced her birthmark, stopping to nibble and suckle at times, she soon pressed her thighs together at the unfamiliar pounding there.

Her skin was on fire, and her clothes felt too tight. As his hand continued to move from her hip, up her ribcage, and back again, her breasts ached, and her nipples throbbed.

What would it feel like to have his hand there?

Her dragon growled. *Ask him.*

Embarrassment rushed through her, and it must've flushed her face, because Bronx stopped kissing her neck to pull away and ask, "What is it?"

"Er…"

He lifted a hand so he could caress her bottom lip with his thumb, back and forth, and everything ached even more, in a good way. He kissed her jaw and moved to her ear to whisper, "Ask me what you want, love, and I'll give it. Don't be embarrassed. Eventually, I want to kiss every inch of your body—and I mean it, every inch—so you'll never doubt how I want you."

At his words, Percy realized she'd been doing exactly that. For too many years, people had made fun of her, rejected her, and told her she was too skinny, ugly, and a freak.

And yet as she moved back to study Bronx's eyes, desire burned brightly in his gaze. Lifting a hand, she traced his jaw, loving the faint roughness of his stubble. She'd felt it on her neck but wondered what it'd feel like other places.

Her dragon grunted. *Ask him. Don't make me take control and do it.*

You would... take control?

I could. Not because I'm rogue, but because I'm bloody impatient.

Her dragon had been locked away for all those years inside the facility, so Percy couldn't really be mad at her beast's impatience.

But it was much, much harder for her.

Yet as Bronx caressed her lip, then her cheek, and back again, she relaxed. This was Bronx. Patient, kind, protective Bronx. He'd never once laughed at her lack of education or knowledge or made her feel ugly or less in any way. It was time to trust him with this too. "I-I want you to touch me other places."

He tucked some stray hairs behind her ear. "Where?"

Before she could let embarrassment stop her, she said, "My breasts."

His gaze instantly dropped to her chest. His pupils flashed rapidly, and he growled, "Are you sure?"

Her dragon said, softer this time, *Be bold with him.* *It's time to start taking what you want, and that means giving him permission to not hold back.*

Her beast was right. So Percy rose from his lap and took a few steps back. Instead of anger or annoyance, he just watched her, still with desire burning in his gaze, but nothing else.

Taking a deep breath, she grabbed the hem of her top and tugged it over her head. He growled at her simple bra, and the sound sent a rush of heat through her.

She rather liked Bronx growling at her.

Emboldened by the sound, she pulled down her bra straps, turned it around, and unhooked it. As it fell to the floor, her nipples tightened even further.

Bronx crooked a finger. "Come here."

While it was a command, she knew he'd allow her to disobey if she wanted.

But Percy didn't want that. Not with her dragonman.

She took one step, then another, the cool air making her even wetter between her thighs. Who knew that a male's gaze could make her so hot?

She stood between his legs and made to sit down, but he put his hands to either side of her ribcage. As his thumbs caressed up to just below her breasts and back down again, she swayed a little toward him.

Bronx continued stroking slowly, his rough fingers delicious against her skin. His voice was deeper as he said, "Tell me I can tease your nipples, Percy." His gaze met hers again. "Please."

The *please* nearly made her cry, but she pushed away the rush of emotions. She refused to ruin this, the first time she was naked with a man of her choosing. Instead, she merely said, "I trust you, Bronx. Do whatever you want with them."

He growled, slowly pulled her closer to him, and flicked his tongue against her nipple. It was nice, but not nearly enough. She wanted... more. Before she could ask for it, he took her taut bud into his mouth and suckled.

Percy threaded her fingers into his hair, leaned more into his teasing, and moaned. When he bit her nipple lightly, she placed her other hand on his shoulder and dug her nails into his skin.

He murmured, "Yes, love. Touch me too."

Shyly at first, she ran a hand over his shirt but then gathered the courage to put her hand under his top, feeling his hard upper back. "You're so warm."

He chuckled, releasing her long enough to say, "You have no idea what you do to me, Percy. I'm on fire for you."

Then, never breaking her gaze, he suckled her. Hard.

She cried out as the pounding between her thighs became even more intense, and she squirmed, loving how her jeans rubbed her in just the right place.

While Percy had orgasmed before, it'd always been the result of some experiment or other.

Bronx must've felt her muscles tense, because he

released her nipple and stood slowly, pushing her back a little in the process.

She wondered if she'd just fucked it all up, then he tugged off his shirt and tossed it aside. At the sight of his broad, muscled chest, lightly covered in dark hair peppered with gray, all rational thought left her head.

He gently took her hand and placed it over his heart. "Feel my heart racing? It's me, Percy. Just Bronx. And my heart wants you just as much as my body." He caressed her cheek. "If that means waiting, I can. Do you want to stop?"

As she stared into Bronx's gray eyes, tears filled hers. "How are you real?"

His eyes blazed. "You're my true mate, Percy, which means I was born for you."

Her heart melted at his words. Yes, a lot of people had fed her bullshit over the years. But right here, right now, none of that mattered.

She had a male who wanted her, who took care of her, who pushed when she needed it, and held back when she was about to break. Percy wasn't exactly sure if it was love, but whatever this feeling was, she wanted to hold on to it and never let go.

To do that, she needed to bare herself and be honest with him. And right now, she wanted her first orgasm of choice to be with him. She wouldn't let her bloody past ruin this moment, no matter how hard it tried to do so.

She ran her fingers through his chest hair, loving how his pupils flashed more and more as she did it. "No, I don't want to stop." She moved backward until she could undo her jeans. For a second, she hesitated.

While she had regular meals now and was gaining weight after so many years of not eating enough, she was too skinny, not curvy enough, maybe not female enough. And once she'd dropped her jeans, Bronx's gaze would turn cold.

"Percy," he growled, and she met his gaze. "You're fucking beautiful. I've dreamed of seeing you naked for a while. And I guarantee I will love whatever is beneath your clothes."

His words rang true. And judging by the bulge in his trousers, he did want her.

Taking a deep breath, she pushed down her jeans and underwear, until she stood naked.

Bronx's eyes roamed her body, heating her as he went. Who'd have thought a male's gaze could make her so wet and swollen?

He growled, "So fucking beautiful, just like I thought."

His words helped push away her doubts, and she closed the distance between them. Cupping his jaw, she murmured, "Touch me, Bronx, and look into my eyes as you do. I want to know it's you, see how you react, and make a new memory today."

He traced her lower lip. "As you wish."

Bronx maintained eye contact as his hand brushed her shoulder, then down to her breast. He tweaked her nipple and then, inch by inch, went down her belly. He stopped just above where she throbbed, and she growled. He smiled. "One day, I'll really make you growl when I worship and tease your pussy with my tongue."

Desire rushed through her at the thought of Bronx

looking up at her as he did what he described. "Do males like that?"

He ran his finger across her lower belly, back and forth, the caress driving her mad. "I don't know about other males, but I can't fucking wait to taste you."

The image of Bronx licking between her thighs, slowly teasing her with his tongue, sent more wetness between her thighs. "Oh."

His finger finally moved lower and lower but avoided her clit. She nearly cried out in protest, but then his finger lightly ran through her center, and she sucked in a breath. As he continued to trace back and forth, she'd never expected it to feel so good.

Still, she felt empty, oh so empty, and wanted more of him. "Stop teasing me, Bronx."

He plunged a finger into her core, and she gripped his shoulders to stay upright. As he slowly fucked her with his finger, she couldn't hold back a moan. "Damn."

His pupils flashed faster now. "So wet and hot, and you grip me so perfectly." He increased his pace, and she dug her nails into his upper arms. "No dream matches the reality, love. And I definitely can't wait to taste you now."

Without thinking, she said, "Do it then."

He stilled his hand. "Are you sure?"

She nodded. "No one's ever done that to me before. And I want my first time to be with you." She bit her lip and added in a rush, "As long as you can control your dragon."

As his pupils flashed again, Percy waited to see what he'd say. She hoped yes, because she wanted to give something to Bronx that she'd never given to another.

And not just out of gratitude. Oh, no, she was greedy to see what it felt like.

Her dragon chuckled. *Good. If we can't have his cock yet, then this might be just as good.*

As if you know.

Neither do you. But does it really matter? Anything with Bronx will feel special.

Her beast was right. And so Percy waited to see if Bronx really meant what he said, about wanting to lick between her thighs.

BRONX HAD NEVER BEEN SO hard in his life. There was something erotic about Percy slowly revealing more and more to him, until she'd let him fuck her with his finger.

And now? She actually wanted him to eat her pussy. He wanted to immediately scream yes, but first he asked his dragon, *You can handle it?*

It's the wrong set of lips to set off a frenzy.

He mentally rolled his eyes. *You're not funny.*

I rather thought I was. Bronx growled at his dragon, and his beast sighed. *Fine. Yes, I'll be fine. Although don't put her mouth close to ours afterward. Because after tasting her pussy, I'll definitely want to taste her mouth.*

I'll be careful.

Shame filled Percy's gaze, as if she regretted asking him for something, and he snapped out of his head. "Don't. I just wanted to ensure my dragon would be okay." He nuzzled her neck and kissed her skin. "I already know I could eat your pussy for hours and never get enough." He leaned back and took her face in his hands. "I want you to sit in the chair and spread your legs for me. Can you do that?"

She bobbed her head, and he gently squeezed her breast before releasing her. "Hurry, love. I'm starving. For you."

Percy rushed to the chair but sat with her legs closed for a few seconds. Even though his cock pounded and he wanted nothing more than to rush over, spread her legs, and make her come, all of this had to be her decision.

Today would set the tone for forever. So if that meant taking things a little slower than he liked, he'd do it.

One beat then another. Then Percy sat up straight, opened her legs, and placed her hands on her knees. She finally met his gaze again, and it took everything he had to focus on her eyes and not finally get his first glimpse of her pussy.

She relaxed at what she saw in his face.

His voice was husky as he said, "I'm coming over now."

He waited for her to bob her head with consent before closing the distance in a few strides. He traced her jaw with his finger before falling to his knees.

Bronx caressed her legs until he could take her hands. He lifted one, kissed her palm, and then did the same with the other. "You're so lovely. And the fact you're sharing your body with me means the world."

She swallowed. "I only want you, Bronx. No one else."

Her words made his cock ache, but he ignored his dick. Right here, right now, it was all about Percy. "And you have me. Now, let me make you feel good, love. And don't be afraid to dig your nails into my head or shoulders and scratch me a little."

He winked, and she laughed, the sound making his heart swell. "I'll remember that."

Bronx pushed her legs even wider and leaned over to kiss her neck, one breast, and then the other. Then he trailed kisses down her abdomen until his head was mere inches from her glistening pussy.

Fuck, she was so wet. For him.

With a growl, he lapped at her entrance and groaned at her taste. And even though he felt her hands in his hair and he wanted to feast for an hour, he wouldn't keep her waiting. At least not this time.

No, he wanted to show her that he could give her pleasure when she asked for it. Maybe someday he'd make her beg or keep her on the edge for hours. But not yet.

After thrusting his tongue into her pussy a few times, he licked upward, until he could flick her clit. Percy groaned and dug in her nails even harder.

He continued to lap, and swirl, and tease her hard bud, loving how she eventually arched into his touch. When she breathed, "Bronx, please," he suckled her clit between his teeth and nibbled lightly.

She cried out. He continued teasing her with his tongue as he lightly thrust a finger into her pussy to feel her clamp her inner muscles around him. Only when she finally slumped and her muscles relaxed did he give her one last lick before lifting his head.

He met her heavy-lidded gaze, and a combination of pride and satisfaction coursed through him. He'd done that to her. Him, and no one else.

She raised a hand and traced his jaw. "That was…" He leaned in closer, leaning his head into her touch. "Brilliant? Amazing? Earth-shattering?"

She laughed. "I suppose. It felt bloody good." She sat up and placed her hands on his chest. "Let me do the same for you."

He stilled. His bollocks tightened, wanting her mouth on his dick more than anything.

And yet, he had to tread carefully. "Your orgasm is payment enough, Percy. I didn't do it to get something in return."

She smiled softly and took his face between her hands. "I know, Bronx. But making you come with my mouth will make me happy. It's what *I* want. No one's forcing me or ordering me to do it." She brushed her thumbs against his cheeks, and his dragon hummed. "You're my choice, Bronx. My first one. Tell me I can."

He placed his hands over hers and squeezed gently. "The fact I'm your choice means the world to me, Percy. I will never take it for granted."

"Then let me pleasure you too, Bronx. Please."

As she leaned in and nuzzled his neck, he groaned. "I don't think I can ever say no to you, love."

She chuckled, her breath hot against his skin. "I'm sure that'll change eventually. But for now? I'm bloody well going to take advantage of it."

Percy nipped his neck with her teeth and then eased

the sting with her tongue. If not for her hands under his, he would've threaded one hand into her hair.

She leaned back. "Now, it's time to switch places. Although make sure you're naked first."

He stood, taking Percy with him. Before she could move away, he held her against his chest and caressed her back, her arse, and up again. "Even without the frenzy, I want you to be mine, Percy. Are you?"

"Yes."

He raised his head, and she did the same. They stared into each other's eyes for a few beats, and Percy leaned closer to him. He knew he needed to lean back, to move away, but she kept his face in place. "Percy…"

"Bronx, I just want to kiss your jaw. Please."

Swallowing, he said to his beast, *Can you handle it?*

Yes. As long as she doesn't kiss our mouth.

He lowered his head a little, careful to keep distance between their lips. Just feeling her hot breath dancing across his skin made him want to groan.

She kissed his jaw, and he did moan, loving the light brush against his skin. Then she kissed his cheek and rose onto her tiptoes to kiss his nose.

But she stumbled, and her mouth pressed to his.

No, no, no. Dragon, behave. Please, behave.

However, his dragon roared, *She's ours. Our mate. I want her. Fuck her. Now. Until she carries our young. Don't fight me, or I'll take control. She's ours. OURS.*

Bronx stepped backward, doing his best to keep his beast from taking over.

The battle wouldn't last long—even the most strong-willed dragon-shifter would lose against a frenzied dragon half—but he had to give Percy the chance to run away.

He opened his eyes and saw the fear on Percy's face. He tried to keep his voice as calm as he could manage while also containing his beast. "Go, Percy. Bram and the others will take you to safety until I can temporarily silence my dragon." She didn't budge. But as his dragon struggled more and more to take over his mind, he shouted, "Go!"

Percy picked up his shirt, tossed it on—it was long enough it covered her, or his dragon never would've allowed her out of their sight. Then she ran out of the room.

Once the door slammed shut, he crouched, gripped his head, and closed his eyes as he struggled to maintain control long enough to let Percy get to safety.

Chapter Twenty-Nine

Percy had fucked up, big time. Bronx had done everything possible to be careful and keep from kissing her mouth. But she'd grown bold, wanting to at least kiss him everywhere but his lips, and then she'd tripped and done it anyway.

She'd frozen a few beats, afraid his dragon would just toss her down and fuck her repeatedly. But then Bronx had said for her to go, and she had.

She'd barely gotten his long top over her head when she opened and rushed through the door. Bram and Brenna sat in chairs across the way. Both stood when she slammed the door behind her.

Breathing heavily, she tried to calm her heart. She was so focused on her task that she missed Bram's first question and only caught it when he repeated, "What happened, Percy?"

"I-I accidentally kissed him."

Bram frowned and gestured for her to go down the

hallway. "Then hurry before you can't contain your dragon any longer."

Her beast spoke up. *Contain what?*

It was only Bram's words that made her realize the truth—she didn't have a pounding need to fuck Bronx and complete a frenzy.

Why?

Brenna rushed to her side and placed a hand on her back. "Come on. Let's get you away from Bronx, and then we can figure out all the details. Right, Bram?"

The clan leader grunted. "You take her, Brenna. I'm calling Dr. Sid."

He took out his phone as Brenna guided her down the hallway. More comfortable around the female than Bram, Percy blurted, "Why doesn't my dragon demand to fuck Bronx?"

Brenna blinked. "There's no mate-claim frenzy pull on your side?"

"No."

Did that mean she'd been pumped full of so many drugs over the years that she'd never experience that?

Her dragon spoke up. *Does it matter? I still want Bronx, especially after today. No other male will do.*

But it ends with a pregnancy, dragon. Surely you remember that?

And that's a problem, why? Bronx will be a good father.

She didn't doubt it—all she had to do was look at Violet.

And yet, she blurted to her beast, *I'm not ready. I want to be more than a broodmare to Bronx or the clan.*

Do you really think that's how he sees us?

Before she could reply, Brenna shut them into a room that looked like some kind of waiting room. "Sit down, and I'll make some tea while you tell me what happened."

Her cheeks flushed. Could she really tell Brenna that?

The other female laughed. "No, I don't need to hear the play-by-play. You're wearing Bronx's shirt, so I have a fairly good idea of what happened. But how did the frenzy start? Did he accidentally kiss you?"

"No." She explained about stumbling and kissing him before adding, "So it's all my fault."

Brenna handed her a mug of tea. As Percy took a small sip, the dragonwoman said, "Bronx knew better than to let you get that close, so I say it's no one person's fault." She sat down in a chair across from Percy. "But have you decided what to do?"

She drank some more tea, needing a minute to answer.

Her dragon spoke up. *Even if it didn't trigger a frenzy with us, you care for him. I know you feel safe around him, feel beautiful, and love his tongue on our pussy, not to mention our clit between his lips.*

Dragon!

Her beast chuckled. *You can't hide that fact from me.* Her dragon turned more serious. *He's not like them and never will be.*

Of course she knew that. Bronx was the polar opposite of anyone from her time inside the facility. And yet, she'd wanted more time with him before thinking of mating or motherhood, to become even more comfortable. Yes, she'd loved being naked in front of him earlier, but she'd probably have setbacks later. Maybe even nightmares. How would Bronx handle them? Would he eventually get annoyed and wish he'd never saddled himself with her in the first place?

Would he never be able to love her? That was probably her biggest fear. She'd never really been wanted by anyone, and yet with Bronx, she felt wanted for the first time in her life.

But even if Bronx could love her, did she know how to do it herself? After all, she'd never been loved in her life and didn't have any example of what it was supposed to look like.

Her dragon growled. *I love you.*

She blinked. *What?*

Just because we were forced apart for years doesn't mean I forgot how it was before. We were best friends, and I hope we can be again.

Tears pricked her eyes. *I want that too. I've always loved you.*

Her dragon sniffed. *So you do know what love is.*

Brenna's voice prevented her from replying. "I don't like to interrupt conversations with inner dragons, but Dr. Sid texted me and said she quieted Bronx's dragon for now. If you want to see him, Bronx said he wants to talk to you."

She bit her bottom lip a second. "Will it be safe?"

"From the frenzy, yes. Without his dragon, it'll be just his human half."

Just knowing she'd caused someone to lose their inner beast, even temporarily, made her stomach churn.

Brenna reached out and touched her arm. "Just be honest with both him and yourself."

She searched the female's eyes. "Shouldn't you be trying to coax me to go through the frenzy so Stonefire can have another clan member, to help bring up your numbers?"

The dragonwoman frowned. "Why? I moved to Ireland with Bram's blessing, meaning he lost a clan member. Does that mean he bans me from seeing my family or is angry about it? Of course not. He's happy for me. Stonefire is about clan and family and friendships, Percy, not just repopulating. Forget about the crap they told you in the past. Stonefire believes in love, no matter what that looks like."

She nodded, knowing Brenna spoke the truth. She'd seen too many happy couples, families, and even people working together to do something as simple as give the young dragons a field trip.

More than anything, she wanted Stonefire to be her home. And not just on her own, but with Bronx. She couldn't imagine any other male being so patient and kind or making her feel so desired and wanted. Not to mention just his lips against her neck had made her hot and bothered.

She wanted him and only him.

The time to run or find excuses was over. Standing, she handed her empty cup to Brenna. "I need to talk with Bronx."

～

As SOON AS the drugs took effect and Bronx's dragon went quiet, he was simultaneously relieved and terrified.

Not because he thought his dragon would instantly come back, find Percy, and fuck her repeatedly. No, he trusted Dr. Sid and her concoctions. But he was worried Percy would want to leave, to put distance between them, all because the choice of wanting a future and a child with him had been taken from her.

The silence in his head was deafening. And to think, Percy had lived this way for years and years; it only made her survival more admirable.

Dr. Sid finished packing up her medical bag. "Absolutely no kissing Percy, Bronx, not even on her skin. And you have two days, maybe three, of silence. After that, I need you to decide if you want to try the experimental drug I have to calm the mate-claim frenzy pull or embrace your inner dragon and claim your mate."

He should ask more questions about the first option, but he couldn't stop staring at the door. Would Percy come?

The doctor sighed. "I see chatting with you right now is pointless. I'll check in on you later." She moved into his direct line of sight. "But I mean it—no kissing anything until you're sure of what you both want. Understood?"

He was slightly older than Sid, and if it were anyone else, he'd tell her to bugger off and stop scolding him. But he knew the doctor meant well. Plus, silencing his dragon was hard for her, given her own past.

So he nodded. "I understand. But I need to talk with her."

She patted his arm gently. "I know."

The door opened. Percy stood there, her gaze locked on to Sid's hand on his arm. She growled, and Sid sighed. "I don't want your male. I have my own, thank you." She moved toward the door. "Just don't kiss him, Percy, and his dragon will remain dormant for a little while."

As soon as Percy entered and Sid left, shutting the door behind her, he said, "You came."

"Of course I came." She searched his gaze. He hated that she still stood on the far side of the room. "Are you okay? I'm so sorry, Bronx. I didn't mean for that to happen."

He shook his head. "Don't apologize. I knew better than to allow your face close enough to mine."

She put up a hand, palm toward him. "No, don't try to deflect the blame—it's my fault. But I didn't come here to argue about that." She took a step closer. "We need to talk about what to do."

Her hesitant tone made his heart squeeze. "I can keep my dragon silent long enough for you to leave and go live with another clan. After a few months, I should be able to keep him calm without any sort of drugs."

She took another step. "Won't that be agony?"

He shrugged. "Maybe. But I won't be the one who takes away your freedom, your future, or your choices from you, Percy. You'd hate me, and I could live with a lot of things, but never that."

Her eyes turned bright, as if she were about to cry.

Before he could say something else, she spoke. "You would do all of that for me?"

"Yes, love." He studied her face, hoping this wouldn't be the last time he saw her.

Just the thought of never hearing her laugh, feeling her in his arms, or even hearing her criticizing the ridiculousness of Violet's soap operas made his heart ache. He admired her strength, her will to live, and even how she'd endured the challenge of learning to be a dragon-shifter at a late age.

She was brilliant and lovely, and he was certain she'd bloom even more as time went on.

Even if it hadn't been long, Percy had come to mean so much to him.

Then it hit him—he loved her.

But it was exactly because he loved her that he wouldn't push for the frenzy. Not because he didn't want it or a family with her—he did. No, it was because he wanted to give her every dream she wanted and the future she deserved, even if it meant hurting himself in the process.

PERCY'S HEART raced as she stared at Bronx. If she'd ever needed more proof about how he was different from any male in her past, he'd just shown it. He was willing to suffer pain for months on end just to give her the freedom she'd always wanted.

And while she never wanted to be locked up again, her old version of freedom seemed less rosy than in the past. Being alone, even with her dragon, wouldn't be as brilliant as she'd once thought.

Because to have that, she'd have to give up Bronx. And just the thought of him finding another female, let alone touching her, made both human and dragon growl.

Bronx's brows came together. "Are you growling at me?"

Her dragon spoke up. *Just talk with him. Truthfully. No more hiding. You said you trust him, but now's the time to fully prove it.*

In other words, she'd have to admit her dream had changed and that she wanted more than her dragon.

She also wanted a future with Bronx.

It was time to tear down the last of her barriers and go after her new dream. "Yes. I was picturing you with another female, and I didn't like it." She took a few more steps toward him. "Can I hold your hand?"

He blinked. "That should be fine, as long as you don't kiss any part of me, love."

Every time he said "love" it made her heart warm a little more.

Nodding, she reached out, and Bronx took her hand. Although it was such a simple gesture, for her, it signaled so much. Taking a deep breath, she stated, "I don't want to leave Stonefire, Bronx." He frowned, but she carried on before he could say anything. "And I won't ask you to leave."

Something flickered in his eyes, some sort of emotion, but she didn't catch it. "If you aren't leaving, and neither am I, does that mean…?"

She smiled as she squeezed his hand. "Yes, I want to stay here with you. As your mate."

"I want to whoop and hold you in my arms, but I need to know—why? If it's some sort of compromise, so you can stay here or to repay me for my help, then I won't accept it, Percy."

She narrowed her eyes. "It's not any of those bloody things, you stubborn dragonman. I-I, well, can't imagine a life without you. And your daughter, of course. But I choose this path because of you, Bronx. You're my new future."

He growled, stood up, and placed her hand on his chest. As he lightly squeezed her fingers, he ran his knuckles across her cheek. She nearly purred at his touch.

Yes, she wanted this male. Far too much.

Her dragon spoke up. *No, you can't want him too much. He's to be our mate. We should want him this much.*

Ignoring her dragon, she focused on Bronx as he said, "I'll do whatever I can to protect you and treasure you and love you, Percy. But I can't guarantee anything when it comes to childbirth. So if we have a frenzy, there is a risk. Dr. Sid offered an experimental drug to calm my beast, to dull the frenzy, and we could try that. This choice I will give to you—either go through the frenzy and have a child, or I try the drug and we wait and see how it goes."

Yet again, Bronx was going out of his way to give her options.

Tears pricked her eyes at his kindness, his goodness, and his all-around honorable nature. Did she even deserve him? Especially given what she'd been forced to do during her time inside the facility?

A tear slipped down her cheek, and Bronx wiped it away. "What's wrong, love? Tell me."

She sniffled. "I'm afraid if I tell you, then you'll walk out that door."

He cupped her cheek as he shook his head. "No. I can't imagine you doing anything that bad."

If Bronx was willing to give up everything for her, she owed him this truth. Taking a deep breath, she replied, "I had to do some bloody awful stuff inside the facility. At first, I was the experimental test subject, the one having things done to her. But in the last few years, they forced me to be the one doing stuff to others."

He searched her gaze. "Tell me."

Percy took a minute to memorize his face, his gray eyes, his firm jaw, and the way his hair had a few gray strands at the temples.

Yes, she loved this male, as scary as that notion was. And she might just lose him forever with what she said next.

Her dragon said softly, *Don't assume what he'll say or do. Just tell him.*

As if knowing she needed the quiet, Bronx merely waited in silence. Eventually, she spoke again. "They ran a bunch of fertility tests on me. Since I'd never conceived in all the years I'd been there, they wanted to see if changing things would get a different result."

Memories threatened to rush forth, but she pushed them back. Staring into Bronx's eyes gave her the strength to do it.

Eventually, she continued, "They wanted to start

tests with me fucking dragons instead of humans. They'd captured older dragonmen—before, they had caught younger prisoners to better control them and their shifts for dragon's blood—and put us together. One reluctantly did it, but only because they threatened his mate back home."

The haunted look in his eyes, plus his voice murmuring apologies to both her and his mate, stayed with Percy to this day.

Shivering, she said, "But it didn't work. They wanted a younger dragonman, one about my age, to see if it made a difference. However, the male—named Kit—refused. Eventually, they gave him something to make him catatonic. They'd, er, prepare his cock and then told me to fuck him.

"I said no. But then they administered something that felt like fire racing through my veins, day after day, until I finally said yes." She swallowed. "The dragonman had no idea of anything, was unaware, and I had to climb on top and fuck him every day for weeks."

Tears ran freely down her cheeks now, but she was too determined to finish this to even bother wiping them away. "Eventually, they stopped it, to move on to different test. But they'd made me like them—they turned me into a rapist."

A sob broke free, and she tried to calm down. But it was as if a floodgate had been released. Sob after sob wracked her body, to the point she could barely breathe.

As soon as Bronx wrapped her in his arms, she burrowed into his chest, breathing in his comforting scent, absorbing his warmth. Because this might be the last time he ever held her, after hearing about this dark part of her past.

BRONX MURMURED soothing words to Percy as he stroked her hair and held her close. The more he learned, the more he wanted to hunt down all the fuckers who'd hurt her and avenge her.

But he knew that would only land him in jail and probably get him executed.

Besides, Percy needed him more. And the fact she thought sharing this excoriating part of her past would drive him away only made him angry and more determined than ever to give her the future she deserved.

Once she finally calmed down and merely hiccupped in his arms, he said, "You were forced into it, Percy. You are *nothing* like those bastards, do you hear?"

"But—"

"No, there's no *but* here. I imagine if you'd continued to refuse, they probably would've just kept torturing you and eventually killed you, right?"

"Probably. But—"

He squeezed her tighter against him. "You are *not* like them. You were merely someone stuck in an impossible situation, doing what she could to survive." He pulled back until he met her gaze. The puffiness of her eyes shot straight to his heart. "From everything I've seen since your arrival, I know you can be kind and patient. Not to mention your determination to save Joey and Ava and how you came up with such a quick-witted plan. And no, don't say it was just a selfish move. Maybe on the surface, you thought so. But would you have allowed the facility doctors to just take them away and do what they wanted?"

Percy shook her head as she whispered, "No."

"You're nothing like those facility arseholes, Percy. If I have to spend the rest of my life convincing you of it, then I'll gladly do it."

She blinked. "You still want me?"

He growled. "Of course I bloody want you. Or did you miss the part when I said I loved you?"

For a beat, she remained silent. Then hope flickered in her gaze. "Are you sure?"

He wanted to laugh but knew it would be the wrong move. Percy had been alone, tossed aside, treated as a thing instead of a person for her entire life; she might never fully overcome her uncertainty.

Infusing every bit of truth he could into his voice, he replied, "Yes, I'm sure. I love how strong you are, and determined, and how you handle my enthusiastic daughter, even when I could see it was a bit overwhelming for you."

She almost smiled. "Violet is lovely. I also think she is my first-ever friend, after my dragon."

He moved a hand to cup her cheek, rubbing his thumb back and forth, removing the last of her tears. "Yes, although if you agree to mate me, you'll become her stepmum. I hope that means you won't team up against me all the time."

Percy smiled, and it made his heart sing. "Not all the time. Just as I won't always side with you blindly."

He nodded. "Good, because a biddable mate would be boring."

Her face sobered. "Are you truly sure you want to mate me, Bronx? What happened just now is probably only the tip of the iceberg. I'm sure the longer I'm free of the facility, the more breakdowns or episodes or nightmares will appear."

"Of course I'm sure. Everyone has their own issues, flaws, or history they have to deal with. I'm sure I'll have occasional bouts of self-pity about my leg, wishing I could keep up like I used to."

She growled. "You're perfect just the way you are. I wouldn't want to mate anyone else."

He smiled down at her. "I love you, Percy Smith. Will you be my mate?"

She bit her bottom lip, and for a second, he panicked. Would she find more and more excuses, unwilling to ever take a chance on him?

But then she beamed up at him and placed her hands on his chest. "I will, and not only that, I think I want to have a frenzy with you. In a few days, if possible. Although I don't want to risk doing permanent damage to your dragon for my benefit."

He pulled her into his arms and buried his nose against her neck. As her arms tightened around him, her small, soft body pressed against his, Bronx couldn't wait to claim her as his mate in truth.

She might not have mentioned love yet, but he was patient. Just the fact he'd found his second chance in the most unlikely of people was enough for now.

Eventually Percy pushed against him, and he released her. She touched his cheek and said, "Let's tell everyone and then go home."

"Home, where?"

"Your home, inside Stonefire, if Bram will allow it."

"I hope so." He took her face in his hands. "I can't wait until I can wake up every day to your beautiful face, love."

"Stop it, Bronx. You don't need to flatter me. I already said yes."

"No, you *are* beautiful, Percy. And I'll add that to my list of things to prove."

He expected her to fight him, but she merely nodded.

Yet again, she was giving him the gift of her trust.

After another moment, he finally said, "Let's talk with Bram and figure out what comes next."

And as she melted to his side, her arm around his back, they exited the room and made plans.

Chapter Thirty

Two days later, Percy plucked at the dark-red material of her gown. Apparently, the slightly revealing garment was Stonefire's traditional dress. It tied over one shoulder and fell in loose folds around her body.

It was simple and a bit cold, but she didn't care. The dress meant she was about to officially become part of Stonefire and Bronx's mate.

The last two days had been a whirlwind. She'd been forced to stay with Brenna and Killian—no one wanted to risk an accidental kiss, which probably would've happened if they'd stayed in the same house, even with Violet there. Still, it had been brilliant. Not constantly thinking of how to keep her distance so she could eventually leave made a huge amount of difference. She was starting to make friends with the other females inside the clan, had even visited the school once to watch the children with their shifting lessons, and had learned she liked assisting the teachers.

Tristan had even suggested she become a teacher's assistant, when she was ready.

To a female who'd always been alone, never had a choice about her future, and been treated as a thing instead of a person, it was all too good to be true.

Her dragon spoke up. *Not this again.*

I can't help it, dragon. I keep waiting for it all to disappear.

We'll work on that. For now, just focus on the ceremony and tonight.

Yes, once the ceremony was complete, she and Bronx would go back to his empty place—Violet was going to stay with her uncle Hudson—and finally kiss properly, which would trigger the mate-claim frenzy.

Bronx had wanted to be prepared, though, and he'd convinced Dr. Sid to give him a dose of the dragon silent drug to use, just in case Percy changed her mind.

It was yet another way he showed how much he cared about her, which made her love him even more.

Her dragon huffed. *Then tell him.*

Eventually.

Why?

It's still new to me, and scary, and I don't want to unlock some more pent-up emotions by finally admitting the truth to him.

Her beast grunted. But before she could reply, there was a knock on the door, and Brenna came in, wearing a dress similar to hers but in the bright-green color of Clan Glenlough.

The dragonwoman grinned and waggled her eyebrows. "Ready to mate your sexy older dragonman?"

Since Brenna had been teasing her about this for

days, she merely rolled her eyes. "I want Bronx. I don't care about his age."

Brenna lowered her voice. "He does have the sexy older-male vibe, though. Not that I'd trade my two-headed dragon-shifter mate for anything. I'd miss his grunting, at the very least."

Percy laughed. "You can have Killian's variety of grunts. I'll take my smiling, more open dragonman any day of the week."

Brenna winked. "To each their own, which is a good thing. If everyone was the same, it'd be boring."

Sarah, Hudson's human mate, walked in. "What would be boring?"

The human was a lot like her, in that they were quieter and more reserved than their mates. That kinship had started a tentative friendship, one she hoped would grow. "If we all wanted the same mates."

"Oh, aye. I couldn't handle someone like Brooklyn or even Tristan."

The middle Wells brother was easily the most outgoing. Percy shook her head. "I only want Bronx."

Sarah touched her arm lightly. "And I'm glad of it, lass. Bronx deserves some happiness, and you make him light up in a way I never noticed before."

Her cheeks flushed. "If you say so."

Sarah nodded. "Aye, I do. But now's not the time to argue. Bronx is waiting in the wings for you. Are you ready?"

She looked from her soon-to-be sister-in-law to Brenna and nodded. "Yes. More than anything."

And as they exited the room and headed for the dais in the great hall, her heart raced.

She would not only officially have a clan of her own soon, but also have a mate and a stepdaughter.

In other words, a family, which was something she'd never had before.

Her beast said, *Don't start crying.*

I won't. And they would be tears of happiness, anyway.

Still, I want to have fun. And Bronx will worry if our eyes are red. I don't want to waste time once we're back at the cottage. I'm more than ready to claim our dragonman.

She smiled at her dragon's eagerness. *Me too, dragon. Me too.*

BRONX TAPPED his hand against his thigh as he remembered the last time he'd done this.

When he'd mated Edith, it'd been in Bram's office. It'd been rushed, and there hadn't been time to organize a big celebration. While it'd been tight to manage it all for today, Bronx had been determined to give Percy the best.

His female had never had a birthday party, Winter Solstice celebration, or any sort of happy event. He wanted their mating to start as he meant to go on, which was giving her everything she'd missed, and for them to make enough good times to replace the horrid ones.

His dragon was still silent, at least until he kissed Percy. It felt wrong not having his dragon present for this, but he'd have to make it up to him later. Percy would officially be his mate before he claimed her.

Violet sidled up to him and whispered, "Are you ready?"

He raised his brows. "Of course I am." He studied his daughter a second before asking, "You're truly okay with this?"

Violet huffed. "I've said yes a dozen times already, Dad. Percy's brilliant." Her voice softened. "And I like knowing you'll have someone to care for and be cared by once I move out eventually."

He put a hand on his daughter's shoulder and squeezed. "Don't remind me. But no matter how old you are, you'll always be my little girl."

She hugged him. "I love you, Dad." She pulled back. Her eyes caught something over his shoulder, and she gestured with her head. "Now, go get me a new stepmum to conspire with."

Bronx turned his head and stopped breathing for a few beats.

Percy walked toward the dais, wearing a traditional dragon-shifter dress. She was always beautiful to him, but it was more than that. They'd discussed the option of her wearing a shirt under the dress, if she didn't want her birthmark showing. However, she wore just the dress, which exposed her arms, neck, and part of her torso. The reddish birthmark covering her neck, one shoulder, and her upper arm was fully visible.

Watching her walk tall toward him, smiling as she did, made him both proud and eager to claim her before some other male tried to.

Brenna and Sarah released Percy into his care, and he offered his hand. As soon as she placed it in his, he leaned over to whisper, "You look gorgeous."

"Stop it. You can flirt later."

As they smiled at one another, it was such a contrast to the first time they'd met, back when she'd mostly sat with her legs pulled up, wrapped in her arms, as if trying to make herself invisible.

Something rumbled in his head, and it kicked him into motion. He couldn't risk his dragon waking up too early.

Once they were on the dais, they each stood to the side of a high, small table that held the mating bands. Bronx had been willing to alter this part, just in case it would make Percy feel as if she were an object again by wearing his name on her arm, but she'd assured him she wanted it. She wanted him.

Even if she hadn't said she loved him yet, he was determined to woo her until she did.

Once Bram asked for quiet, Bronx took out the smaller silver arm cuff, the one engraved with his name in the old dragon language. "Percy Smith, when you first appeared in my life, I had no idea what was to come. I had been determined to never take a mate again, had resolved myself to being only your teacher, and to help you become the dragon-shifter you were always meant to be before walking away. However, as we spent more time together, shared more secrets, and even endured some ridiculous soap operas to make my daughter happy, I started to want more, so much more, with you.

"And I had no idea if it'd ever happen, especially as all you wanted was your inner dragon and the ability to shift. But somewhere between that first meeting and you agreeing to be my mate, I fell in love with you.

Because you're brave and strong, and the stubbornness that served you so well to survive will probably cause a few hiccups along the way. But I'll gladly take all of it, all of you, because you are my future, Percy, my second chance. And I hope to spend every day reminding you of how much you mean to me." He raised the arm cuff. "I stake my claim on you, Percy Smith. Do you accept?"

She nodded, and he slid the band around her upper bicep then traced the engravings a second before lowering his hand.

Percy took out the remaining cuff and never took her gaze from his as she said, "If anyone had asked me even a month ago about taking a mate, I would've brushed it off. Not only because I hadn't known anything about true mates to begin with, but also because I'd been raised to believe that I was less for having a human mother. And then with no inner dragon, I wasn't even sure I could be called a dragon-shifter. However, it's because of you that I've learned so much, come to accept I am as much a dragon-shifter as anyone, and that there are good people in the world. You make me laugh and smile and enjoy life in a way I've never done before. More than that, you taught me that it's okay to trust, to allow people in, and that I'm worthy of love and being loved."

She swallowed and paused a second, her pupils flashing, before she continued, "You may have started out as my teacher, Bronx Wells, but you've become so much more than that. I want you as my mate, as my best friend, and as my shoulder to lean on when I need it. The road may still be rocky, but I know I can face anything with you by my side. I stake my claim on you, Bronx Wells. Do you accept it?"

"Yes," he stated clearly.

She smiled, slipped the arm cuff onto his bicep, and then took one of his hands in hers. Bronx leaned down to hug her and nuzzle her neck—he wanted to kiss her but couldn't yet—and reveled in how she hugged him back.

As soon as they stood tall again, the great hall erupted into cheers, and Percy smiled shyly as she leaned against his side.

He put an arm around her shoulders, and they went to the main floor so they could be congratulated and celebrate with the clan.

And every second, he kept waiting for the chance to sweep his new mate away. When it finally happened, he took her hand and tugged her along, and they half-jogged toward his cottage.

Chapter Thirty-One

Percy's heart raced as they entered Bronx's cottage. As soon as he shut the door, he hauled her against him and nuzzled her neck. "Please tell me you're ready, love."

She hugged him and murmured, "Yes. Make me yours, Bronx."

He pulled back and searched her gaze. Cupping her cheek, he said, "I love you, Percy Wells. My mate, my second chance."

She smiled. She'd debated sharing her feelings during the ceremony but had decided she wanted it to be their moment, and theirs alone.

Her dragon huffed. *About time.*

Hush.

Her beast fell silent, and she placed a hand on Bronx's cheek. He leaned into her touch, which only made her heart soar. "I love you too, Bronx."

He stilled. "What?"

She grinned. "I know you're older than me, but I

didn't think you were ancient enough to lose your hearing already."

He smacked her arse lightly, and the touch sent a rush of heat through her. He growled, "I heard you perfectly well. But I wasn't expecting it."

She placed a hand on his chest and leaned against him. "I wasn't even sure what love was before I came here. Although my dragon reminded me that I had experienced it before—with her—and I realized that I felt just as strongly about you. Except for one thing."

"Which is?"

"I don't want my dragon's tongue between my legs."

He laughed, and the sound made her heart even warmer. It would take time to get used to such happiness and not constantly worry about how it might disappear. But Percy was determined to keep hold of what she had with Bronx and to fight to keep her new dream alive.

Bronx's gaze went from laughing to molten, and he stepped back enough so he could give her body a once-over. His gaze was slow and deliberate, and judging by the approval in his eyes, he liked what he saw. His voice was deeper when he said, "You're so beautiful tonight." He leaned over and nuzzled her neck, right where her birthmark was. "I'm glad you shared your outer dragon with the world."

Though it was hard to concentrate with his delicious scruff rubbing against her skin, Percy managed to reply, "It wasn't easy, but I was tired of hiding. This is who I am. And as I discover more and more of myself, I need to embrace it, be proud of it, and forge my own path. Besides, I rather like having an outer dragon to go with my inner one." She ran her fingers through Bronx's hair, loving how he growled. "However, that's enough talk about my outer dragon. Right now, I just want to kiss my new mate."

He pulled back to meet her gaze again. "Are you sure, love?"

She wrapped her arms around his neck and smiled up at her dragonman. Yes, she rather liked thinking of Bronx as hers. "More than anything. I want your kiss, your dragon, and the frenzy. I know about what happens, and how you've given me options to stop it. Even the doctors have given me numbers to text, and the list goes on. But I know I won't need it."

He brushed hair from her face. "How?"

She leaned into his hand on her cheek. "Because it'll be with you, Bronx. Our inner dragons are a big part of who we are, and even in the throes of a frenzy, I trust you and your dragon."

"Percy…" He paused, cleared his throat, and added, "Then come with me. I want to have a proper bed for our first time." He lowered his voice to a loud whisper. "Although we can try against a door whenever you're ready. Just say the word."

She snorted but followed him up the stairs to his bedroom in silence. Her heart raced, and her dragon paced back and forth inside her head. Her beast spoke up. *His dragon better give me a turn.*

We'll see. His beast is older with more experience. Not to mention no one knows where we'll fit on the dominance scale.

She'd learned about that over the last few weeks too, how dragons had a sort of hierarchy. Dominant ones tended to be leaders or Protectors, while more submissive ones were usually caregivers or the glue that held the clan together. Everyone had been adamant that no one was more important than anyone else, though.

Although people might think she was toward the bottom at first glance, Bronx was convinced she'd be farther up toward the top. Otherwise, she never would've had the resolve to survive as she had.

Her dragonman had such faith in her. It was yet another thing she loved about him.

They reached the bedroom, and Bronx stopped them near the edge of the bed. "Get undressed first, love. I want to make sure you're ready."

She remembered how Bronx had "readied" her in that conference room with his hands, his mouth, and his tongue. Her entire body heated, and her dragon grunted. *Yes, yes, about time.*

She stepped back and slowly undid the tie over her shoulder. The slinky material slid down her body, baring her. She didn't even have on underwear.

Shivering, her nipples tightened and Bronx's gaze zeroed in on them. He licked his lips, and wetness rushed between her thighs. He hadn't even touched her yet, and she was ready.

He undid the kilt-like fabric around his waist. The material fell to the floor, revealing his very hard and very long cock.

Percy had wondered if she'd panic, hesitate, or be bombarded by memories. However, this was her mate, her dragonman, and she would never be afraid of any part of him.

Taking a deep breath, she closed the distance between them until they stood about six inches apart. She looked down and reached a hand toward him. When she hesitated, Bronx said, "Touch me anywhere, everywhere, however you like, love. I'm yours."

His words made her bold, and Percy encircled her fingers around his dick. He was warm, hard, and yet soft at the same time. She tugged upward and back down, and Bronx groaned as a drop of liquid emerged from his cock.

She repeated her actions, and he gripped her wrist. "Keep doing that, and I'm not going to last long, Percy."

She pumped her hand again, loving how Bronx threw his head back and moaned. Right here, right now, she had so much power over him.

A kind of power she'd never had before.

Her dragon growled. *Why are you taking so much time? Kiss him and let him fuck us.*

You almost sound like you're in a mate-claim frenzy.

He's our mate, and I want him. That's enough.

She released Bronx's cock and ran her hand up his chest. Tilting her head upward, she whispered, "Kiss me, Bronx, and claim me as your mate."

He cupped her cheek lightly, leaned down, and stopped a hairsbreadth from her mouth. "I love you."

With that, he pressed his lips to hers and wrapped his arms around her. She'd expected him to merely toss her onto the bed. But he teased her bottom lip, and when she opened her mouth, he delved inside. Percy groaned as he licked, lapped, and suckled her tongue, as if starving to memorize every part of her, taste her, and devour her.

Percy had never been kissed before, apart from the brief pressing of lips with Bronx days before, and it was better than she'd ever imagined. She soon mimicked his tongue, taking her time to explore his mouth. With his warm, solid body and scent surrounding her, Percy grew hotter and hotter, and the pulsing between her thighs kicked up.

He finally broke the kiss, his pupils flashing rapidly. Bronx's voice was strained as he said, "My dragon is allowing me to make love to you first, but we can't take too long. Crawl under the covers whilst I remove my prosthetic. I'll hurry under with you, so you don't have to see my leg."

She'd barely paid attention to his leg when surveying him earlier. But as he gestured toward the bed, she shook her head. "No. I want to help you take it off. You told me not to hide, and now it's your turn."

Even with his flashing pupils, Percy noticed the vulnerability in his gaze. "Are you sure?"

"Yes." She pointed to the bed. "Now, sit down."

He smiled at her order and complied. She knelt in front of him and looked to his leg.

It was missing just below his knee. She could see where the sort of cupping part at the top kept it in place. "Teach me how to remove it."

After a beat, he explained how to tug it off. When she finally removed it, he shifted, as if nervous.

But Percy wasn't having it. She leaned down and kissed the bottom of his leg, where it ended.

She felt Bronx tighten under her lips. "Percy, you don't have to do that."

After kissing him again, she looked up. "I know. But I need to convince you that I love you, all of you, Bronx Wells. And I'm going to keep at it until you believe me."

He smiled, yanked her up until she stood between his legs, and said, "I love you. And I would like nothing more than to make you come again with my mouth, and then my fingers, and then finally claim you. However, my dragon's barely keeping it together, love. So tell me how you want to do this, and let's start the frenzy."

She looked down at his still-hard cock, leaned down, and stroked it a few times. As Bronx groaned, she said, "Just like this. I've never done it with someone sitting upright before."

He leaned over and suckled one of her nipples until she forgot how to speak, taking his time nipping, laving, and all around driving her crazy. She threaded the fingers of one hand into his hair, to keep grounded and not collapse from how bloody good it felt.

Then he ran a hand through her pussy lips, the light touch making her crave more, so much more. She widened her stance in invitation.

He continued to lightly caress and tease her opening, never quite moving up to her clit. Who knew a few fingers could make her so crazy and desperate?

She couldn't wait to see what else he could do when he was finally inside her.

As he continued to use his magic fingers, Percy moaned. Soon, a light sheen of sweat covered her body, and she was moving her hips, almost begging him to touch her where she needed it most.

Bronx removed his hand, and she nearly cried out.

Then he put his finger into his mouth and sucked it clean. The sight strangely made her hotter, especially when he growled, "So fucking sweet."

Her dragon huffed. *Why aren't you riding his cock yet? I want him. Now.*

Bronx placed his hands on her hips, and a jolt of lust rushed through her.

And to think, at one time, she'd been afraid of his touch. Now she craved it more than anything.

Bronx lightly strummed his thumbs against her skin and pulled her closer. "Straddle me, love. I want to be inside you, but give you the chance to take me at your own pace."

His pupils kept flashing rapidly. "Will you be able to handle that? I don't want to make your dragon mad."

Her beast sniffed. *He should be the one trying to please us.*

Ignoring her dragon, she focused on Bronx's words. "I can, if we don't take too much longer. Come."

After he patted to either side of him, she straddled his body, her hands on his shoulders to keep her balance.

Staring into Bronx's eyes, she whispered, "Claim me, Bronx. Now."

With a growl, he kissed her again. As he licked, lapped, and teased, she felt the head of his cock at her entrance. She widened her legs further, almost desperate. This was her choice, her male, and she wanted to start her new life already.

He broke the kiss and whispered, "Lower down

on me."

She maintained eye contact as she slipped inch by inch onto his dick. He stretched her and filled her, and by the time she had taken him to the hilt, all she wanted to do was move her hips.

So she did. Percy didn't really know what she was doing as she'd never been in charge, but she rocked, and swirled, and did whatever made her feel good. Something was building, a pressure like when Bronx had made her orgasm before, and she reached for it but could never quite get there.

Then Bronx caressed her clit, and she gasped. He murmured, "That's right, love. Let me help you."

Her grip on his shoulders tightened, and she continued moving her hips. Combined with Bronx's loving, hot gaze and his pressure on her clit, she finally let go and cried out as wave after wave of pleasure crashed over her.

Bronx moved her hips with his hands a few times before stilling and groaning. As he spilled inside her, another orgasm washed over her, so intense, it nearly hurt.

Only when she finally came down from the high did she collapse against him, her head on his shoulder, and say, "Bloody hell, I didn't know it could be like that."

He tightened his arms around her. "Didn't they tell you how when a dragonman is your true mate and he comes inside you, you get an instant orgasm?"

She shook her head. "I think I missed that lesson. I'm glad it works even if my dragon doesn't recognize you as our true mate."

Bronx stroked her back and murmured, "It doesn't matter what your dragon thinks. You're mine, Percy Wells. All mine."

She wrapped her arms around him and hugged him tightly. She loved belonging somewhere, and most especially to this dragonman. "As long as you know you're mine too. I've waited my whole life to find someone to love, even if I didn't know it, and I'll do whatever it takes to keep it. I'm rather good with a knife, so others better beware and stay away from my male."

Bronx chuckled. "Even if they try, they won't succeed. Save your knife skills for self-defense lessons." He kissed her ear and murmured, "My dragon will come out soon, Percy. I took it slow and controlled with you, but dragon halves are more demanding. Are you ready for it?"

His words shattered the warm, fuzzy bubble she'd been in, and she tensed at the idea of being fucked roughly and quickly. Her dragon spoke up. *Let me take control. I can give his dragon a run for his money.*

At her dragon's confident tone, she mentally laughed. *That might be a good idea. Let me tell Bronx first.*

She explained her dragon's plan, and he pulled back to meet her gaze. "Maybe we should do that for the whole frenzy—human halves in control at the same time, and dragon halves in control at the same time. Sound good?"

She nodded, kissed his lips, and said, "Yes. Now, shall we let the dragons out to play?"

"You first."

Percy said to her beast, *You heard our plan, so do you agree?*

Hell yes. I want to show his dragon a thing or two.

All right. But when you tire him out, let me have the human turns.

Agreed. Now, don't fight me.

As her dragon came to the front of her mind and gently pushed her toward the back, Percy complied. It was strange being present and yet not. She could see and feel everything but didn't control her body.

For a second, she wondered if this was a good idea.

Then her dragon said, *I'm not rogue. I will give you back control later. Trust me.*

Since her dragon was one of the few she trusted, she nodded.

Then her beast crawled them off Bronx's lap and said in a slightly deeper voice, "Where is he? I want your dragon to try to take control of me."

Bronx's pupils remain slitted as he looked up at them. "You are my mate. Mine. And I'm going to fuck you over and over again until you carry our young."

Her dragon placed their hands on her hips. "Try it."

Bronx's dragon pulled her onto the bed and they tumbled and rolled, constantly changing who was on top, until he finally pinned her hands against the mattress. Her dragon then lifted a knee and gently rubbed his dick. "I'm still going to win."

In the next second, he flipped them facedown on the bed. He raised their hips and positioned his cock. "Now you're mine, female."

Her wanton dragon spread her legs and arched her

back. "Then hurry up and fuck me."

He complied, thrusting hard and rough, over and over again. Percy waited to freak out or trigger a memory. But even though she could see and feel it all, she knew her dragon was in charge, would protect her, and would never let harm come to them.

And so she merely enjoyed the feel of Bronx's dragon half taking them hard, shaking the bed, and driving them closer and closer to orgasm. She fully expected his dragon to just take and be done with it, given his need to impregnate her. However, even his dragon half found their clit and pinched.

She came hard, his thrusting while she did so driving her even crazier. As her dragon dug her nails into the bed, he finally stilled and triggered another orgasm with his own.

When they both finally relaxed, breathing heavily, her dragon said, "I want a rest. Let them have some time."

"No."

She crawled away from him and turned around. "Yes."

As they stared at one another, Percy waited to see what would happen. Eventually, Bronx's dragon grunted. "Fine. But don't always think you'll get your way."

Her beast smiled. "We'll see about that."

Her dragon said to her, *Take a little rest. If his dragon tries to take you before it's his turn, wake me, and I'll deal with him.*

I kind of like this side of you.

Well, he's cocky. If I'm not firm now, he'll be bloody

unbearable later.

She mentally laughed. *Okay. Let me have control again.*

They switched places, and it was strange to finally have control of her limbs again. Without thinking, she asked, "Is it always this weird to come back?"

Bronx's pupils were round again. He smiled. "No, with time, it becomes second nature." He reached for her, and she melted against his chest. "Are you all right?"

She nodded, reveling in his comforting scent. "Maybe one day I can handle your dragon on my own. But I think for the frenzy, my dragon will do a better job of it."

He leaned back and cupped her cheek. After kissing her gently, he said, "We have years and years to do that, Percy. As long as I can have you to myself, I'll be happy."

"But won't your dragon be upset?"

He shook his head. "He has experience with being patient."

She murmured, "Because of your late mate."

He caressed her cheek with this thumb. "Yes."

Searching his gaze, she found the courage to ask, "Will you tell me about her?"

He frowned. "Now?"

She shrugged. "My dragon is taking a rest, and I need one too. I'd rather spend the time learning more about you." Placing a hand on his chest, she rubbed back and forth across his chest hair, loving the springy texture against her palms. "I want to know everything about you, Bronx." The corner of her mouth ticked up. "And you have more years to share than me, after all."

He gave her arse cheek a squeeze. "You're a cheeky minx when naked."

She ran her hands up to his shoulders and then to behind his neck. "It's something I didn't really know was in me until I met you. But I like it, so you'd better get used to it."

His gaze turned warm and caring. "I love everything about you, Percy. And I can't wait to see what else pops up along this journey, as long as we do it together."

Tears pricked her eyes. "That's so lovely."

"Well, I can occasionally be romantic."

She smiled. "Good. Now, before our dragons wake up and want more sex, hold me and tell me some more of your past. I really do want to learn all about you."

And as he did exactly that, Percy snuggled into his side and listened to his deep voice as he shared his life before her. Although she'd expected jealousy, it never came. Bronx was perfect for her precisely because of his experiences. After all, she might never have fallen in love with a version of Bronx that had never loved his first mate and raised Violet.

Besides, her past wasn't exactly rosy, and he bore it whenever she talked about it.

This had to be more of what it meant to love someone—to take them as they were, flaws, pasts, and all. In the end, they were better together than apart.

It wasn't long before she fell asleep in the arms of the male she loved.

Which was exactly where she belonged and intended to stay.

Chapter Thirty-Two

Nearly two weeks later, Bronx held a sleeping Percy in his arms, torn between waking her up with the news and giving her the well-earned sleep she deserved.

His dragon yawned. *I don't care. She carries our young, and I need a nap. Don't wake me for a while.*

He chuckled mentally. *Percy's dragon most definitely gave you a run for your money.*

His beast sniffed. *I let her win most of the time.*

Right, tell yourself that.

I'm sleepy.

And his dragon curled up inside his mind and passed out instantly.

Bronx studied Percy's sleeping face. She looked so young like this, with her hair fanning out in a tangled mess behind her, her mouth slightly open as she snored softly. She could be free of her past when asleep—unless she had bad dreams—and could simply let go.

Their frenzy had been a bit longer than some,

which had given them more time to talk and get to know each other. Percy had even shared more about her time inside the facility. Sometimes she was angry, sometimes she cried, and sometimes sadness just weighed her down.

But day by day, he liked to think she was lighter. Just the night before, she'd been teasing him, acting playful, and had slept peacefully throughout the night.

True, it wouldn't always be like this—she had a long road ahead of her still. But he'd seen the glimmer of the female she would become one day, and he couldn't wait to be at her side when she finally emerged for all to see.

Bronx didn't know how long he stared at his mate before she moaned and slowly blinked open her eyes. Her voice was heavy with sleep as she said, "You're staring at me again."

He brushed some hair off her face and used his thumb to remove the drop of drool at the corner of her mouth. "You're my mate, so it's allowed. Besides, I have a contest—to see if you snore before the drop of drool finally escapes your mouth."

She lightly hit his arm. "Stop it. No one wants to be reminded of how they drool."

Taking her hand, he kissed her palm. "How do you feel?"

Her brows came together. "Tired, but otherwise fine. Why?"

One of the things they had solidified during the down times of the frenzies was to tell the truth, and he wasn't going to change that now. He said softly, "The frenzy is over, Percy. You're pregnant."

He studied her face closely, in case it triggered some memories or overwhelmed her.

But after a few beats, she smiled, rolled onto her back, and placed her hands over her lower belly. "Our little one to protect."

Her words made his eyes heat with tears. Clearing his throat, he placed his hand over hers. "Yes. And to love. Just let someone try to hurt our son or daughter, and see what happens."

Even his beast grunted his drowsy approval.

Percy finally met his gaze again. "It feels… different than I thought it would. I didn't expect to be happy. And yet, because it's little parts of you and me, I am."

Bronx moved to put his face above hers and kissed her gently. He squeezed his hand still over hers. "He or she will be our family, Percy." He kissed her again. "Although until they arrive, I'm most definitely going to make the most of every day with their mother."

She smiled, raised a hand to his face, and lifted her lips to meet his. "Good. Although I hope I can rest for a day or two. Your dragon is insatiable."

He chuckled and nipped her lower lip. "Yours is worse."

They grinned at each other before laughing. His dragon growled. *Hers is worse. I swear that female tried to kill me.*

He chuckled and shared his dragon's words with Percy. She pushed at his shoulder until he lay on his back and she could straddle his waist. As she ran fingers across his chest, his cock twitched. She murmured, "Although I wouldn't mind one last time, I think. Before we have to face the world."

Lightly strumming her half-hard nipple, he said, "The world won't be that different, though. Mostly more lessons for you on how to work with your dragon, maybe some training for a job at the school, and then learning how to be a stepmum to Violet. Oh, and auntie to quite a few nephews."

"I can't wait. For a female who never had family, I'm going to have more than I know what to do with now."

He wiped the tear that slid down her cheek. "Yes. You're part of the Wells family and part of Clan Stonefire. Soon you'll be begging for some peace and quiet again."

She laughed. "I doubt that. But if it gets that overwhelming, I have the perfect teacher to show me how to cope."

He slid his hands to her arse cheeks and squeezed. "I'd rather spend time teaching you a few other things first."

She cocked an eyebrow. "Oh?"

Sliding one hand around her front, he teased just above her clit. As Percy sucked in a breath, his cock turned to stone. "Like how much more intense you'll come if I tease you for hours first."

Percy arched her hips. "Then maybe you should show me a preview now, while we're still in our bubble."

He lifted a hand and pinched her nipple, loving how her eyes turned molten. "Then let's start your lesson, love. The first of many."

And as Bronx took his time, slowly driving her wild before finally letting her orgasm and then finally coming himself, he felt whole in a way he hadn't for a long, long time.

As he cuddled Percy in his arms, he couldn't believe he had a mate he adored, another child on the way, and Violet to go home to. He might not be able to lead rescue missions or easily jump into the air in his dragon form like before, but all of that didn't matter. His family had always been the most important thing to him, and Percy had reminded him of that.

With her, he had a second chance, a fresh start, and he would make the most of it and never take anything for granted again.

Epilogue

Several Months Later

Percy eyed Bronx, who was already in the air, hovering in place, waiting for her.

Today was the day she'd try flying for the first time.

Her dragon spoke up. *Don't be nervous. We've had loads of shifting practice.*

Yes, but we've never really done more than jump into the air, hover, and land.

We can do it. And best of all, we can share our first flight with Bronx and meet up with Violet near the lake.

And there's definitely no one else I'd rather share this memory with.

Besides, we need to fly whilst we still can. Once we're too pregnant and fat, the doctors won't let us.

And once the doctors gave the order, Bronx would make sure she followed it. Even though Dr. Sid and Dr. Innes had assured him Percy was strong and doing well, he worried. When it came to their baby, Percy had to be the strong one.

Not that she minded. She couldn't wait to add to their little family.

Placing a hand over the slight swell of her belly, she waved at her mate. He swished his tail, mimicking a wave, and she said to her beast, *Okay, then let's try this.*

She tugged off her dress—resisting the urge to stare at her recent dragon tattoo yet again—and closed her eyes, uncaring that Dr. Sid, Nikki, and the dragon teacher, Ella, were watching her.

Being nude in front of anyone was still new to her, and everyone had made accommodations, ensuring only females were present when she shifted. It made her feel less like some bug being watched, like when she'd been inside the facility.

Well, most of the time.

Her dragon sighed. *Stop stalling.*

Allowing her dragon to come to the forefront of her mind, she imagined her fingers extending into talons, wings growing from her back, her nose elongating into a snout, and her body stretching, growing, and shifting into her dragon form. Once she finished, she opened her eyes and snapped open her wings.

Even though she'd been in this form dozens of times now, it still amazed her to see scales instead of skin, or a tail and wings instead of just her human back and bum.

Her dragon grunted. *Come on. Let's fly.*

Crouching, Percy readied herself for the all-important first jump. Without enough lift, she wouldn't have room to move her wings.

One second then another, and she finally used her powerful rear limbs to launch into the air while simultaneously beating her wings. For a second, she faltered and thought she might crash, but she caught herself in time. Up, and up, and up she went, until she hovered right next to Bronx. He gave a low roar of approval and then gestured for them to head toward the lake.

Even if it wouldn't be a long flight today, she didn't care. It was time to cross one of the last hurdles to becoming a fully-fledged dragon-shifter.

She dove down a little and then beat upward until she could find enough wind to coast on. Once she located it, she spread her wings and took in the landscape below. Everything was so tiny. The people were mere specks, the cottages looked like toys, and even the small children practicing their dragon shifting in the schoolyard looked like a dream.

So engrossed in the scenery, she didn't realize for a second that Bronx had caught up with her. He grunted, and she swiveled her head. Seeing her mate flying, his majestic form glinting in the sunshine, made her incredibly proud. She had the handsomest dragon for a mate, and he was the sexiest one in his human form too.

He dove down, down, and then pulled up at the last moment. Percy wasn't ready to attempt that trick. But she loved watching Bronx perform his maneuvers from this vantage point instead of from the ground.

The lake came into view, and Violet's green dragon form jumped into the air to meet them. She was smaller than her father, but not much bigger than Percy.

Her stepdaughter roared her greeting, and Percy did the same. Then they all headed toward the final destination—one of the hills dotted around Stonefire's lands. She needed to skillfully land at the designated spot, where she'd be evaluated by Tristan and Kai. Only once they gave her the all-clear could she fly without supervision.

The two males finally came into view, and Percy took a few deep breaths. She didn't want to fail.

Her dragon spoke up. *You won't.* We *won't. We're ready.*

Bronx nodded at her before settling to the side of the teachers. He had gotten better about compensating for the fake dragon foot and remained upright. Violet followed her father, and they both watched and waited for Percy to land.

Slowly, she hovered and descended. If she came in too fast, she'd crash. Too slow, and she might still tumble and lose her balance.

The grass was a few feet under her, and she finally maneuvered her wings and slowly placed her rear limbs on the ground. She did wobble a bit as she folded her wings against her back, but she managed to stay in place. She roared her success, and both of the males in human form smiled at her.

Tristan spoke first. "Yes, you did well, Percy. You have the green light from me."

Kai nodded. "As long as you stay close to Stonefire, you have permission to fly whenever you wish. Although you need to pass a few more tests before you can attempt longer flights, such as to Lochguard."

While the longer flights were her next goal, she didn't care if she could only fly close to home for now —because she *could* fly whenever she wished.

The two males gave their goodbyes and headed over the crest before the two jumped into the air—one black dragon and one golden one.

Once they were gone, Percy closed her eyes and imagined her wings melting into her back, her snout shrinking into a nose, and her limbs becoming arms and legs again. Once she finished, she opened her eyes and saw that Bronx and Violet were already in their human forms—Bronx in trousers and Violet wearing a loose dress.

Violet rushed over with something for Percy, and she put on her own dress. Once she was done, Violet hugged her. "You were brilliant, Percy. I told you that you'd pass on the first try."

After squeezing her stepdaughter one last time, she pulled back and nodded. "You were definitely one of my biggest cheerleaders. I'm glad I didn't disappoint you."

Bronx grunted, right behind his daughter. "You'd never disappoint us."

She jumped into his arms, and Bronx held her close a beat before taking her lips in a deep kiss. Once he finally allowed her up for air, he studied her face. "But you're sure you feel okay?"

Rolling her eyes, she took his hand and placed it over her belly. "I'm fine. I'm still allowed to shift, as Dr. Sid told you about a million times."

His hand lightly rubbed her abdomen. His voice was soft, for her ears only, as he said, "I know. But I still worry."

She cupped his cheek with her free hand. "If I feel ill or unwell, I'll tell you. I always do."

He smiled, kissed her gently, and nodded. "I know. I just love you so much."

"And I love you. But it doesn't mean I'll let you coddle me whenever you feel like it."

"I know, love. And I'll keep trying not to worry so much."

She was about to kiss him again when Violet's voice broke through. "Come on, you two, or I might eat the entire picnic Tristan and Kai brought for us."

Bronx frowned. "You know Percy needs to keep up her strength."

Violet raised her brows. "She eats plenty. After all, who's been teaching her to cook more and more?"

Percy bit her lip to keep from smiling. The pair always argued about who would teach her something next. It was adorable, really, to watch Bronx and his teenage daughter stand toe-to-toe.

Her mate pulled her to his side and wrapped an arm around her waist. "Let's just eat and not argue. I'm starving."

Violet shook her head then raced ahead to the basket filled with sandwiches, biscuits, fruit, and drinks.

After she'd laid out the blanket and then unpacked the food, Percy turned to face Bronx and wrapped her arms around his neck. "It's okay to share duties with Violet. It doesn't mean you love me any less."

He grunted. "I should do it. You're my mate."

"As long as I'm taught by a dragon I trust, that's good enough. Besides, I like spending some of my time with you in an entirely different way."

He pulled her closer. "Hm, and what could that be?"

She lightly ran her fingers through the hair at his nape. "The kind where I stay naked and try not to wake your daughter."

He laughed and then kissed her. As he explored her mouth, his familiar taste comforting and hot at the same time, she sighed and enjoyed what her life had become.

As they finally sat down to eat lunch, they laughed and shared stories about the area or just chatted about things that didn't really matter.

Surrounded by love, Percy couldn't believe this had become her life. Never in a million years had she envisioned being happy, let alone with not only her inner dragon, but also Bronx, Violet, his family, and even all of Stonefire by her side.

She finally belonged somewhere. More than that, she was loved in return.

All it'd taken was the male at her side to teach her how to trust herself, her dragon, and him. His daughter hadn't taken long to earn the same.

And most importantly, she was no longer alone. As she laughed at Bronx and Violet's latest teasing argument, Percy placed a hand over the small bump of her belly and felt whole. She'd found her family and her place, and she was going to hold on to it tightly and never let go.

TURN the page for a bonus epilogue…

Bonus Epilogue

Many Months Later

Percy leaned against Bronx's side, their son in her arms, as she watched Violet play with her cousins on the grass.

It'd become a tradition for the Wells family to all gather at least twice a month for either a big dinner or a picnic. The weather was warm again, and it felt good to have the sun on her face, even if she was exhausted. Phoenix was teething, and that meant Mr. Fussypants kept her up at all hours.

Her dragon sighed. *And he used to be such a well-behaved baby.*

Her son had slept through the night earlier than most, according to Bronx. And in a way, she'd been glad of it.

Motherhood had been both amazing and hard.

When she'd first held Phoenix, she'd burst into tears—because she'd finally met her little one and because she couldn't imagine ever giving him up, like her mother had done with her.

Thank goodness for Bronx and his steady presence. Most of the time, she barely had nightmares or bad memories take over. But if they did, her mate was always there, her rock, never complaining about how she was still a little bit damaged.

Her dragon huffed. *We're not. We're bloody brilliant.*

You always say that.

Because it's true.

Bronx nuzzled the top of her head as he fixed the blanket around Phoenix. "Penny for your thoughts?"

"I'm just hoping Phoenix will start sleeping like a rock again."

"This won't last long, love. Enjoy it. Because once he starts running around, that's when the true exhaustion begins."

She eyed her mate. "That sound ominous."

"Well, given how old and decrepit I am, you'll be the one running after him."

He winked, and she laughed. They often teased each other about their ages, but she knew in truth it didn't matter. Bronx was her true mate and best friend; no one else would ever come close.

She tilted her head. "Hm, well, if you're too tired for that, then I doubt you'll have the energy for me to ride you until you groan."

He nipped her ear. "Minx."

She grinned. "And you love me anyway."

He cupped her cheek, and she leaned into his touch. "Always."

"And I love you, even when you have to go away and help other clans with rescue plans."

Bronx had grown more and more comfortable in his teaching and strategic role with fire and emergency rescues. All of the dragon clans in the UK, and even Ireland, wanted his help, when possible.

Although Percy was greedy and would always miss him when he was gone, no matter how much good he was doing.

He kissed her slowly and carefully, so as to not wake their son, and she finally pulled back to say, "But you promised to help with the next camp for human and dragon children. Are you still able to?"

He nodded. "Barring any major emergency, I'll be there."

It was to be her first time as the head camp organizer. Percy had found that she worked well with children and liked planning activities for them, almost as if she could relive her missed childhood through watching their joy and experiences.

She was about to kiss her mate again when Violet ran up to them. She sighed dramatically. "I swear, you two are never going to stop kissing all the time, are you?"

Bronx put an arm around Percy's shoulders and grinned. "Nope."

Violet rolled her eyes and looked at Percy. "Can I tear you away from my dad long enough to convince my cousins that badminton is just as brilliant as football?"

Mark—her sister-in-law Sarah's son from her first marriage—ate, breathed, and dreamed football. She wondered if he also slept with the black-and-white ball in his arms at night.

Percy was one of the few adults he listened to without too much grumbling, probably because she'd roped in his help with the last few human-dragon camps. The boy liked being busy and in charge.

She gently maneuvered Phoenix into Bronx's arms and held her breath a second. But their son merely snuggled against his father's chest and conked out again.

After kissing her mate and then her son, she stood and threaded her arm through Violet's. "Right, let's see what I can do."

Soon Percy was playing badminton as Violet's partner against Mark and his stepdad, Hudson. The boy forgot all about his protests and played as if his life depended on it.

When she and Violet won—just barely—they all headed toward the picnic laid out on a large blanket.

As she approached, her son stirred and put his arms out toward her. She picked him up, kissed his cheek, and balanced him on her hip.

And as everyone settled down and battled for the food—the Wells family apparently always battled for food when all together—Percy laughed, ate, and played with her son, stepdaughter, and nephews. She couldn't wait until her niece, Hudson and Sarah's daughter, would finally be able to play and even the ratio of females to males a little bit.

When Percy finally leaned against her mate's side

again, her son in her lap and her stepdaughter at her side, she recognized how lucky she was. The female who'd once been alone, so very alone, was now surrounded by more love than she knew what to do with.

Author's Note

When Percy first showed up on the pages of *Trusting the Dragon*, I knew she needed to find a happy ending. And who else should help her but yet another Wells dragonman—Bronx. I think they fit together well, and while there is a huge age gap, that also works for the pair, in my opinion. Percy desperately needed stability and support, and Bronx gives her exactly that!

And yes, I know some people are going to comment about how quickly Percy "healed" from her experiences. However, part of the magic of romance novels is that they happen much faster and (often) better than real life. This book is the second longest dragon book I've written to date (only Finn and Arabella's story has a higher word count), and the pacing would've slowed way down make it any longer. So I used some author magic to bring about their happy ending!

The next Stonefire Dragons book will be *Charming*

the Dragon, about Hayley Beckett and Nathan Woodhouse. Originally, their story had been planned to be #15. However, Percy snuck into the end of #14 and I had to write her story first. :) It should be a lot of fun because we finally have two single people without children again (it's been awhile, lol). Plus, Nathan is super grumpy, and Hayley is a little scatterbrained and random, which is going to charm the dragonman's pants off, even if he doesn't want it. Their story will release in 2024, but I'm not sure when, exactly. I have a few other dragon books to write first. But I will always keep an up-to-date reading list on my website (JessieDonovan.com) and send updates via my newsletter.

As always, I have a few people to thank with regards to getting this book out to my readers:

- The editing team at Red Adept Editing were amazing and helped remind me of a few of my bad habits, which I'm grateful for! :)
- My beta readers—Sabrina D., Iliana G., Ashley B., and Mel M.—are amazing women who volunteer their time to read, comment, and find the minor inconsistencies and/or typos for me. I truly value and appreciate their hard work.

If you want to stay up-to-date with release information and news, then make sure to subscribe to my newsletter on my website.

As always, a huge thanks to my readers for their support. Without you, I wouldn't be able to write these wonderful stories and revisit characters that have become like family to me. Thank you and see you at the end of the next book!

Also by Jessie Donovan

Dark Lords of London

Vampire's Modern Bride (DLL #1)

Vampire's Fae Witch Healer (DLL #2)

Fae Witch's Vampire Guard (DLL #3)

Vampires' Shared Bride (DLL #4 / Late 2023)

Dragon Clan Gatherings

Summer at Lochguard (DCG #1)

Winter at Stonefire (DCG #2 / August 3, 2023)

Kelderan Runic Warriors

The Conquest (KRW #1)

The Barren (KRW #2)

The Heir (KRW #3)

The Forbidden (KRW #4)

The Hidden (KRW #5)

The Survivor (KRW #6)

Lochguard Highland Dragons

The Dragon's Dilemma (LHD #1)

The Dragon Guardian (LHD #2)

The Dragon's Heart (LHD #3)

Stonefire Dragons Shorts

Meeting the Humans (SDS #1)

The Dragon Camp (SDS #2)

The Dragon Play (SDS #3)

Dragon's First Christmas (SDS #4)

Stonefire Dragons Universe

Winning Skyhunter (SDU #1)

Transforming Snowridge (SDU #2)

Finding Dragon's Court (SDU #3)

Tahoe Dragon Mates

The Dragon's Choice (TDM #1)

The Dragon's Need (TDM #2)

The Dragon's Bidder (TDM #3)

The Dragon's Charge (TDM #4)

The Dragon's Weakness (TDM #5)

The Dragon's Find (TDM #6)

The Dragon's Surprise / Dr. Kyle Baker & Alexis (TDM #7 / TBD)

Asylums for Magical Threats

Blaze of Secrets (AMT #1)

Frozen Desires (AMT #2)

Shadow of Temptation (AMT #3)

Flare of Promise (AMT #4)

About the Author

Jessie Donovan has sold over half a million books, has given away hundreds of thousands more to readers for free, and has even hit the *NY Times* and *USA Today* bestseller lists. She is best known for her dragon-shifter series, but also writes about magic users, aliens, and even has a crazy romantic comedy series set in Scotland. When not reading a book, attempting to tame her yard, or traipsing around some foreign country on a shoestring, she can often be found interacting with her readers on Facebook. She lives near Seattle, where, yes, it rains a lot but it also makes everything green.

You can also sign-up for her newsletter.

Printed in Great Britain
by Amazon

23108284R00209